A DARK THRILLER
The Fly Guy

A DARK THRILLER

The Fly Guy

COLUM SANSON-REGAN

WordFire Press
Colorado Springs, Colorado

THE FLY GUY
Copyright © 2015 Colum Sanson-Regan

ISBN: 978-1-61475-194-6

Cover design by Emma Michaels

Art Director Kevin J. Anderson

Book Design by RuneWright, LLC
www.RuneWright.com

Published by
WordFire Press, an imprint of
WordFire, Inc.
PO Box 1840
Monument CO 80132

Kevin J. Anderson & Rebecca Moesta, Publishers

WordFire Press Trade Paperback Edition April 2015
Printed in the USA
wordfirepress.com

"… *Man is not truly one, but truly two. I say two, because the state of my own knowledge does not pass beyond that point. Others will follow, others will outstrip me on the same lines; and I hazard the guess that man will ultimately be known for a mere polity of multifarious, incongruous and independent denizens.*"

The Strange Case of Dr. Jekyll and Mr. Hyde – Robert Louis Stevenson

"*Ultimate horror often paralyses memory in a merciful way.*"

The Rats in the Walls – HP Lovecraft

CHAPTER ONE

Martin Tripp put his dream in the ground. At the end of his tiny garden he dug a shallow grave in the sticky brown clay, just deep enough to bury a child. The soil clung to his spade, and in the darkness steam rose from him as he sweated and dug and dug, scraping and pushing the reluctant earth away. Moonlight reflected off the plastic bundle he laid in the earth. He straightened, and his heavy breath and sweat made a cloud around him, rising like a spirit in the night. In his shadow his dream glowed. He felt it begin to grow again like a whisper getting louder inside his head. He grabbed the spade and covered it in darkness.

Since that night Martin felt the darkness cling to him. That was months ago and now his weekday routine at the printing office was like a blunt iron thumping inside the walls of a tomb. On the day he started Alison kissed him at the doorway and said, *Remember, this is the start of something real.* Now every morning he auto-piloted the noisy little tin can of a hatchback to the third floor of a grey building sandwiched between a life insurance company and a debt repayment specialist. In the office the days ran to the rhythm and clunk of the printing machines. Brief static phrases of processing and the soft slide and swish of page after page after page pushed time forward slowly.

Martin had a cramped office space opposite the café, and this morning there was a small man sitting at one of the café tables. In a glance Martin felt a pinch and tug at the base of his skull. He knew this man. Here was Henry Bloomburg. Although he could see him, Martin knew how impossible it was. How he could not be sitting there sipping from a tiny espresso cup.

Martin turned away and ordered his coffee. When he looked again he expected the seat to be empty, for the ghost to have vanished, but Henry remained. He wore a black suit with a thin black tie and trilby hat, exactly as Martin had written him. The pinch grew more intense, but Martin looked away again before Henry could make eye contact.

Today was an important day and he didn't want distractions. He tapped the counter and shifted from foot to foot. When his coffee came he spilled some as he turned. He crossed to his office and didn't look back.

He was tired, that was all. His mind was playing tricks. Henry would disappear, of course he would. He had to concentrate. There was a pre-proof press that had to be sent this morning, and it could land him with a series contract. This would be something he could bring home to Alison. Something real.

"The series?" she would say, beaming at him. "Darling that's fantastic!" and she would close her laptop and stand up and say, "Let's celebrate!"

The file opened and he looked again at the cover note. Goodbooks *presents a series which revisits the most read religious texts of all time and offers a new, easy way of reading them, and a way to understand their teachings in relation to the modern world.*

The title page loaded and Martin moved lines and angles, like manipulating a bird's wing. The text floated and stretched, grew and shrank. Martin tasted sweat on his upper lip. He was mumbling to himself, *Sell it on the first page, sell it on the first page.* He pressed print. When he stood to go through to the print rooms his shirt was pasted to his back with clammy sweat.

As he stood by the printer he glanced out the window to the car park below. Henry was there looking up at him. Henry was so out of place, standing there. His arms were limp at his sides and his head cocked at an angle, like a bird listening for a reply. He was perfectly still. His stillness was magnetic, as if everything that moved revolved around him, in his gravity. As he looked Martin felt something come from him, a swell, a wave about to break.

The metallic drone of the printer's buzzer broke his reverie, and he picked up the cover page from the tray. *The Old Testament— Today.*

The first page of his future was in his hands. It looked good. Maybe now was the time. The first chink of light through the walls. He looked again down to the car park. Henry was gone.

He went back into his cramped office and started to type. To the drones and clicks of the printers Martin revised his proposal for *Goodbooks*. All day he lined up numbers, knocked them down, and set them up again.

During dinner Martin said nothing. Halfway through Alison went to the fridge and took out a bottle of chilled wine, stopping for a moment to check her teeth in the mirror.

"Yup. A big chunk of salad. A green tooth, you could have told me."

She sat and poured the wine. The bottle felt cool in her hand. She closed her eyes as she drank. When she opened them Martin was looking down moving the food around his plate.

"Not hungry? Did you eat earlier? Martin?"

She forked some salad into her mouth and chewed, waiting for him to look up.

"Well, if you're not going to talk—" She reached for a magazine and pulled it next to her plate.

"It's just this meeting tomorrow, it's on my mind. The contract."

"I'm sure it will be fine, I'm sure it will. You know what you're doing, don't you?"

"Yeah, I think so. If this works I will get a cut and I can start paying you back."

"I know, you said already." She turned the pages. "Don't pin everything on this one contract though."

As soon as Alison put her fork down he picked up the plates and took them to the sink.

"Do you want any ice cream?"

"No, I'm fine." She turned another page. She wasn't reading, she was scanning for anything interesting. Nothing there. Another page.

"Sally is huge," she said. Martin spooned ice cream into a bowl. "She won't find out if it's a boy or a girl though. I mean, wouldn't you want to know? How can you have the answer there in front of you, but choose to remain in the dark?"

Martin sat down. "I don't know. It's hard to say till it's happening to you I guess. This contract could set me up for a while."

Alison took a spoonful of ice cream.

"You said already." She put the spoon in her mouth.

"I'm just going up to go over the proposal."

She handed the spoon back to him. "Go on then, abandon me. Leave me alone with my wine."

"Come on, it's—"

"I know, I know, go on. I'm kidding, go on," she said as she poured another glass. "I'm not going to stay up late, I have meetings tomorrow, too. The docklands plots are moving, The Bucket O' Blood is ready to sign, but I'll believe that when I see it. So we'll both be busy tomorrow."

Martin leaned over and kissed her forehead. Then he picked up his bowl and went upstairs.

O O O

Martin sat and turned his computer on. He put the bowl on the clean desk. Months ago he would have had to hold it in his lap or balance it on a tower of loose paper, or clear away old coffee cups and post-it notes splattered with brandy splashes.

In one afternoon, Alison had cleared away nearly three years of words. He remembered the sweaty determination on her face when he came home and found her taking down the sketches from the walls, the figure drawings, the hand-drawn maps and words in capital letters inside circles within circles. All of the pages with scribbles in the margins and arrows pointing chaotically were stacked neatly into storage boxes. Now there was even a coaster for him to put the bowl on so that it wouldn't mark the clean desk. *My god,* he thought, *she must have scrubbed and scrubbed that desk to get it so clean.* She had even replaced the bulb in the room for a brighter one.

Martin clicked on his documents folder and opened up his paper-sourcing outlines. As he read, he felt a voice, like a whisper being pressed to his cheek—*not her.* He caught a movement in the corner of his eye and snapped his head around. He was alone.

The next morning, Martin saw Henry again by the lights at the big junction. He looked the same as he did the day before, motionless. It was as though he had blinked out of existence in the car park, only to reappear here.

The lights changed. The fat man in his vest in the grimy van behind Martin beeped his horn and chewed on thick curses. Martin pulled off, looking in the rear view mirror at the thin figure on the side of the road, just standing there. The pinching and nagging at the back of his head got worse.

Martin tuned on the radio. At this time every morning there was a DJ with an over-enthusiastic voice who did a rundown on the issues of the day, but all Martin could hear was static with a faint indistinguishable voice behind it. He tried tuning the radio up and down, but nothing changed. He turned the volume up to hear the voice. It was no good. The car was filled with grainy aggressive un-directed noise, caught in a storm of swirling ground masonry and shattered steel. Behind him another angry driver beeped and waved her arms around behind the glass as if she was sinking. Martin realised he had slowed down again. He turned the radio off and picked up speed.

As he pulled into the car park he saw a woman step from one of the cars. She moved elegantly toward the main entrance with the confident stride of a model in a catwalk. Martin parked up and half ran across the car park, slowing to a walk as he reached the door. She was waiting for the lift. Martin stepped beside her. She shifted slightly and gave him a brief smile.

"Hi," said Martin.

"Hello," she replied. Martin recognised her voice. Her look suited her voice perfectly. When they had spoken Martin leaned into her luxurious tone, pressing the receiver harder against his ear, wanting to get closer to this voice, serious but sensuous.

"Can I ask, are you here to see Mr. Tripp?"

"Yes. Yes, we have a nine o'clock."

"I'm Martin," he said extending his hand.

"Aha! Nice to meet you. I'm Susan—"

"—Purvis. Hi. Yes we spoke—"

"—on the phone."

Martin said, "So, em, there's a café upstairs. Do you want to grab a coffee and—"

"Oh yes," she said, smiling. "Let's grab a latte and chat an outline before we get to specifics."

Martin let his eyes slide down over her for a moment before he said, "I'm sure we can provide everything you need here, but as you say, the devil is—"

"—in the detail."

The lift door opened.

There was Henry, looking straight at him. His face was rugged, there was a scar running from his nose under his right eye. Susan Purvis stepped into the lift. Martin forced himself to move. As he stepped in he heard Henry ask, "Which floor?" Martin looked from Susan to Henry and back to Susan who was looking at him expectantly. Martin felt his insides turn to ice as she said, "Well, I don't know. Mr. Tripp? Which floor?"

"That's, em, I thought ..." Martin felt the blood drain away from his face and the floor begin to tilt. Susan put her hand on his arm.

"Mr. Tripp, are you alright?"

"Yes, I ... I, em ... floor three, third floor."

Henry pushed the button and Martin turned to face the doors. His stomach began to churn with anxiety. Behind him was Henry Bloomburg, who he had buried all those months ago. Martin had seen him before, yes, but he was always in his head, wasn't he? But he had spoken and Susan Purvis heard him. Henry had pressed the button and here they were, going up. The scar on his face, where did he get that? He never gave Henry a scar. The churning anxiety rose to his heart now, and he could feel it reaching up and tugging at his face. Martin's mind was spasming, kicking against the inside of his skull. He wanted to bend over and clutch his head.

When the doors opened it was like breaking the surface and he rushed forward, almost falling on his shaking legs. Susan came to his side.

"Mr. Tripp? Are you okay?"

Martin took a breath. He forced his face into a smile and said, "Yes, I'm fine, I'm fine. Just a bit ... just dizzy for a moment. I'm fine ... let's sit down"

As they ordered coffee Martin glanced around. Henry was not there. Susan was talking, "—We see ourselves as facilitators of spiritual literacy—"

"Well, people are always looking for, well, the—"

"Creator. Whether they know it or not, that is what they need in their lives. It's not just Christianity, we look at all spiritual texts—" Martin nodded his head in interest, trying not to grimace as he stuffed Henry Bloomburg into a dark space in the corner of his mind. He swallowed hard, forcing the pressure down, down.

With coffees in their hands they sat at the table.

"What if Jesus was your homie?" she said.

Martin laughed, then changed it quickly to a cough. He felt himself frown, so he raised his eyebrows and tilted his head to one side.

"What, like in the 'hood?"

"Exactly. Jesus in the 'hood."

He considered her face. It was open and earnest. He could see how thick her make-up was.

"Well, I guess … I'd be lucky. I'd be hanging with Jesus."

"Jesus, as he is now, is all 'thees' and 'thines.' We want to give him a modern voice. You can't be saved if your saviour is trapped in an ancient text. You shouldn't need a preacher to explain it to you."

Martin agreed and glanced around the room. Had Henry been there? Maybe it was in his head. But yesterday Henry was sitting at this table, and today in the lift he was real. As real as this elegant and effortlessly seductive woman who was saying, "Punchy parables. Instant insight. Easy access to the word of God."

When Susan spoke she spread her fingers wide and her hands rotated from her wrists, like a magician inviting agreement; look, there's nothing there.

CHAPTER TWO

When Alison first joined the company, she attended a rooftop meet and greet. The autumn day was bright and cold, and she could almost taste the vivid blue of the sky. Way up high the crisscross of contrails was like floating ribbons cut free from a bridal veil.

She smiled through the introductions to her new bosses' partners and colleagues, and their partners, and their friends and partners, and their business associates. She wished she had brought a shawl to put around her shoulders, she felt exposed. As she listened, she drank and soon the glass in her hand was empty. She had to stop herself bringing it to her lips as the conversations moved around her. *Relax, relax, relax*, she said to herself as she nodded and smiled. Her face was beginning to ache.

The group drifted to the edge of the roof. Various properties and planning proposals in the city were pointed out and discussed. A forest of rooftops and buildings stretched out beneath them. Alison felt queasy as more and more of the city came in to view. She stayed still until she was at the edge of the group and then went back to the drinks table.

"More champagne?" the man behind the table asked.

"Yes, please," and she held out her glass.

He poured slowly. His hands were elegant and slim. He was clean but frayed. He was younger than her, in his mid-twenties she guessed. His hair seemed a bit too long, there were bits at his fringe and behind his ears which were breaking free, as if it wanted to be curly, and couldn't wait till his shift was over.

He finished pouring and handed her the glass. His eyes took her by surprise. They were grey, with tiny flecks of black and green, like a sheer cliff face. Suddenly she knew she had been looking too long, and looked away. Her glass was full but she didn't move away from the table. She took a little sip.

After a while he said, "It really is quiet up here considering we're right in the middle of the city." And for the first time she listened beyond the voices of the people around her talking about acquisitions and interest peaks and equity rates, and listened to the stillness of the high air. Somewhere in the distance was the hum of traffic. Beneath them were stories and stories of people talking, explaining, negotiating, selling, buying, discussing. It was odd to think that so many people could be so close and yet unheard. None of what was going on below could disturb them up here.

The more she listened the quieter it became. Even the talk from the rooftop fell into the background and started to disappear, as if they were all extras on a movie set whose noise would be dubbed in later. The camera was trained on her and this handsome stranger now, the rest of the set had to act in silence.

She stood for a moment and a smile came to her face, her sweet natural smile, before she said, "Yes, actually it is." She still didn't move away from the table. She forgot about feeling cold.

That was the first time Alison met Martin.

Every time she went back for another glass she found out a little more about him. He bartended and wrote articles for online publications. He never shopped at the big stores because rows and rows of clothes made him feel uncomfortable. He preferred spring to summer. Brandy was his favourite drink, and the bigger the glass the better. Heights didn't bother him but speed did.

He asked about her. She told him she had just started with the firm and had been introduced at a level she hadn't been expecting, and was still finding her feet.

He said, "You should be busy hobnobbing with the suits then."

"I don't know them. I've never been in a group like this before. I don't know what to say."

"Just compliment them, then ask them about themselves and let them do the talking," he said. "They'll access parts of you that you hadn't considered talking about."

"I'm just not that interesting." As she said it she held out her glass and slightly turned her head away, keeping her eyes fixed on him and pushing her lips into a pout.

"I bet you are," he said with a smile and poured. "Anyway, don't worry about being interesting, be interested."

She wanted him to walk with her, to stand with her while she joined in the conversations about market expectations and whether Julie's nanny was making the right choice by moving to Chorleywood. She asked him where else he worked. ICE 49 on the weekends. ICE 49 was near her apartment.

The champagne worked, and soon there were voices raised in good humour rising into the afternoon air, explosions of laughter resounding around the rooftop. Alison was welcomed by everyone, and she moved easily through the back slapping and promises of goodwill and lasting business bonds. She couldn't help but glance over at the drinks table. If he wasn't pouring he would catch her eye and a quick smile would flash between them, like a brief electric signal. It felt good. Alison felt an excitement run from her legs up her back every time it happened. ICE 49. She repeated it, keeping it for later.

O O O

The following Saturday she was at ICE 49 with two of her friends. She hoped she sounded natural when she suggested it. It was quiet when they got there, only a few groups drinking quietly in the booths. At the long bar they were greeted by a tall, lean barman who put both hands on the counter and said, "Before I get anything for you lovely ladies, can I see some ID?"

There was an outburst of giggles and a flurry of bag rummaging as the barman leaned on one elbow and smiled. Alison scanned the bar for Martin, and there he was, right down at the end, loading bottles into a fridge. As she produced her ID she kept an eye on him. She ordered her drink, and as the barman walked away, Martin looked up and she smiled at him. He smiled back and went to the other barman who was preparing the drinks.

"Ozzy, man, let me get these." Ozzy stopped.

"Really? Why? Do you fancy your chances?"

"I know one of them."

"Which one?"

"The blonde with the green top."

"Right." Ozzy looked over his shoulder. "The plain one. When you say you know her...?"

"I've met her once."

Ozzy poured crushed ice into the glasses. He put mint leaves in front of Martin. "Well, whatever you do, don't bring her back to your place, man. Unless you've got a new bolt on the door."

"Ozzy, come on, what are the drinks? I got this."

"Well, at least you are playing within your league. If there's any movement, get me over, her two friends are hot."

As soon as Martin brought the drinks Alison's friends knew there was something up. They watched as Martin and Alison smiled at each other for a bit too long, and Martin asked, "How did the rest of the day go?"

"I was pretty drunk. Was I embarrassing?"

"Not at all, you were fine, really."

Alison paid and she and her friends turned away from the bar. They immediately teased her about him being too young for her, and she felt butterflies in the stomach, like a schoolgirl with a crush.

By the time they left the bar, she and Martin had agreed to meet up the next day to go and see an exhibition. When her friends quizzed her what it was an exhibition of, she squirmed. *Something to do with cultural art?* They all laughed and she flushed.

Alison and Martin never got to the exhibition. At seven o'clock they were still in the bar they had met in at three, still talking. By then Alison knew that she would never meet anyone like Martin again.

o o o

As Martin walked back to his apartment that night, the rain started. He hunched his shoulders and looked at the ground as he walked, running through the evening with Alison. She hadn't asked him anything about his past. He didn't have to avoid any questions.

They talked and laughed and drank, and when she said she had to go, Martin put his hand on hers. In that moment something within him moved, as if shocked to life, and he could still feel it twitching inside. He straightened up and saw the rain make halos around the streetlights as he turned the corner of his street.

Sitting on the wall in front of his room there were the usual thin shapes of hooded youths, smoking and pushing each other, and jeering passers-by. He saw the legs of the Carson girl amongst them. The closer he got, the more he saw of her. She was twisting her wet bleached hair and thumbing her phone as the boys sold a plastic baggie of weed to a dark shape in a car that had pulled up, engine still running. He walked past her. She ignored him and he caught a glance at how the rain hit her long pale legs ending in tatty worn sneakers before he turned and disappeared into the dark alley behind her. He stepped through the puddles and empty beer cans and piss pools, and up the steel staircase to his door.

The air in the small, dark one room apartment was stagnant and cold and chilled his lungs as the door clicked closed. He heard the rain falling on the pools of water on the flat roof. The streetlight outside shone brightly through the thin curtains, showing the creases and thread marks like veins on a bat's wing.

Through the window he saw the Carson girl was still there getting more and more wet, and there was no sign of the boys. Maybe they had gone with the guy in the car. He took a blanket from the bed and hung it over the rail to block out the streetlight. From the window the walls of the room angled in on each other, narrowing like a coffin to the head of the single bed. He took his jacket off and lay down. He wanted peace to cover him like a soft cloud, but instead a vibration of anxiety welled inside him. The cracks on the ceiling made him wonder how long he had left before this vibration grew strong enough to collapse everything.

He had told Alison that he was a published writer. He had one story with an online magazine. All she had to do was search online and she would see he was a fraud, exaggerating how much he had done. He pulled himself off the bed and turned on his lamp. He opened up his laptop and without thinking started typing.

Henry knew the guy was lying, but wondered which truth he was trying to hide. He could bet it wasn't the one he was looking for.

Martin continued writing until he felt empty. He stood up. Standing to the side of the window, he moved the blanket aside just enough to see out. The Carson girl was still there, her shoulders hunched over and her head down. She looked like she was crying.

He opened his door and walked down the metal steps and through the alley, through the discarded powder wraps, and cigarette and joint butts; the detritus of the street life of these kids. He thought he was being quiet, he felt taut as a fishing line dragging a prize, but she looked over her shoulder and saw him come from the shadows. She screamed and ran. He stepped back into the darkness and watched her pale legs run down the road before turning and going back to his room.

He sat again and typed. The wallpaper bulged and sagged and slipped from the corners, creating new shadows on the walls, and the green mould continued its slow silent spread around the room.

The squeal of the metal shutters from the mechanics garage below told him it was morning, and soon he heard the clanking and grind of machines as Carson and Son got to work. He pressed Save again and lay down, covering his face with the pillow.

Every time he started drifting off to sleep the muffled monosyllabic shouts of the mechanics or the smell of oil and burnt rubber yanked him awake. He closed his eyes tighter, but couldn't shut his ears or his nose.

There are too many ways into my head, he thought. He reopened his laptop to reread what he had done. When he got to the end, he attached it to an email to *Noire*, the online magazine, with the heading "Henry Bloomburg" and pressed send. He sent a text to Alison. *Thanks for last night, I had a great time. Let's do it again.* He buried himself in his bed and at last sleep overtook him.

O O O

The next time he saw Alison, Martin was able to say that he had submitted another story. It was two days later and he was sitting on the wall waiting for Alison to pick him up. Behind him the Carson girl was arguing with her father in the shadow and grease of the garage. Her shouts rebounded off her oil-stained father and his deep, thick-necked threats rumbled past Martin out onto the street. Alison pulled up.

"Where's your place, then?" she asked as he got in the car. He pointed to the room on top of the garage, squeezed between two houses like an embarrassed afterthought.

She looked up at the window and said, "You not going to invite me in?"

He smiled, leaned across, and kissed her. She backed away for a second and looked into his eyes before closing them again and pushing her lips to his. She was holding her breath. He put his hand to her cheek and stroked her face gently as they kissed. She felt herself relax. He could still hear shouts from the garage as the mechanic's voice grew louder, and then they both looked up as the Carson girl ran out past the car and down the street. They smiled at each other before they pulled off.

"What are we going to do? Is there anywhere you really want to go?" Alison asked.

"No, whatever you want."

"Okay, well I have a plan."

Martin leaned back and watched the city pass.

That night they were at Alison's sitting on the sofa. Alison's holiday video was just finishing. It was footage of her stay at her parent's new boat-house which was on a lake out in the country. The stillness of the water and the lushness of the trees was beautiful, and the picture faded on Alison's smiling face, waving into the camera, with the sun set throwing a wash of rich colour onto the lake behind her. Martin sat straight with his arm around Alison, who rested her head on his shoulder.

"That looks fantastic," he said.

"It's so special up there. You'd love it." The screen went blank. "Tell me about your story then. What's it about?"

"What's it about? Well, you can read it, I can send it to you."

"No," she said, getting closer, "tell me about it. I want you to tell me."

"Okay. Well, there's Henry Bloomburg, a detective—"

"Ooh, it's a mystery." She traced her finger across his chest.

"—and he is hired to find this kid who has been missing for ages, so long the police have stopped looking. The parents of the kid hire him. And anyway, Henry finds him, he has been kidnapped—"

Alison sat back, sitting upright and putting her hands on his leg.

"—by this creepy old guy who has been keeping him in his attic, and like, abusing him for years."

"Oh no! That's horrible. What age is he? Do you want more wine?"

"Em, okay. The kid was about six when he went missing and now he's about ten or eleven—"

Alison got up from the sofa and went through to the kitchen. Her bare feet left heat prints on the bare wood floor for a moment before vanishing. As she opened the fridge she called in, "Keep going, I'm listening."

"So Henry finds him and he's locked in this attic, and in the attic with him are one hundred puppets."

Alison padded back into the room with two full glasses of chilled white wine. "Puppets?" she said, handing him a glass and sitting down.

"Yeah, so, he has made friends with them all over the years and he's cared for them, and they've cared for him, and now they won't let him go."

"They're alive?"

"He's given them life, they've been his friends for years. He doesn't want to leave them either."

"Martin, that's creepy."

"Yeah. Well it is for a website called *Noire*."

"And the boy in the story, do you describe what the old guy does to him?"

"Some of it, but nothing too—"

Alison put her glass down on the side table next to the neat little pile of property and fashion magazines. She pulled her feet up under her and folded her arms, then covered her mouth with her hand to hide the grimace she felt pulling at her lips. A young innocent, a prisoner, abused. His reality stolen. A whole childhood, the most magical and fun-filled time of life, robbed. A life damaged and twisted out of shape forever. And Martin, sitting alone in front of his computer, writing this, creating this.

"Hey," Martin said, "it's not as bad as you think. You should read it, really—"

"No, no, Martin, I don't want to read it. It's horrible. I mean, I mean, I'm not good with horror stuff. I'm too …"

"I know what you mean. Don't worry, it's okay." He reached out to her and she leaned into him. She felt the tension roll off her like a refreshing rain on a hot and humid day.

O   O   O

Martin started spending more and more time at Alison's. She gave him the door code so that after his shifts at ICE he could go back to her place. He'd knock on the apartment door and listen for the soft padding of her bare feet. The door would click open and she'd smile at him, squinting, her hair ruffled and her nightdress loose, a strap hanging from one shoulder, before going back to bed as he undressed and showered.

As he climbed into bed, Alison turned around so that he could spoon her and mumble a happy consent when she felt his arms around her. Martin always found it hard to sleep. He was tight and on guard. He lay listening to Alison's breathing deepen and slow.

Sometimes the window was open allowing a soft breeze to drift into the dark room, and the sounds of the city at night washed gently through, as if they were on a midnight boat and the wind carried the sounds of the land over the waves. With his eyes closed, the clean smell of the apartment and Alison's skin, warm and sweet, filled his head and seeped into his body, worked its way into his muscles. His guard dropped, his grip loosened, and sleep overtook him.

In the mornings, Alison kissed Martin as he slept and softly closed the door.

O   O   O

An email came through from *Noire*. They liked the new Henry story and it would feature in the next edition. During the day Martin sat at the kitchen table and wrote. He tried not to be excited by the news from *Noire*. Henry would probably be buried right at the back of the magazine. But someone liked what he was doing. He didn't have a plan for a story, but he wanted to write. He sat at the blank screen, flicking back to his email every few minutes. Nothing came in. He was uncomfortable. He put his fingers on the keyboard and tried to be still, to let whatever was in hiding come out.

Henry Bloomburg answered the phone. A voice slid into his ear. It was neither an adult's nor a child's, it was neither a whisper nor a shout, it was disconnected, it came from no shape that Henry knew. He felt it writhe as he heard the words, "Bloomburg, you need to sssstop me."

Martin stopped for a second as the voice faded, then started to write.

Hours passed and Martin didn't move from his position at the table. His coffee was cold beside him as his fingers typed and typed. Usually he prepared and cooked so that when Alison came through the door after work the table was set, the smell of food was in the air, and a bottle of white wine was chilling in the fridge. Today when she came back he was still writing, staring at the screen. As she put her bag on the counter, Martin stopped.

"Sorry," he said. "I will put some dinner on now."

"Don't worry," she said coming close to him and kissing his head. "I'll do it. Why don't you freshen up? Have you moved all day? You look pale."

"I'm okay. Yeah, I'll have a shower." Martin walked to the bathroom on legs that felt like wooden blocks, stamping his feet to get some circulation going again. Alison glanced at the computer screen as she took off her coat. It was Henry Bloomburg approaching an apartment.

He just wanted to ask this lady a few questions, that was all, about the guy she had shown around the city properties. If she had answered his call or responded to his message he wouldn't have had to find out where she lived. But people don't know what the most important thing is. They think they do, but they've almost always got it wrong.

Alison sat down and read more.

The door was off the lock, slightly open. Henry took a second and listened, then gently pushed the door. As Henry walked into the apartment, the description was exactly like the door she had just come through. She could see the sunlight he described as pouring through the window, reflecting on the metallic clock, making a butterfly of light on the opposite wall.

She looked up. There was the silver butterfly in front of her, trapped in a shimmering moment. There was a CD in the player, still playing. It was the show tunes CD she used to cheer herself up.

Henry looked around the apartment, taking in the little pictures of cats with humorous quotations underneath that were pinned to the noticeboard and stuck to the fridge.

She turned in her chair and saw the pictures described there in front of her. She had put them there so long ago she hardly even saw them anymore.

Alison's heart started to race. What was Martin doing? He had brought Henry Bloomburg into her home. She stood up and checked the front door. It was closed. She could hear the shower from behind the closed door of the bathroom. She sat back down at the computer, scanning back over the description with a growing panic before scrolling down.

Henry turned and walked to the bathroom. As he opened the door the CD started to skip just as track seven was ending, the last line of the song repeating and repeating—the guy's only doing it for some doll ... for some doll ... for some doll ... for some doll ... for some doll ... *and there, where she stood naked every day, was a pretty blonde slumped backwards, almost sitting up on the floor of the shower, naked with her stomach split open and intestines spilling out. There was blood on the wall and the shower curtain and in a crimson pool under her body. One of her hands was practically inside her stomach as if she had been trying to push her guts back in as she died. Her blue eyes were still open. Looking straight at him. Straight at her. As Henry stood and calmly took in the details of the scene*—

Alison heard the shower stop. She fumbled with the keypad, trying to get off the page, away from Henry.

Martin's mail page opened, and there was a new mail, in bold black lettering with the subject line: **check out the site.**

When Martin came out of the shower, rubbing his hair with a towel, she had calmed down and started to prepare some food, chopping vegetables while a pan of water came to the boil.

Martin sat and clicked, then stood straight up again.

"I don't believe it! Look! Look!"

She ran to the table, the knife still in her hand. On the opening page of the website, there was an illustration showing a puppet, like a crazed court jester, with an army of similar shapes behind him, sinister eyes and teeth glowing in the darkness. In the background stood a silhouette of a man in a trilby hat, with his hands at his sides holding a gun. Underneath ran the title: "The Puppet Master—A Case From the Files of Henry Bloomburg, by M. Tripp."

Martin threw his hands up in the air.

"Front page! Front page!"

Alison let out a little squeal. "Front page!" she joined in. "Oh that's fantastic! Martin, that's fantastic!" Martin started a little twisty dance which she joined him in, before he broke away, sitting back down at the computer, and talking over his shoulder at her, his voice a little loud. "I've got to read this now, this is really important."

Alison went back into the kitchen and continued chopping. She tried to shake off the uncomfortable feeling left over from reading what Martin had written. After all, she told herself, he's got to get his ideas from somewhere. I just won't read any more.

That night as they were finishing the bottle of wine at the table, she congratulated him again.

"In the email, they said they loved Henry and to send in more stories, so that's what I've got to do."

"And it's great that you don't have to work tonight," she said, putting her hand on his leg. "We can get on with a story of our own." She leaned forward and pressed her lips to his, then opening her mouth, seeking out his tongue with hers.

He responded and she moved over onto him, straddling his lap, kissing and grinding, pushing her breasts against his chest. She wanted to break through his mind, get beyond whatever story he was wrapped up in, so that all of his concentration was on her. She felt him get hard against her as he unbuttoned her shirt. She gripped the back of his head and pulled him to her, and he started grabbing her, tugging her bra aside and taking her breast in his mouth, hitching her skirt up around her waist and squeezing her backside pulling it even closer. *Now I know where you are,* she thought. *Now I know where you are.*

CHAPTER THREE

Henry heard the voice over and over again, squirming around in his head. It pressed up against the inside of his skull like a larva feeding and growing. He had no way of tracking the source of the voice.

He was investigating a property investor whose money had come from drug trafficking, when he started coming across bodies of women. They all had something missing. An estate agent whose stomach had been removed, a party girl found behind a club without a tongue or eyes. Henry knew the voice had done this, and inside his head it bulged and pulsed, and he knew he had to stop it.

He was searching an area where another girl went missing, a teenager who had vanished between the fast food restaurant where she worked and her home, when he saw a skinny man with oversized sunglasses. His black hair was thin on his scalp, brushed back and oily. He walked oddly as though he had three knees in each leg, more of a jerk and a twitch than a stride; as if constructed from scrawls in a child's flip-book. Yet no-one else seemed to notice him, he moved unseen; sliding in and out of the city's gaps without drawing a look.

Henry followed him to the docklands. This was the city's forgotten dream, an abandoned beginning, where the houses stood like old broken promises. Some buildings slumped against each other like starved prisoners, chained together and close to death; others crumbled into the ground, collapsed into their hollow selves.

Henry followed, watching the man's strange movements, and every jerky step he saw loosened something inside him, like a screw unwinding at the front of his brain. Colours bled from their outlines as he saw the odd man push open a door of a derelict house and go inside.

As soon as he pushed open the door Henry covered his mouth and nose, but it was too late, a sharp rotting smell hit him hard. Tears streamed down his face and he gagged and heaved as his stomach turned.

The strange figure disappeared down a dark stairwell, and Henry followed. His skin was stinging from the stench as he crept down to the basement. As he crouched at the bottom of the old stone steps in the shadow of the doorway and watched, he felt his insides freeze over.

A single light bulb hung from the damp ceiling, casting a pus-hued light onto the stone walls and the cold stone floor. In the middle of the room several bodies were piled in a heap. They were all naked. He saw the face of a young girl, eyes closed at peace, and mouth open in an eternal scream, but it was hard to tell what it was connected to, the bodies were dismembered and jumbled together.

Henry held his breath as with sharp, spasming steps the bizarre man circled the gruesome heap. Squeezed organs and entrails oozed and leaked, lank clumps and strands of different coloured hair sprouted and hung from the tangle of limbs, wounds, blood, shadows, hands, bruises.

Every instinct within Henry told him to run, to get as far away as possible from this horror. His stomach heaved, sending waves of gripping cold through him. His eyes burned. He backed away. The man then started to undress.

Henry froze.

Like a nightmare slowly opening, he watched as thin hands with fingers like gnarled roots peeled clothes off, and grey skin fell in loose creases on the skeletal frame. His limbs were too long. His torso was the size of a child's, with a tiny ribcage and a distended belly, the one place where his smoky skin was tight. Where his navel should be was a nipple, sticking out like an arrowhead, and leaking drips of yellow sticky pus. Between his legs a lumpy growth hung like a rotten piece of fruit. His neck, thin like the stalk of a plant, bowed under the weight of his oversized head. His mouth was small and perfectly circular. He stood there in the cold yellow light, a hideous distortion of the human form, naked but for his big sunglasses, and when he took them off Henry saw the eyes of a fly.

Then he crawled onto the dead bodies. He pushed his face into the bodies to feed. He chewed in a frenzy, violently, his head shaking as he pushed deeper. Henry backed away again, feeling behind him for the steps. The Fly Guy lifted his skinny neck from the broken and open chest of a bleach-blonde girl, turned his head, and looked directly at Henry. It was a pale face that was spattered with blood and skin, its mouth like a vicious O with tiny razor sharp teeth, and its eyes, black domes separated into hundreds of tiny circles, flecked with spots of blood.

It spoke, and Henry felt the voice inside him again.

"Sssstop me. Bloomburg. Sssstop me."

Terror overtook Henry; a screaming lightning bolt through his brain, and he turned and fled.

Henry didn't sleep that night. The horror turned and twisted within him. His heart raced, and he rolled and wrapped the sheets around him. Soon they were damp with sweat.

As soon as light soaked through his curtains, he dressed and returned to the derelict house. But there was no house. There in front of him was an old parking lot, where weeds and tendrils reached up from the cracks in the concrete, like hands reaching up from an urban grave. He walked up and down the desolate street, searched for the house, the door through which he had followed The Fly Guy, but could not find it.

That day and the next he searched. He scanned the papers and police radio for reports of missing or murdered girls, but there was nothing. Henry drove back to the docklands again and again.

He began to lose confidence in the reality of this creature. Henry hadn't seen anyone cast a glance to this weird misshapen man in their midst. Was he the only one to see it? Henry couldn't decide which scared him more, the monster being real, or the monster existing only inside him.

Day after day he waited for The Fly Guy to reappear. No new cases came in. He wandered around the city, looking into windows, standing on street corners, until he gradually began to fade into the city.

O   O   O

Martin was frustrated by the way the story just dissolved.

When Alison got home, she found him sitting at the table in front of his laptop holding his hands behind his head as if surrendering. By now he spent all of his time at her table. Where she used to put bills, there was now a pile of newspapers and dog-eared property magazines with red and orange circles around apartments and houses big enough for two. On the corkboard next to pictures of her parents was the first check he received from *Noire* and Martin's favourite bits of feedback from fans of Henry Bloomburg. A man in Budapest said the stories were nightmarish parables. A woman in Burnley wanted to take Henry home and give him something of her own to investigate. A man in Detroit had read "The Puppet Master" at the hospital bed of his comatose lover who opened his eyes for the first time since an accident six weeks previously just as Henry witnessed the puppets come to life.

Alison put her bag and a bundle of magazines and folders on the counter and switched on the kettle.

"Having problems?"

"Hi, babe. I just don't know if this story is finished or not."

"Is it long enough to send?" She hung up her jacket and took off her shoes, rubbing the soles of her feet and her heels. All day she had been walking around properties, showing clients around big old city houses with high ceilings and kitchens the size of her apartment.

"Yeah. I guess … it's long enough. I don't think it's finished, but yeah, it's long enough."

"Send it then. It can always be the first part of something. How long have you been sitting in front of it?"

"All day."

"Press send, sweetie."

Martin attached it and sent it to *Noire*. He got up from the table and went over to her, putting his arms around her waist.

"I didn't get dinner ready again, sorry," he said.

"That's okay, let's get something on now, I'm starving."

"Why don't you come into ICE tonight? To keep me company? It's such a drag."

"Won't Ozzy be working?"

"Yeah, but it's still a real drag of a job."

"Martin, I'm tired, I don't want to sit in ICE while you and Ozzy work."

"Call your friends, come on."

She broke away, turning to open the cupboard and reached in for a pot.

"I'm tired, I'm not going to come. Can you get the pasta out, and that paste we like? I'll mix up something nice and easy."

She hadn't been to ICE for months. The dark bar and drunken conversations shouted above the noisy music seemed light years away from where she was during the day.

In the office she was taking every opportunity she could, volunteering for everything that the bosses threw onto the front desk. She made a point of finding out who was buying what, which investment companies were bulk-buying repossessed properties. *Be interested,* she kept telling herself. She made notes on index cards which she secretly kept in her purse. At lunchtime she went up to the rooftop terrace and pointed out into the cityscape, locating buildings and matching them up with companies, names, saying the name of the property and who owned it out loud, then checking the cards, reprimanding herself if she got it wrong.

She was getting better and better at it, slowly but surely becoming fluent in this new language. She came home with copies of council planning drafts, road proposals, and reclamation notices. By the time she had eaten and looked through these, she just wanted to sit on the sofa and watch TV, drink wine, and be comfortable. The thought of the bar, the clash of loud music and half heard conversations, bumping people and squeezed dancing was something she wanted to get beyond. And she was working hard to do it.

After dinner Martin turned on his computer. Alison scanned another property magazine.

"I don't believe it. That was quick." Martin murmured.

"What's that?"

"They've read 'The Fly Guy' story already and it's going to be in the next edition but …" he trailed off as he read.

"But what? Martin?"

He turned the laptop around and slid it across the table. She put the magazine aside, open on the page with New Acre in bold italics at the top, and pulled it closer. The email read: *Hi Martin. 'The Fly Guy' is a wonderful piece, really creepy and unsettling. We will definitely feature it in the next issue. You have a great tone and the positive feedback on your stories is pouring in. We were just discussing that you should try a full-length piece. Have you ever tried that? A novel? Both Rich and I have worked in publishing for years and we both know agents and publishing houses that would love your work. We could pass their details to you when you are ready to present something. You should think about it. In the meantime, keep sending us the stories!! Best regards, Bubba and Rich,* Noire.

Alison looked up. Martin was beaming.

"So you're—"

"I'm going to write a book!" Martin said loudly. He drummed his hands on the edge of the table. "I'm going to write a book!"

Alison laughed. "You're going to write a book!"

"Ozzy is going to get a kick out of this. He thinks the stories are freaky enough, wait till he hears there'll be a whole book!" Martin jumped out of his seat. "Chapter one. I'm going to get changed for work." He laughed went into the bedroom.

Alison read the email again. A book.

That night when he climbed into bed next to her, she turned to him.

"I've been thinking," she said as she put her leg around his hip, "we should get somewhere together. This place is too small." She kissed him. "Mmm, you are nice and fresh. I do like it when a freshly showered man climbs into my bed. What do you think?"

"Have you seen somewhere?" He rubbed his hand along her thigh, following the contour of her leg.

"Somewhere you'd like to be?"

"I think so. I'll show you. Maybe you could stop working at ICE? Concentrate on the book? It takes me forever to get across town to work from here. This place is on the right side of the city. You hardly ever go back to yours anyway."

"I'd be happy never to back there again," he said. He reached down. She took his hand and pulled it back up, kissing him lightly.

"Hey, mister, take it easy."

"Wherever you are, that's where I want to be," he said.

"Since we've been together," she said, "everything has gone right. So, let's just do it."

"Let's do it," he said.

She kissed him again and turned over. Within minutes she was asleep. Martin lay awake and stared into the darkness.

O   O   O

Alison and Martin drove out from the city, away from the high-rises, the city towers, the endless concrete rows. Out on the motorway the countryside opened out for them. It was summer. The green hills basked in the sunshine, rolling away into the distance like a painting from the brush of a romantic artist. After the roundabout the road rose before them and as they climbed, Martin saw the land undulate below them, the rows of hedges dividing the fields, the freshly dug earth overturned, and the livestock grazing lazily in the lush pasture.

"This is beautiful," Martin said.

"It's in there," Alison replied, gesturing out her window. All along the other side of the road was a grey corrugated fence. Over the top of the fence Martin could see the arms of diggers and the tops of trucks. When they turned into it, they went under a big archway with NEW ACRE across it in embossed metal. Martin pushed himself further back into his seat when he saw what the men and the machines had done. The road turned to a flattened dusty path, and the shells of houses were being constructed. Big lorries with extendable arms trundled past men with fluorescent jackets and helmets.

"They're nearly all sold," Alison said excitedly. "Another six weeks and the whole estate will be finished. Can you believe that? It's so quick."

Scaffolds stood like brittle iron frames, thick pipes were snug in trenches, piles of earth like sentries guarding the plot. All of the houses looked exactly the same, regimented like a newly constructed army, red brick and narrow, roofs tall and steeply angled, standing to attention side by side with just enough room for a cat to squeeze between them. The thin porches over the front doors were like the visors of blackjack dealers. Next to the driveway was a thin rectangle of grass, a bright green ticket beside the smooth black tarmac.

"It's so nice out of the city. Wait till you see inside. It's this one, number eleven."

Martin and Alison got out of the car and walked to the front door. She took out a set of keys and let herself in. Straightaway they were in the front room, with a staircase right in front of them.

"The front room gets all the light, there's no entrance hallway to eat up space and light. Isn't it nice? This staircase gives you a great storage area underneath and on this side, we can have a feature wall. You know? Some really nice textured wallpaper to contrast the walls."

Martin was uncomfortable, like he had wandered into a shop he didn't want anything from but couldn't see an exit. It had the personality of a new cardboard box. They walked through the front room and to the kitchen at the back.

"Oh look, the kitchen is already fitted, and it's bigger than you'd think, isn't it? From the front?"

Through the window he could see the back garden; a narrow stretch of grass with a wooden slat fence around it. There were young trees planted at the end, their branches thin and small, trunks as thin as his wrist, except for one in the middle, which was thicker, whose green branches swept down toward the ground, like the skirt of a girl that was being twirled.

"It's got three rooms upstairs," Alison said. "You can have a room for your writing." Martin followed her up the stairs and looked out the window of the back room, down onto the back garden and over the fence into the other gardens with the same young trees growing at the end of the green strip. This was the only one with the thicker, taller tree. Alison was still talking from the other room.

"This one is definitely the master bedroom. The wardrobes are sunk into the walls."

From here he could see the layout of the estate and the countryside beyond. Martin knew that all of the construction he could see from the window was all based on plans which would result in buildings identical to the one in which he stood, slotted together like the cells in a beehive.

Alison's voice came to him again. "It's great, I love the fact that it's brand new. I will have to show you the contract."

Martin considered this. This space where he stood now, elevated from the ground, had not been occupied before. The first ghosts to haunt this place would be theirs. Martin began to see the potential of a soulless shell. They could fill it with themselves, grow a new soul within it. There was nothing here to connect him with a past, only a future.

"And the attic, the attic is perfect for converting. It could be another room, or maybe that could be your writing room, and the bathroom has a lot of light, no bath, but we don't do baths anyway, do we?"

He looked out the window at the other houses, all standing to empty attention around him. They would all be filled, filled with the potential of the lives within them. Each person in each house will leave their own ghost behind. The houses may look identical on the outside but soon their insides would all be different, changed forever.

Alison came in behind him and said, "Did you hear me? About the attic? Have you seen the bathroom?"

Martin didn't turn around, just replied, "I know how I'm going to start the book."

CHAPTER FOUR

Lucy. Martin changed her name twice in three different drafts. Anna. Nicola. *Lucy*. He watched her, writing as a breeze from the opened window stroked her hair and shadows moved across her sleeping face; her delicate hands trembled as she held the syringe and all the tension of the moment; her echoing hours, waiting for Gregor.

O   O   O

She hears a knock. Where is it coming from? Somewhere in the distance. Focus. In the room? No. Again, two knocks. Archie will answer it. She feels around for the thin cover and pulls it over her. Archie's feet thump down the hallway. She can let her mind slump back, and everything slides away from her, like the tide going out.

Archie looks through the spyhole. In the dark corridor is the skeleton of Bradley. The blue tracksuit hangs like plastic bags on a scarecrow. He picks the loose skin at the side of his face. He shifts his weight from foot to foot. Archie pulls back the bolt lock and opens the door.

"You took your time," he says.

Bradley just looks back at Archie and scratches his face. That's the wrong answer, his eyes say. Archie puffs his chest out. He is in his vest, underpants, and socks, with remote control in hand.

"What? You needing another hit? You going to come and get it then? This shit won't just walk out of here and sell itself."

Bradley takes a step back. Archie steps into the hallway, the carpet sticking to his socks. Bradley turns his head and closes his eyes, his face contorting to a grimace. *Fucking junkies,* Archie thinks. He reaches his hand to Bradley's shoulder to pull him inside, then sees movement from the corner of his eye.

A bright light of pain blinds him, his right knee explodes, and everything in his head is sharp and jagged. As he falls he is caught by strong arms and his mind wildly flips to the cover of a romance novel. He looks up at the face of his attacker. Gregor, with a lump hammer, dragging him one-handed back into the flat.

Archie throws his head around desperately looking for a way to break free, he reaches out to catch the doorframe, but the pain has broken up his senses and his arms flail uselessly. In the corridor he sees Bradley still standing like a plastic Halloween figure with a frozen fear in his eyes. Bradley mouths, "I'm sorry."

Gregor kicks the door shut.

Archie's looks up again to see Gregor's face in grim concentration as he raises his arm. Archie tries to turn away but Gregor's elbow lands on his nose. Blood fills his mouth and he chokes and tries to cough it out. Bolts of pain rush up from his leg and he gasps and gags. Gregor drops him to the floor.

Gregor pushes the door to his left. Old water stands in the bath, grey with a thin film of brown and white scum on the surface. He turns. There is a door on the right. He steps over Archie who writhes around in his own blood, gurgling and coughing.

He listens at the door for a second, then steps back and kicks it open. In the dark the blonde girl screams. She is crouching on the other side of the bed, the sheet twisted around her, trying to hide behind it. He strides across the room and grabs her arm. She is wearing only a pair of boxer shorts and the sheet trails behind her as he pulls her screaming to her feet, out of the dark and into the light of the hallway. When she sees Archie lying there like roadkill, twitching and bleeding, she falls silent and pulls the sheet around her to cover her breasts.

Gregor pulls Archie to his feet and juggles him down the hallway. Archie spills into the main room, illuminated only by the television.

Archie moans hoarsely, "Fuck, fuck."

Gregor shouts at the blonde, "Get in here."

She jumps, then starts to move. He points at the lump hammer at her feet. "Bring it," he commands.

She picks up the hammer as she comes into the room. A shouting and knocking on the wall starts from next door. Gregor points next to Archie.

"Sit down."

She sits and Archie whimpers and reaches out to her. She recoils, disgusted by his broken face. Gregor stands over them. The television screen behind Gregor fills the wall. It's on pause. A bikini-clad woman in heels is walking through a warehouse toward a group of white men. Archie coughs more blood onto the floor and sees his knee for the first time. A bone sticks out from beneath it, poking through his skin. He screams.

From next door the sound of the television being turned up full comes through the walls, the sound of cars and sirens and gunshots swimming around the room. Gregor squats down in front of Lucy. His eyes are deep brown, and his short hair is greying at the temples. His hands are tanned and smooth as he takes the hammer from her, placing it out of reach. He reaches inside his black leather jacket, and with a single movement and a sound like a whip pulls out a flick knife. Its blade reflects and shines. It is smooth at the top and serrated at the base. He holds it in front of the blonde before turning to Archie.

Archie tries to struggle away, but Gregor grabs his chin and holds his face still. Archie's face is cracked in the middle like a ripped photograph and his cheekbones are swelling up beneath his eyes. One of his eyes has turned red. It looks like the blue pupil is floating on a ball of blood. Gregor presses the edge of the blade to Archie's face.

"Where is it?"

Archie splutters and grabs Gregor's forearm to try and break his grip. Gregor grips his face tighter and pushes him back on the floor, turning his head and holding his face to the floor with his knee. The girl leans forward, her eyes widening as Gregor pulls Archie's ear tight and with one cut, slices through the cartilage. Archie's mouth opens wide and a tremulous shriek rushes out, a higher pitch than before, the rasp in his throat like a drill behind the screams.

33

The volume from next door's television ramps up and noise swills around the room. Gregor turns to the girl, the piece of ear in his hand. Drops of blood are spattered on her face.

"What's your name?" he says.

"What?" she shouts back.

"What is your name?" he shouts.

"Lucy," she yells. She sees him say it to himself, as if trying it out.

He closes the flick knife and puts it back in his pocket. As Archie's scream subsides, Gregor takes his knee from his face and pulls him up to a sitting position. He holds half of Archie's right ear in front of his face.

"Where is it?"

Archie clutches the side of his head, coating his hand in a bloody glove.

"The coke is all here, right by the table."

"Not the fucking coke, Archie, you know what I'm talking about."

"I don't know. I don't know what you want."

Gregor yanks his head back as though preparing him for slaughter. Archie's face is sticky with blood and saliva and mucus, and he is spitting as he breathes, heaving foul coppery breath.

"Where is it?"

"What? What? Tell me what the fuck … I don't know what the fuck—"

"Spiral, Archie. Where is it?"

"I don't know, Gregor, I don't …"

Lucy shouts and points. "The sink. Under the sink. The bag."

She speaks with an accent, a sharpness which Gregor recognises as deep Eastern Europe, maybe Russia. He knows why she is there, sleeping in Archie's bed. Another junkie.

But there is something more about her. How was she so calm? Once she saw Archie was down, she stopped screaming. She knows him for the lowlife that he is.

Gregor lets go of Archie, who flops back. The channel in the room next door has changed and now there is an excited voice, bells, and applause. He moves over in front of Lucy again. She is young. There is a strength in her which cannot be taught. He takes hold of her face. She doesn't resist but holds his gaze. He considers her for a moment like a breeder considering a new animal. Then he turns and goes to the kitchen.

In the dark space under the sink among detergents and plastic bags there is a dark hold-all. He unzips it and looks into it before zipping it back up and coming back to Archie. He pulls Archie's limp body back up.

"Is it all here?"

Archie is choking as he tries to respond. His voice is a rasp.

"Where did you ... that bag is not mine, I don't know man. Gregor, please, I never saw the fucking—"

"You always have been shit at lying. Don't lie to me Archie."

He flicks the blade out again, next to Archie's bloodied ear. Archie shakes. His head rolls back and he splutters, "Please, no, no, it's all there, take anything, anything ..." Gregor lets him fall back onto the floor.

He stands Lucy up and slides his coat off his shoulders and onto hers. The noises from the neighbours disappear. It is quiet for a moment as she feels the warmth of Gregor seep from his jacket into her skin. Then the silence breaks, she hears laughter and applause from next door. Gregor zips up the jacket.

"Have you got shoes?"

Archie blubbers, "Bitch ... you fucking bitch...."

Gregor hands Lucy the bag and picks up the lump hammer. He stands over him.

"You always were a fucking low life piece of shit, Archie. What a favour I'd be doing the world to just take you out now."

Lucy stands beside him, wild-haired and spattered with blood. "Go on, do it," she says.

Gregor grabs the hold-all and takes Lucy by the elbow away from Archie and into the corridor. He lets the door stand wide.

Archie stays on the ground, turning on his side, heaving and retching through his swollen face in the light of the television screen. Lucy waves to him over her shoulder as she and Gregor head for the stairs, and out onto the street. They walk together through the noise and uneven light. Outlined in dull pulsing neon, they pass, as if ghosts, along the peopled street.

CHAPTER FIVE

Martin looked out the window of the back upstairs room—his writing room. The house didn't seem as far out of the city as the first time. From the outside, as they drove away from it, the city seemed smaller, not bigger. Alison's flat seemed squashed, layered with a grime which could never be removed, just the build-up of so much living. It was as if the city was encased in a plastic dome, filtering the light of the sun, only letting through enough light essential for survival.

Outside the dome, in the open country, the light was fuller, more vital. The air moved differently, it didn't feel like it was recycled. It wasn't heavy with smells and sounds of the street, it moved over the fields and through the trees around the estate and then it blew on, further away, followed by fresh winds and new air.

From the back bedroom window Martin could see the fields beyond the red brick estate. On a hill in the distance was the edge of a forest; the trees were dark and thick and covered the brow of the hill. At the other corner of the window, away on the other hill in the distance, stood four wind turbines, their propellers spinning, their thick white trunks jutting out of the hillside like the inner machinery of the earth revealed. When the clouds moved, Martin could see their shadows move across the hillsides like giant ghosts moving silently over the land.

When they moved in Martin only had a suitcase of clothes, a bag of books, and a laptop. Alison had boxes and boxes of clothes, toiletries, property magazines, office papers, ornaments, and her favourite dish set. It seemed like a lot when they had packed it, but when they got it in to the new house, the boxes made a little pyramid in the middle of the front room, taking up hardly any space at all. They had so little that it only took them a day to move in their furniture, unpack, and arrange everything.

Martin planned to bring his table from his bedsit to write on, but Alison offered to buy him a new one as a housewarming present and he accepted. He only stepped into his old bedsit to empty the wardrobe and the bookshelf. It took him five minutes, and then he closed the door and walked down the iron steps into Alison's car. She looked surprised.

"One bag?"

"That's it," said Martin.

"Are you leaving anything behind?"

"No. Just a past that doesn't want to be remembered."

She started the car and pulled away. "So poetic. Still, though. One bag?"

O O O

Thanks to Alison's position at the property agents they were the first to move in. The estate was finished and the trucks and diggers were gone. On that first night, neither of them could sleep, so Martin and Alison got out of their new bed and walked around the empty New Acre Estate. It felt like a film set, unused, unreal. It still could be dismantled and taken away, and another scene set up. The moon was bright and the sky was clear and the street lights were on, shining just for them. It was just them and their shadows moving through the brand new streets.

They chased each other like children and shouted *Hello!* down the road, listening to the echo roll and bounce around. They walked down each identical cul-de-sac, and Alison said how easy it was to imagine that they were the only two left, that the world was deserted except for them. Martin said he was getting cold and they headed back to their house.

It did feel like time had stood still, like they were outside of the normal laws of the world. They had not heard a single sound besides their own voices.

When they got back to number eleven and closed the door Martin was glad to be inside. He could relax. He had become nervous outside. The black windows, without curtains or lights had the pattern of faces looking at him as he passed. There was something inside the houses, just out of sight. The darkness within the empty houses was swollen and alive.

Over the days and weeks that followed, the houses filled with couples and families, and the darkness was pushed from the houses and streets, forced further and further back into the fields and hills behind the estate. He watched the vans filled with possessions unload as the streams of people's lives ran to identical doors. Furniture was tilted and squeezed through doorways, appliances were flipped on, boxes opened and unpacked.

Martin watched all of this from the upstairs window. Neighbours did not come out and help or greet the newcomers. No-one called next door to say hello and introduce themselves. They unpacked their cars and emptied the removal vans, then went inside and closed the door. At night, no-one walked outside. The furthest anyone would walk was to the door of their car. All of the lives on the New Acre Estate were being lived behind closed doors, tucked safely into the new houses on the hillside.

Martin continued to write the story of Gregor Alskev. Every day Alison caught the train into the city and he filled the computer screen with words. He didn't have to clear away his notes or shut down his computer when Alison came home, he just moved downstairs and spent the evening with her. Gregor Alskev stayed up in the writing room.

CHAPTER SIX

G regor and Lucy drive away from the heart of the city, with the great broad river to their left. Old spreading trees shelter the road and the houses hide behind ornate walls. Above the branches Lucy sees thin clouds passing over the stars like smoke from a distant fire. She imagines that it comes from Archie's filthy flat, that everything in that place is now ash. She closes her eyes and imagines flames curling up the side of the wall-sized plasma TV, melting the image of the woman. She imagines the blood on the floor heating up, the thick red pool bubbling.

Gregor turns the car suddenly right. She opens her eyes and sees a long shadowed driveway, with dense hedges on either side. In front is just blackness.

"Where are we going?"

Gregor doesn't answer.

O O O

Martin stopped writing. Through the window behind him the sky had darkened to a deep charcoal blue and the glow of the computer screen in front of him was the only light in the room. He turned off the computer and went downstairs.

He was still watching the car pass through the city as he kissed Alison's cheek and asked her how her day was. As Alison put their plates on the table and sat opposite him he was on the bonnet of the car, looking at Gregor and Lucy through the windscreen, rocking and bumping with the rolls of the road, the warmth of the engine beneath him, feeling the city wind in his face.

As Alison told him about where she had been thinking of going on holiday this year, Martin heard the rattling drone of the engine, the wheels on the street, the buzz of the city. He saw the pale drawn skin of Lucy, watched the changing reflections of the passing shop windows in her eyes, studied her wide mouth and angular cheek-bones, her thin nose and the dark long lashes. He leaned in through the windscreen to see the colour of her eyes, green with flecks of silver, like sunlight shining on a shallow coral reef. He followed the line of her profile as she looked out the side window, so defined, her sharp chin and elegant neck. He saw her turn to Gregor and he heard her voice as she said slowly, "I want to go to Mexico." Alison was filling his wine glass and saying, "It's expensive, but wouldn't it be something?" Lucy turned away to look at the passing city and said quietly, "Mexico looks so good."

O   O   O

The headlights show a set of tall gates which open as they approach. An old Georgian style house is revealed, with an arch over the front door. Gregor pulls up and walks around to her side of the car, opening the car door. Cold air hits her and she pulls the jacket closer around her, bringing her knees up to her chest.

"Come on," he says, "it's warm inside." He takes her by the arm and they walk across the gravel to the front door. He switches the light on and the hallway appears. It is big enough to hold Archie's apartment, with warm amber walls and a wooden floor. A gloriously patterned rug with swirling patterns of shimmering gold on deep violet runs all the way to the foot of the stairs. As they walk across it Lucy looks at her dirty bare feet on the thick weave and finds herself squeezing Gregor's arm. She stops. He glances at her, then walks ahead.

"We'll get you some clothes upstairs."

As she follows him through the grand hallway she sees a door ajar, opening to a parlour room. The stairs are elegant with a carved banister, which is smooth and warm to touch, like recently bathed skin. There is a little landing area and the stairs turn back toward the front of the house. Lucy follows Gregor as he goes up another flight, turning lights on as he goes. At the top, the walls are a yellow cream from the ceiling down to a dado rail and beneath the wooden rail is wallpaper, textured ridges of swirling paisley patterns encrusted with purple and silver.

"Do you live here alone?"

"Not anymore."

There are four doors and Gregor leads her to the furthest one on the right. He opens it and gestures inside. Lucy walks into a bedroom. A mound of pillows and cushions cover the double bed. On the wall is a painted portrait of a little girl, her blond hair tied into pretty plaits. Her painted face is on the verge of tears. Lucy touches the canvas.

"Who is that?"

Gregor is still standing in the doorway. "Who does it look like? It looks like you maybe?"

A large window is sunk into the deep outer wall, with a cushioned sill. Lucy can see the driveway and the black four-by-four, the gate and beyond. The lights of the city pulse in the distance, from the high rises and the houses, like every building has a fire inside, hollowing it out. She turns and Gregor is standing in the doorway with a blue tracksuit in his hands. He hands it to her.

"Here, try this," he says, "we'll get you fixed up in the morning. I'm going to get some food. Make yourself at home."

Then he is gone, padding away down the hall. The front door shuts.

Next to the bedroom door Lucy sees a circular mirror, the ring frame of which looks like it is spun from golden strands of silk. Half-closed eyes squint out from dark pits and her cheekbones protrude above hollow cheeks. Gregor's car rumbles down the rattling gravel, past the iron gates, which then whir slowly closed. She is alone. A grey ghoul stares at her from the golden frame. Is this what Archie has done to her? She turns away from the mirror.

She puts the bottom half of the tracksuit on and pulls Gregor's jacket tighter around her; she is getting used to its smell. She goes back out to the landing and opens one of the doors to a pristine bathroom, white tiled with a large corner bath with steps into it. Towels are folded neatly over a rail on the wall, matching the pale blue colour of the sink and toilet. Through another door is a large room with a running machine and a weights bench, a blue mat on the floor and a TV screen that fills the wall. She tries the other two doors but they are locked.

She kneels and runs her fingers over the swirling silver and purple on the bottom half of the walls. Then she stands and goes back down the stairs. At the bottom of the staircase she turns right through to the TV room. There are two large sofas, a big screen television, and a wall of books. As far as she can make out they are all biographies: Winston Churchill, Nelson Mandela, Ted Bundy, Dennis Nilsen. Heroes, statesmen, and killers side by side.

Lucy walks through double glass doors into the kitchen. She flicks the light switch and a smooth light grows from the bulbs embedded in the ceiling revealing a mesh of the old and the new: a stone sink with a hand basin that looks like it has been carved from an ancient mountainside, and a sleek coffee machine with a green digital display. The cupboards are muted green and stretch from floor to ceiling and match the colour of the pots and pans hanging from hooks on the opposite wall. In the centre of the room a stone plinth like a derelict Greek column rises and is topped with green marble, smooth, glossy, and embedded with the crisscross of fine white threads.

Lucy touches the smooth surface. She sees it as a piece of a distant planet, the reflections from the bulb above like the glow of a sun, the web of white lines scars on the rock surface and dry river beds, a landscape she will never experience.

Every surface in the kitchen is clean. There are no crumbs, no coffee cup rings on the worktops. The fridge, tall and silver, stands in the corner. Lucy sees her distorted reflection. Her head looks tiny and squeezed, the jacket she is wearing bulges and grows, and her blue track-suited legs look short and fat. As she moves, her reflection elongates and slides, her body follows her head, squashed and stretched, and she walks to the back of the kitchen through an archway and into the dining room. There is a long table of thick old wood and sturdy wooden chairs sit heavily on the stone floor. Off to the left another archway shows the first steps of a staircase curving out of sight.

On the other side of the table are glass sliding doors, and Lucy sees herself again, skinny and grotesque. She walks toward herself before cupping her hands around her eyes and peering through the glass. She sees grass and overgrown flower beds, old trees, and a statue of two lovers in an embrace, their two bodies joining at the hips and melding into one, curving gracefully into the earth. Lucy pulls at the doors but they are locked.

She walks back through the kitchen and out into the hallway where she came in and she sees the door of the parlour again, half-open. Inside is a room painted white and a large sleek table, dark polished wood with office-style chairs around it. On the wall hangs a painting, luscious but elusive, a web of blues, greys and reds, with streaks of light and shapes appearing and disappearing behind each other. The more she looks at it, the more the colours move and shapes slide across the canvas. Lucy is overcome, and a dizziness sways her.

She backs out of the room to the hallway until she feels the thick rug beneath her feet. Then she lies down. There is not a sound. It is a silence inside a beautiful ornate box, sealed tight. With her cheek on the violet weave with golden spirals, she closes her eyes. She sees again the flames rise in Archie's little flat, burning, burning.

CHAPTER SEVEN

Now that he had his own writing space, Martin could let Alison go to bed and work. If she wanted to watch something on TV that he didn't like, whereas before he would have stayed on the sofa with her telling her what a waste of time the programme was, now he could go up to his writing room and close the door.

In the six months that had passed since they moved in, Alison noticed that he was talking less. To her anyway. Sometimes she would come to his door before saying goodnight and hear him muttering. She would open the door a bit and he would jump up to kiss her goodnight.

"You not coming to bed then?" she would say.

"In a bit, babe," was his usual reply. At the threshold they would hug and then he would close the door again and she would turn and go to the bedroom.

There on the bedside table were the magazines and catalogues of things to make their new home more comfortable, more beautiful, more individual. She would browse through them until she felt tired enough to turn the light off. In the hallway a thin strip of light escaped from beneath Martin's door, and Alison could hear the *tap-tapping* on the keyboard.

This was how it went on, Martin in his room with the door closed and Alison on the outside hearing the *tap-tap-tapping*. Martin wrote and wrote until he had completed a first draft. He sent it through to *Noire*.

Alison stood in the doorway. "Does this mean I'll get you back? You need a break anyway, it can't be good for you to be locked away in that room all day and night. When will you know?"

"When they've had time to read it, I guess."

"Well they can take their time, so I've got you all to myself."

O   O   O

The first time Alison had ever heard Martin mention Lucy it was a Friday night and Alison had still not changed out of her suit. When she got through the door from work she was ready to just get changed and go out for some food and some drinks. She had texted Martin to tell him not to bother with dinner, that they would go out, so she was expecting him to be changed, for the place to be clean, for her evening to be ready to begin. Instead Martin was still in his slacks and his dressing gown. He was sitting at the kitchen table with the laptop open in front of him. She knew there was something wrong. He showed her the email from *Noire*.

Gregor Alskev is great, it said, but what has happened to the detective? Henry Bloomburg is the one we fell in love with through your stories in Noire. *We were expecting a story about him.*

"But that's okay," she said, "that's positive. Look, they fell in love with the detective. In love. Sweetheart, that's great." She really wanted to get out of her shoes and her suit. "You just have to figure it out. Let's go out and talk about it at Giorgio's or the Mexican place. Come on, get your things on."

"But it's Lucy's story," he said. She stopped with her foot on the stairs.

"Who's Lucy?"

He didn't answer.

O   O   O

They went out to Giorgio's. There was a wait for a table, so as they sat at the bar, Alison asked again.

"Who's Lucy?"

Martin rubbed his forehead and closed his eyes. "She's involved with Gregor."

"And it's her story?"

"Yeah, it's her story."

"Well, everybody's got different ideas about stories, don't they? You can't expect them to think exactly the same way as you. Do you have to do a new one? Can't you just change it? Can you do it that way?"

A smiling barmaid slid a small plate of black olives in front of them, each one speared on a cocktail stick. Her hair was brown and tied back in a ponytail. Her complexion was tanned and her teeth seemed almost to glow white in the low light of the restaurant. Alison smiled back. Martin shifted on his bar stool.

"Your parents are still together," he said.

Alison nodded. He knew they were. He had met them both at their house. Well, their house-boat. They had spent two days there, on the lake. Alison had felt so happy, finally bringing a man she could say she loved to meet her parents, and she knew Martin would love it. He did.

It was a two storey wooden house set on a floating platform. For the first twenty minutes or so, Martin just stood in front of the wall of glass that looked out on to the lake and the mountains beyond. The water came right up to the base of the wall and swans and ducks floated past, just a few feet away. The sunlight hitting the water bounced through the window and around the room, throwing intensities of light like a diamond turned in the hand of a jeweller.

Her mother said to her as they prepared dinner, "He's very sensitive, isn't he? Quiet. Just lovely."

Martin and her father didn't have much to say to each other at the start. By the end of the second day they were playing chess and drinking brandy while discussing the politics of the impending energy crisis.

"Your parents are still together because their story stayed the same. Mine broke up because I changed their stories. For my mother, after I was born, the story was now about me, do you see? Everything was now in relation to that. But for my dad the growth of a child was too slow, too predictable a plot."

Martin had never gone into much detail about his family. Like Alison he was an only child, but his upbringing was very different.

His father had left and come back several times, and each time his mother had accepted him back. Alison got the impression that he was a womaniser who probably had more than one family on the go, but Martin still held an obvious affection for him. His mother had several relationships with different men, and Alison knew that Martin resented that. But each relationship ended as soon as his father came back, and then within months he would be gone again.

In all the time Alison had known Martin he had never talked of contacting either of his parents. She thought it odd that he was talking about them now. She was chewing on the olives and placing the sticks neatly in a row at the side of the plate.

"Hmm, it seems like they changed their own stories. I mean, you didn't consciously do anything to make them act the way they did."

"No, but the very fact that I was there changed everything for them."

"I don't see what you're driving at. What has this got to do with the story you are writing?"

"If Bloomburg comes into it, just the fact that he is there will change everything. Everyone's story will change." The smiling bar lady was back and asked them did they want to top up their glasses. They did, and while she poured the wine she apologised for the wait. She was pretty sure that a table was coming free any minute now. It is usually very busy on a Friday. She spoke with a thick Australian accent.

Alison said, "Thanks. We usually book, but tonight we just came out."

"I know," said the waitress, "it's not like you can plan everything is it? I mean, look at me. I was only going to stay here two weeks. That was two years ago." They laughed.

"Something must have caught your interest then," Martin said.

"Well, something or someone," she replied, raising her eyebrows and smiling her neon smile. "I will let you know soon as that table is free, guys," and she walked away.

"But Martin, you are in control. It's up to you what happens," said Alison.

"Ah, that's it, that's not the point. The point is, the point is—" Martin ate another olive and placed his little stick down across the neat line Alison had created on the side of the plate, like a bar in a fence, "—the story is about Lucy. If Bloomburg comes along, everyone's story will change." He pushed the plate away and turned around in his bar stool, scanning the restaurant.

Couples and small clusters of people ate and talked and poured each other's wine and water. *How many stories were changing right now, in this room? How many people would rise after this meal, wipe their mouths with their napkin and pay the bill, with their lives altered? None,* Martin thought. *Because even when people made decisions it was not until the action was carried through that change actually occurred. And actions can be deferred. How many life-changing moments are there in a lifetime?* He saw a waiter place a fresh tablecloth and wine glasses on a table for two near the door. He turned back to the bar.

Alison said, "You're making this hard for yourself. Just give them another story then. Change it. Or start a new one. Give them what they want. They love the detective, they love him." She chewed the last olive and put the little stick next to the others, and moved the one Martin had placed across so that it was standing in line.

The bar lady was back.

"Table six is ready now," she said. "Sorry again about the wait."

As Alison gathered her bag and her wine glass, Martin said, "And you, are you still with the person you stayed here for? I mean, did it work out?"

Alison looked up sharply, and said, "Martin, that's none of your—" but the bar lady cut her off.

"Oh no, it's okay," she said. She was blushing, crimson showing on her tanned cheeks. "It didn't work out with that guy. He turned out to be a total loser, but I'm with an amazing fella now that I would never have met if I hadn't stayed in the first place. So it did work out. Not the way I thought it was going to. Not quite a fairy tale, but—"

Alison put her hand on the bar lady's arm and said, "Really, I must apologise for him."

The bar lady just smiled. The redness was fading from her cheeks now. "That's okay, really. Number six is over there by the door. Enjoy your meal."

As the evening turned, Martin couldn't help but look around at the other diners. He watched them chew and mumble, saw heads tilt and eyebrows rise as they listened and were listened to. He saw one woman put down her fork, reach across and put her hand on the hand of the woman sitting opposite. The man at the next table was twisting and twisting his napkin in his hands just below the table edge. He and Alison talked about the present, guessed about the future, and laughed about the past. Maybe he was wrong about no-one in this room having life-changing moments.

A lifetime is long. He was thinking too quickly. He was thinking of change as being something instant, but change can happen at a creeping pace. It depends on the pressure. Change takes pressure and pressure needs to build. That build was one long moment, he just didn't know when it would end.

Later, while Alison was looking at the dessert menu, she said, "If you do continue the Lucy story, don't kill her off."

Martin sat back in his chair, then forward. "What? Kill her off?"

"Well I've only read a few of your stories, but it seems like if there's an attractive girl, she gets killed off."

"Come on. How can I kill her off if it's her story?"

Alison shrugged. She looked back at the menu. Martin leaned back again.

"I'll just have a coffee, I'm full. You go ahead."

"What age is Lucy?"

"Em, about your age actually, but I've been thinking of making her younger."

"And what does she do? She doesn't work in property, does she, Martin?"

"No, no, of course not. That would be far too … no, don't worry, babe. I can be creative you know."

"I know, I know."

CHAPTER EIGHT

When Gregor comes through the door, he picks the sleeping Lucy up and carries her into the lounge, putting her on one of the sofas. He disappears and then comes back with a blanket which he puts over her. He disappears again.

Lucy hears the sounds of plates and cupboard doors, something being poured. Gregor comes through from the kitchen with a tray full of food, all in little silver trays. The smell makes Lucy's stomach leap and she sits up. Her head feels too heavy for her body. She is suddenly aware of a great hollowness which has opened up inside her. Gregor puts the tray in front of her and passes her a plate.

"Go ahead," he says, "it's late, I know, but it's really good, especially this."

He takes a pancake roll from one of the trays and starts to eat. Lucy does the same. Inside the soft pancake is spinach and goat cheese, with the woody, fleshy meat of mushroom. The taste sends shivers to the bottom of her skull. She finishes the rolled pancake in two mouthfuls. She picks up a handful of light batter parcels and feels her teeth crunch into sharp explosions of anchovy and garlic.

Lucy starts to eat voraciously, grabbing some thinly sliced fried potato in a tomato dressing, feeling the kick of peppercorns send spikes of flavour through the roof of her mouth, up behind her eyes, and directly into the front of her brain, knocking at the inside of her forehead. She is picking up prawns in oil, tearing soft fresh bread, taking food from the foil dishes in both hands, luxuriating in the strong flavours, the salty roughness of cured pork, the juices of cherry tomatoes are dripping from her mouth down her chin.

She looks up to see Gregor sitting on the floor, cross-legged, with his rolled pancake still in his hand, watching her devour this food, but she doesn't care. A pressure has been released. Oils and juices coat her fingers and smear across her face as she wipes her cheeks, as she cries and laughs and eats.

O O O

The next day Lucy wakes under the warm weight of a thick duvet. Her clothes are still on. Her face muscles ache, her jaw is stiff, and her head pounds as she squints around the room, at the brass lamp on the bedside table, the little girl on the wall, and the window, through which she can now see a blue sky.

There is a dressing gown on the window seat. She takes off the tracksuit leggings and boxer shorts and puts it on. She goes downstairs, following the smell of fresh coffee to the kitchen. She walks through the door then steps back again, stepping behind the frame.

Inside, Gregor is standing at the centre plinth with two other people. There is a black case on the green marble top. He has seen her back out of the doorway and gestures her in. The other two turn to face her. One is a woman, short and stubby with a massive shock of thick dark hair which is standing at impossible angles. She greets Lucy with a big smile. The other is a man, lean and angular, with a shaven head, slim glasses, orange t-shirt, braces, and a suit jacket. The woman stands as if to attention, and the man seems to be leaning against an invisible wall.

"This is Ula, and this is Franz," he says. "Ula will take care of your hair and stuff, and Franz will fit you. Tell them what you would like, anything. I trust them. You can."

He hands her a coffee and points to the table near the glass doors. Outside the doors the garden is green and glistening with freshly fallen rain. Next to the table there is a rail of clothes and on the tabletop sits a pile of materials.

"There's food in the fridge. I have to go out."

Gregor takes the black case and points to a mobile phone on the green marble.

"If you want to call me, call me. It's the only number." He turns to Ula and Franz. "Whatever she wants."

They nod, Ula enthusiastically, and Franz languidly. Gregor walks from the kitchen out to the hallway. The door shuts.

Franz looks her coolly up and down, and Ula comes to her, arms outstretched. "Gregor is right, you are beautiful. We'll take care of you. You are going to look amazing sweetie," she says. Lucy holds her dressing gown tight around her.

"I have nothing ... nothing to wear."

Franz says, "I've got it darling. Let's start comfy, the high fashion can wait. Let's find out what you like. We can have some fun with it. While the cat's away."

He turns to the dining table and picks up an armful of clothes and materials. He is smiling now, patting and stroking the clothes on his arm.

"Take your coffee darling, shall we adjourn to your boudoir? Ula, can you bring some of those sweet pastries? We can do fitting and pastries. Upstairs?"

O O O

Gregor stays the first two nights with her in the house, both nights wishing her good night before going into his room and closing the door.

When he is in the house, he is walking in circles around the central plinth in the kitchen talking on the phone, or typing on his computer in the TV room. Once she opens the door of the upstairs gym room and sees him on the running machine, his muscular frame keeping a steady rhythm, sweat making a V down his broad back, while some singing woman is being judged by four people behind an elaborate desk on the huge TV screen.

The rest of the week, he is gone.

During that first week Lucy spends a lot of time in bed, sleeping for hours and hours during the day, moving from one side of the double bed to the other, waking up sideways, looking from underneath the thick duvet at the cream walls, the cushioned window seat, the portrait of the little girl on the brink of tears. Her muscles ache and her head pounds.

At night she goes downstairs and sits in front of the big flat screen switching between channels. At these times, late at night in the empty house, she gets an urge to call Archie, to score a baggie or some pills. In her mind, he's still lying in a pool of blood in his vest and pants, his nose cracked in the middle, fire rising up the walls around him as he blubbers and moans.

She wishes sleep would come. Hours stretch. She wants something to surrender to, something to drown in. When sleep does come, she dreams, and when she wakes, she remembers her dreams. It's been a long time since she has, and she doesn't want to. She longs for the dreamless blackness, the escape from her mind.

By the third night alone, she's been through every drawer in every open room, searching for something to take. The vain hope that Gregor has a stash of something keeps her looking, and she checks and rechecks, but she finds nothing. On the shelves are books and art pieces, and when Lucy opens the drawers they're all empty, but for the instructions for the television entertainment system in the TV room and a pair of leather gloves still in plastic wrapping. In the kitchen behind the cupboard doors there are stacks of plates and rows of glasses, upside down, never used.

On the evening of her fourth day alone in the big house, Gregor is back, preparing some food and putting clothes through the wash. There is a box on the marble plinth in the kitchen. Popping out of the top of the box are celery stalks, foil wrapping, and the tops of wine bottles.

Lucy takes a bottle and opens it immediately. Gregor sees this and smiles, taking glasses from the shelf. Lucy pours and starts drinking. Gregor picks up his glass and takes a sip.

When the spinning of the drier finishes he takes the clothes out and checks them, looking closely at the fabric before shaking his head and taking them out to the garden. He takes the grill off a barbecue bowl and puts the trousers and shirt in and splashes them with lighter fluid. He throws in a match, and as the flames catch, strolls back through the glass double doors, into the kitchen and stirs the pot.

"I need more clothes," she says.

"In the morning Franz will be back with a selection of clothes for you. This is smelling really good, I hope you're hungry."

"You don't have any music in this house."

"There's the TV."

"That's not the same."

"What do you mean? There's music channels on the TV."

"You don't own any music."

"No. I don't own any music. There's music on the TV if I want it."

"If you hear something you like don't you want to own it, to hear it again?"

"No."

"When you do watch TV, you only watch crappy reality shows."

"True. Not all crappy. Some are really good."

"How about good movies? Or horrors, or comedies?"

"Well you get all that in real life. Why bother looking at or reading something someone's made up when you can see something that really happened? Isn't that more interesting?"

"There's something wrong with you. Something missing."

Gregor laughs and stirs the pot some more, leaning his head over the steam to smell the aromas. He puts in a handful more of herbs. Through the glass double doors she can see the flames leaping up from the barbecue bowl.

"What kind of music do you like?" Gregor asks.

"Old stuff, swing."

"Old stuff? Like what?"

"Swing."

"I don't know what that is."

"You don't know swing? Like Frank Sinatra? They don't play it much on the radio."

"Wasn't he an actor? Black and white? I didn't know he did music. How did you get to hear it? Aren't you way too young to be into that stuff?"

"My daddy used to play. What age do you think I am?"

"I think you are nineteen or twenty. What age do you think I am?"

"I don't know. Too old for me."

Gregor laughs again, still stirring the pot.

Now she changes the tone of her voice, the words get longer, more needy. Her accent becomes more pronounced as she says,

"Gregor, I don't feel good. I need some medicine."

"That's okay. It's okay not to feel good for a while. Give yourself a few more days. As long as you eat well, really, that makes all the difference. Come on, we will eat at the big table."

Lucy watches as he lays out place mats and knives and forks and spoons on the thick wooden table, before going back and stirring the pot again. She's finished her glass of wine. She pours some more.

"My mother showed me how to make chicken casserole when I was a boy. Of course, back then she picked the herbs from the garden and the verges. She made special dumplings but I've never been able to get them right. I did try, but I've given up on them, but the casserole ..."

He lifts the stirring spoon to his lips and tastes.

"Well, you'll see, it's really something, even without my mother's herbs. It's missing something, ha ha, like me, but it still tastes ... mmm, it's nearly ready."

"I'm not hungry. These lights are too much. I need something else, not food. Everything's sharp. Every corner's ... cutting me. I need something. You know? Wine isn't enough. Do you know? Have you ever felt like this?"

Gregor dims the lights and takes her by the elbow, walking her across the room to the big wooden table.

"Food. Really, the secret is in good food."

As she sits she sees that the flames outside are dying down and night is coming in.

"Franz will have some great clothes for you, I can guarantee it. He knows what looks good. That'll make you feel better, won't it?"

He pours the rich red wine into her half-empty glass, filling it back to the top.

"I will be away tomorrow but I can come back late. He'll be here during the day and I'll get back later. You'll feel better tomorrow. Come on let's eat."

"You don't know anything about me. Do you even want to know anything about me? You haven't asked about my family, or where I'm from, or Archie, or anything? Don't you want to know about me?"

"You can tell me whatever you want to tell me. I know about Archie, and I know that you are too good for a lowlife like him. But you didn't like him either, did you? I mean, you wanted me to cut his throat."

Lucy doesn't say anything.

"You know," Gregor goes on, "you haven't asked about me either, so we will discover each other. How about that?"

He goes back into the kitchen and serves the food onto two plates.

"You tell me about your daddy playing swing and I'll tell you about my mamma cooking casserole." He sets the dish in front of her.

As he walks around the table she says, "When are you going to let me leave the house?" The neediness, the whine has gone from her voice and the question is short and staccato, and stays in the air.

He sits opposite her, blocking her view of the darkening garden. The dying flame in the barbecue bowl flickers on his shoulders. The statue of two-becoming-one to his right is disappearing into the thickening night.

He eats a mouthful of the chicken casserole while looking at her. Lucy does not pick up her fork. He motions to the plate in front of her as he chews. She doesn't look down, but holds his gaze. He stops chewing and swallows a mouthful of wine. Still looking at her, he replaces his glass on the table and turns the stem in his fingers. The sound of the glass revolving on the wood of the table is the only sound in the room. He stops. For a moment neither of them moves. This is the longest they have looked into each other's eyes.

Gregor says slowly, "If you want to leave, you can leave."

Lucy holds his gaze for a second more, then picks up her knife and fork and starts to eat. A rush of flavours hit her palate. She wonders as she chews whether she has ever eaten so well, or if the withdrawal is heightening her taste. Gregor is eating across the table, with his eyes closed and a pensive expression as if trying to conjure the memory of the taste. They continue eating in silence.

Behind Gregor it is dark now, and the fire in the garden is out. Just the ashes of the clothes remain. Outside has disappeared and the glass doors now reflect what is on the inside.

CHAPTER NINE

As the months went by Martin continued to write, to redraft what he had sent. The story grew. It began to fill the writing room. Martin hand-wrote potential plots and stuck them to the walls, with wall planners depicting timelines to make sure the episodes he was writing would make sense. About once a week Alison went inside and collected the empty cups and glasses, the plates and biscuit wrappers. She never touched the bundles of paper or stacks of books. Once she stopped and picked up the top page of one of the bundles.

Gregor was holding a syringe to someone's neck. The person was tied to a chair, with tape around his mouth and dirty sweat covering his face. His eyes were wide with terror as Gregor was advising him not to move, lest he miss the vein and cause some damage. He was wondering aloud if this amount was enough to overdose on.

"It's a combination of meth and DMT, so it's hard to predict. It all depends on your tolerance," he was saying. *"Of course it could just go straight to your brain and cause a fatal seizure. It also depends on how clean the rig is. So let's give it a go shall we? Remember hold still. If this kick doesn't kill you, you'll be on one hell of a ride; this is after all a cocktail of our best amphetamine with our best hallucinogen. It's a shame Lucy isn't here to see this,"* he was saying. *"But she will. You see I'm going to film you, so that she can see. It's only fair, you saw her. You thought that was a good experiment? Now let's try this experiment, let's just see what happens."* He touched the point of the needle to the eye of the tattooed scorpion, right on the jugular. *"Hold still,"* he whispered. The needle punctured the skin and a thin cloud of blood seeped into

the chamber of the syringe. Gregor pushed the plunger all the way down.

Martin started coming up the stairs. Alison hurriedly replaced the page on to the top of the bundle and picked up the empty cups. She was walking out the door just as Martin reached the top of the stairs. She felt flushed and avoided his eyes as she stood aside to let him pass into his room. Martin didn't turn around. He just closed the door. Alison stood for a moment, then went down the stairs. At the bottom step she turned and called, "I was talking to my folks. I was thinking of going up to the lake for the weekend. What do you think?"

Martin's voice came from behind the closed door, "That sounds great. You go."

"I go?"

"I can't leave this now."

Alison stopped still for a few moments with her hand on the stair rail, looking up at the light coming from underneath the door. "I go," she said.

o   o   o

That Friday, walking up the hill from the train station, Alison thought about how she would confront Martin. All day at work she hadn't been able to concentrate. The open plan of the office meant that she could see everyone else tapping on their keyboards and talking into their phones, and she wondered what their home lives were like. None of them lived with someone like Martin, she knew that, and she cherished how different he was. But it wasn't working out. Where was the life they had looked forward to together? Surely they hadn't been together long enough to start ignoring one another?

By the time she was in front of the house she was ready to go upstairs and tell him to stop his writing until they had talked this through.

When she opened the door the warm aroma of fried garlic and spring onions mixed with fresh bread filled the house and Martin came out from the kitchen. Before she could say anything he apologized. His head was so deep in the book, he was sorry, he would make it up. He took her jacket from her and hung it up.

The table was set. Alison sat down in front of a smoked salmon and fresh salad with a walnut mustard and goat cheese dressing. She picked up her fork and tried to remember what she was going to say to him, but he got in there first, talking as she took her first bite. He appreciated how hard she worked and he knew that it must seem like he didn't do anything. He admired her for how hard she worked, how she put up with him, all that she was doing for them together.

As he talked he went back into the kitchen and took the freshly baked bread rolls from the oven, putting them in a basket and bringing it to the table. He must look like a total loser from her point of view, sitting up in his room, only thinking about a world which wasn't real, trying to describe and rationalise actions of people who only existed in his head.

He sat opposite her. Thank you, he said, for putting up with me. I will make it up to you, he said, I promise. He picked up the wine bottle and went to pour. She put her hand over her glass.

"I'm still driving up to the lake tonight. Are you coming with me?"

He put down the bottle. "Ah," he said. "No."

They looked at each other. There was silence for a moment.

"I can't now," he said. "I'm right in the middle of it, I've just got to get through this next episode. I don't want to break the rhythm."

"Okay," she said. "But we need to do something together soon. Okay? I need for us to do something together."

"We will, I promise we will, and I don't want to let you down. But I need to do this." Martin looked at her imploringly.

Alison tapped her hand on his and drew it back to cut her salmon. "Don't look so upset. Maybe a few days apart will be good for us anyway."

As she ate she regarded him. It was hard to remain angry at him when he took things so deeply. Maybe all they needed was a bit of space. She looked out the window. At the end of the garden, the trees had grown and thickened, and she saw their tops against the darkening sky. They leaned and nodded gently toward each other, their branches reaching and missing, then touching, then missing again.

"I should leave soon if I'm going," she said. "I don't want to drive all the way in the dark. That was lovely."

Within ten minutes he was waving goodbye, and the driveway was empty. He stepped back into the frame of the front door. He saw lights come on and curtains close in the windows of the houses on the opposite side of the street. A flock of crows passed overhead. He looked up and watched them fly. Against the fading sunlight he saw their fluid unity, he listened to the echoes of their sharp coarse calls shifting and changing with the shape of their flight as they flew to roost in the dark woods beyond.

Martin stepped back inside the front door and closed it. He stood for a moment as the silence established its momentum, and then sat down on the bottom stair. He took his phone from his pocket. *Will be there within the hour,* he texted. He pressed send.

O   O   O

Twenty minutes later Martin was on the train into the city. The carriage was half-full. This train had come a long way before it had stopped for him, and the people on it were tired and quiet.

Outside the shadows were claiming the countryside. In the distance the lights from the high rises were peering at him like guardian eyes at the edge of the city. He was coming from the new streets and clean walls of his estate, where even now the loose leaves stuttering their way across the dark smooth tarmac between the houses were making patterns on the streets which had never been made before, and he was entering the city, where the concrete was stained and aged, where every road had been crossed in every way it could be, where the shadows had been filled with every dark possibility, and where the street lamps were pushing old light through dense used air.

Martin wondered what it would be like to unthink something. Once something developed in your mind, once a thought had created shape, it could never be undone. The best you can do, he decided as the train sped toward the city and the night, is isolate it.

O   O   O

The last time Ozzy had seen Martin he was waving good-bye to him out of the back window of a police car. It was a matter of bad luck. It could have been either of them being taken away, but the way it worked out it was Ozzy in the back seat and Martin left with the long walk home. They had been out for the night, Martin talking about quitting the bar and just writing, Ozzy saying that if he quit the bar he wouldn't have any decent material to write about. Martin teased Ozzy that he was just trying to get him to stay because he would miss him, and Ozzy said that was bullshit, that Martin going meant just there was a vacancy which could be filled by somebody much better looking with a better pair of tits.

They had been drinking for hours, with Martin threatening to go home as he finished each drink, either back to his damp bedsit or back to Alison's warm bed. Ozzy said that he was nuts to even see it as a choice—how could he not go back to Alison's? Martin's rationale was that he didn't want Alison to think he had no life beyond her, he had to have some level of independence. The bedsit was dark and damp, but it was his space at least. On the other hand, he really didn't want to go back there. He couldn't decide, and the more he drank the less he cared about the choice. Then Ozzy suggested scoring some weed.

After a taxi ride to the wrong place and then a long drunken walk they finally reached the street where Ozzy's dealer lived. Ozzy went in and Martin waited on the street. It was mostly shop fronts with the shutters down and doors in shadows. Ozzy finally came back out smiling and saying they were going to have a great night.

They walked for about thirty seconds when two young guys came up behind them, pushed them against the wall, reached into Ozzy's jacket, took the bag of weed, and ran. Ozzy and Martin ran after them. They followed them down a narrow lane and saw them jump over a fence. They followed, Ozzy shouting after them, and Martin falling behind and rolling through flowerbeds as they ran through back gardens and yards, climbing over fences and wire. Martin watched as Ozzy clambered over a fence and dropped down on the other side. He heard a moan and cursing. Then barking and growling.

"Don't come over!" Ozzy called. Martin looked around the back yard he was in. There was a gate. He opened the gate and was out in the back alley. He walked to the fence of the garden Ozzy was in. The fence was high. He called over.

"Are you okay man?"

"There's no fucking way out!" Ozzy shouted back. "It's deeper than the other gardens, I can't climb out!"

"Is there a dog?"

"Fucking damn right there's a dog! He's not happy. It's okay, there's a good boy."

The growling increased in volume.

"Where did those two guys go?"

"Fuck knows."

"How about climbing up on something? Is there anything?"

"No, nothing. Oh, shit, there's a light coming on. Shit, shit—they've seen me—shit."

There was a minute of silence, broken by the occasional growl, before a window opened and a woman's voice said, "We've called the police. They're on their way."

Ozzy called back, "Hey I'm not here to, well—I'm here by accident, I don't want to steal anything. I'm not—if you could just let me—" The dog started barking again and the window shut.

"Ah, come on, I'm here by accident! Please? You miserable old bitch? Please?"

"You got to be more friendly, Oz," Martin called over the fence. "Don't scare her off. Ask her for a cup of tea."

So Ozzy was stuck in the yard and the police were on their way. With Martin on one side of the fence and Ozzy on the other they figured out what they were going to do. They reckoned those kids probably did that to guys coming out of the dealer's place on a regular basis, the little bastards. They changed the story. Ozzy threw over his phone. He had been chasing two guys who had stolen his phone. That was the story.

Soon Martin could hear Ozzy petting the dog on the other side saying, "There's a good boy, good boy. He's fine now, Martin, he's wagging his tail. There's a good boy." In another few minutes they were laughing. "At least I'll get a lift back into the city centre," laughed Ozzy.

When the police did turn up, Martin walked around to the main road and watched as Ozzy was brought out the front door and loaded into the police car. As the car pulled away, Ozzy flashed Martin a smile and little low wave out the back window. He saw Martin get smaller and smaller on the empty street.

Now, as Martin walked into the club, Ozzy could see he hadn't been taking care of himself. He was wearing a faded check shirt and blue jeans. His unruly, wavy hair with the occasional curl was down to his shoulders and he had a beard, wiry and unkempt, creeping up to his cheekbones. His belly was pushing into his shirt. He smiled when he saw Ozzy.

As he walked over Ozzy threw his arms in the air, "Shit! Just 'cause you're trying to be a fucking writer doesn't mean you have to try so hard to look like one! What are you writing, a cook book?"

"Well, it's good to see you too, and I see the hunger strike is still in place?"

"This is just muscle, pure muscle and bone. I'm not carrying any extra around," he said, poking Martin in the stomach. "What's with the wild west look?" He tugged at Martin's beard. "You should have gone for the power goatee." He stroked his own moustache and goatee like a villain considering how long his victim has before the train comes.

"Yes, I see you've got the pirate look down," replied Martin, pointing at the red bandana covering Ozzy's hair.

"Well, at least pirates get to plunder. Cocktail?"

"Just a beer for the moment, Oz. How's Sal?"

"Sal?"

"Your girlfriend. Sally?"

"Oh! Sally! Sal, yeah. No she's not on the scene any more. Um, no, yeah, that stopped working out. Zoe is here, though. I been seeing her for a few weeks now."

"Where is she?"

"I think she's off hassling the DJ. She'll be back now. She is fiery, man. So how about it? How are things?"

"Alison is away for the weekend, so …"

"So party! Aha!"

"You know, just been …"

"Here she is."

Zoe approached them. She was short and bleach blonde with leather trousers and a black netted top through which Martin could make out a purple bra pushing her little breasts into an unnatural cleavage.

"Any joy?" Ozzy asked.

"Nah, the guy's a prick with a prick's iPod full of music by pricks. We can't hang round here. I'm fucked if I'm listening to this wanky shit all night."

"I was just going to get another round in."

"Don't bother. Is this your mate then?"

"Yeah, Martin, Zoe. Zoe, Martin."

"Well where will we go then?"

Martin said, "I never liked this place anyway."

"Don't know, but let's get out of here," Zoe said, and Ozzy pursed his lips around his straw and drained the last of his cocktail from the glass. Then they left the club, walking out into the warm city air.

"There's always the Alabama," said Martin.

"No fucking way," said Zoe "Not after the last time."

"What happened last time?" They stopped at the corner, waiting for the lights to change.

"Zoe got done in the face," Ozzy said. The traffic whizzed past.

"What? Someone hit you?"

"Fucking damn right someone hit me. This tart smashed me in the face with her stiletto." The traffic stopped and the green man flashed and beeped. They stepped onto the road.

Martin shook his head and asked, "Why? Why did she hit you?"

"Fuck knows. I didn't do a thing, didn't even see her before she started giving me a hard time, then I tell her to fuck off and she reaches down and then she's got her stiletto in her hand and she fucking hits me with it, straight in the fucking face by my nose. Here look, you can see it. Look." She stopped and turned to Martin, pointing to her face. He leaned down to see. Her skin was covered in a greasy film of a tan foundation. He couldn't see any marks, just smears where the make-up was too thick.

"I, um, I can't see...."

Cars started beeping. The lights had changed. They were still in the middle of the road. She was still pointing at her face.

"It's right there, right there, a big mark from where she stabbed me with her heel! Bitch."

The cars beeped again, someone was shouting out their window. Zoe turned. "Fuck off!!" she shouted, pulling up her top to expose her bra, then continuing to the other side of the road. Martin gave a wave of apology before following her. As the cars drove past they gave long aggressive beeps. Ozzy was waiting on the footpath rolling a cigarette.

"Not the Alabama then. How 'bout J.D.'s?" He licked the cigarette paper and rolled it tight, then put it between his lips, smiling. "They got happy hour till ten."

"J.D.'s," Zoe said, and took it from him, putting it in her mouth, pouting her lips, and closing her eyes. Ozzy held the lighter and lit the end. She inhaled deeply. The tobacco glowed. Ozzy put his arm over her shoulder and they both turned and started to walk.

Martin followed them. Ozzy was much taller than Zoe, and as he rested his arm across her shoulders, she held onto his hand with both of hers and every now and then pressed her cheek against it. His jeans were low around his waist and his loose white t-shirt wasn't doing much to hide his skeletal frame. His hair was black and lank, half covered by the red bandana. She was wearing Doc Martins. Her trousers were black leather, old worn leather, like an old couch. Martin could see the dark roots of her hair, could see rolls of skin bunching above her skirt through her netted top.

Ozzy leaned over and kissed the top of her head. She squeezed a bit closer to him. She came up to just below his shoulder. Despite the size difference, they seemed to walk in step. They looked comfortable together, passing the rolled cigarette back and to, before tossing it on the footpath.

The night was coming down into the city, but it didn't feel cold. Taxis pulled over, emptying groups of guys and bunches of girls onto the street. The guys were puffing their chests out and the girls were keeping close to each other, laughing and clutching hand bags. It was just the start of the night, and the lights of the club signs were just starting to come into their own, just starting to stake their place, to make sense in the clutter of light of the city centre.

As they approached J.D.'s Ozzy turned his head and said, "No pussying out now, you've got no excuse. We haven't been out in ages. Yeah?"

Inside J.D.'s they ordered more double cocktails despite Martin protesting that he only wanted a beer. When Zoe went to the toilets, Martin said, "Shit that's terrible what happened at the Alabama. Was she really hurt?"

Ozzy shook his head. "Not as bad as the other one was. What was she telling you?"

"That some girl hit her in the face with her stiletto for no reason."

Ozzy nearly spat his drink out. "Ha! No reason! Zoe had wound her up so far that the girl snapped. She was calling the girl a slag and a bitch and yeah, she took her shoe off and went for Zoe. I don't really know what the fuck it was all about, I think that it had something to do with Zoe's ex, but really …"

"Didn't you ask her what it was all about?"

"No, I don't give a shit! I mean, it's got nothing to do with me, has it? And she's been going on and on about it, but I still don't know what the fuck it was all about. Anyway, the other bird got Zoe once in the face but it ended up with her on the ground, face down, Zoe kneeling on her back whacking the back of her head with her own stiletto heel. There was blood, but I don't think it was Zoe's. I dragged her off and then we were pulled outside by the bouncers. Just as well, because from what I heard, she ended up being taken away in a fucking ambulance. Nah, man, the reason we're not going to Alabama is because we got no hope of getting in if we're with her."

"Jesus. How did you hook up with her?"

"She used to come into the club with a guy, massive guy, looked like a boxer. Always lined up tequilas, like, six shots at a time between the two of them. I thought she was hot then. Then she started coming in without him. I asked her about it, she said they'd broken up. I said there must be a queue of guys waiting to take his place. I told her that her drink was on me, that she could get me back on my break. Half an hour later she was giving me head in the staff car park."

"Holy shit, the life of a pirate."

"Arrggh." Ozzy growled and leaned forward conspiratorially. "That's nothing mate. We've been going to a club. A sex club."

"A what? Like a, a swingers club?"

Ozzy winked and smiled. "Oh yes," he said. Zoe appeared.

"What happened to your face?" she said to Martin. "You look like you just saw your mama have a wank."

"Em, I ..."

Ozzy butted in, "I was telling him about the Sugar Club."

"Ooh, I didn't know you were that kind of friends! Bum chums are we?"

"No way, Marty is as into pussy as I am, babes."

"Well there's lots of that, and cock too, if you fancy trying it out. You look like you might, Martin. Eh? Go on, tell me I'm wrong."

Martin took a sip from his cocktail. "Well, it would take a lot of these, I can tell you."

They all laughed and drank some more.

The night started to loosen up. J.D.'s was getting full of girls in heels and guys with gelled hair. There was a queue outside the door, a steady stream coming in, all wanting to have a good time. The DJ was playing Motown remixes, and the beats were crisp and the bass and horns were pushing grooves, releasing regular movement into the air, which was making people move. Even if it was just a nodding of the head or the slight sway of the hips, no-one was standing still.

It was past ten and happy hour was over, but there were more drinks lined up on the bar than before. In this crowded space, in this big ground floor room in the city, there was a constant movement of fluid; the bar staff pouring and pouring and pouring, glasses filling up and emptying, people filling up and lining up for the toilets. In between they danced and laughed, moved around each other in group orbits.

Martin saw all around him the tight shirts and fake tans, the make-up and false eyelashes, the plays for attention, the back and to of friendships and unsaid wishes for something closer.

"How's life at ICE?" he asked.

"Same as when you left. Billy is still a wanker, but you get on with it."

"I don't know how you work there," Zoe said, "if he was my boss he'd be hanging by his balls by now."

"Well, babes, he's just a duty manager. Everyone wants so bad for him to fuck up, but he never puts a foot wrong. He thinks he's so above the rest of us. If only being a bastard was a sackable offence. I'm sure everyone has complained about him at least once, but he's hanging on in there."

The more the club filled up the louder they had to talk, until within an hour Zoe was shouting in Martin's ear. He had his head down, leaning into her and she was on her tiptoes with her hand on his shoulder. Martin had to close his eyes so he could concentrate on what she was saying, to keep the beats and swirling music out and to keep the words in, to stop them from disappearing as soon as they were spoken. It seemed like they were the only ones standing still, keeping their place in the club; around them the people danced and pushed past.

Every time Martin opened his eyes he was surrounded by people he hadn't seen before, laughing and shouting at each other, making faces and exaggerating gestures. Martin couldn't see Ozzy. He had started bantering with a group of lads and girls and been carried away with them in the tide of people and alcohol. He had by now probably hooked up with another cluster of revellers. Martin had stopped looking out for him a while ago. He was concentrating on what Zoe was shouting into his ear.

They were gradually getting pushed closer and closer together until now their bodies were against each other, his arm around her waist and her face was against his neck, and as he listened to her he could feel the vibration of the heavy dub beats travelling through her body. She was telling him about her last relationship.

"He totally did one on me. One year. He was always telling me how much he loved me. He bought me things and told me how much he loved me. One year. Then I got pregnant."

Martin shouted back, "Did you want that? I mean, were you happy?"

"When I was a teenager I had cysts on my ovaries. They told me I could never have kids. So it was like a miracle. But one I hadn't wished for, I had accepted the no kids thing. It took me fucking ages to work out, you know? But I decided that it must be fucking destiny or something. This might be the only guy who could ever give me kids. It's now or never. And when I made that decision then I really wanted to go ahead with it. Full blast. It didn't matter if I was ready or not, life happens, you know? I mean, fuck it, it's a baby. It's a life inside me. One I never thought I would have. So that's that. Then he turns around and says he doesn't want me to do it. So it's like, the child or him. I mean fucking hell, you know? So he talks me out of the baby, promises me all sorts, all about our life together, what we'll do, the stuff we'll be able to do and have if there isn't a baby in the way. On the Sunday—the abortion is booked for the Tuesday—on the Sunday I check his phone."

"Why did you check his phone?"

"A feeling. He had been on the phone a lot, texting a lot; I just had a look through his messages when he was in the shower. It only took a minute before I found a whole bunch of messages. Two girls. Two other fucking girls he was fucking. Two."

Martin opened his eyes to look at Zoe. Her face was so close to his now that when he turned his head her nose was touching his cheek. He couldn't focus on her she was so close. He leaned back and looked her straight in the face. His neck was sore from bending down to listen. She really was much shorter than he was. Her eyes were welling with tears.

All of a sudden he could see her as a fifteen year old, cheated on for the first time by an older boyfriend. A boyfriend who had told her he loved her, that she was the most special girl in the world, that she was the only light in his dark sky. He could see her as a six year old whose teary-eyed mother had explained, as the back door shut and the car engine started outside, that no matter what happened between Mommy and Daddy they both still loved her.

He took a swig of beer from his bottle and saw Ozzy in the middle of the room, surrounded by a circle of guys. He was leaning back with his arms triumphantly aloft and his mouth wide open and one of the guys in the group was holding a jug of blue neon liquid above his face, tilting it slowly as the group began to cheer. Martin leaned down to Zoe again, putting his lips close to her ear, breathing in her sweet perfume and acidic hair spray. On her shoulder there were tattoos of bird silhouettes flying in a V formation.

"Shit. What did you do?"

"I went fucking ballistic. I wanted to rip his balls off."

"I mean what did you do about the abortion?"

"I went through with it."

"Fucking hell."

"I know. Fucking hell."

"What did Ozzy say when you told him all this?"

"Who? Ozzy?"

"Yeah, I bet he offered to track the guy down and do one on him or something."

"Ozzy? I haven't told Ozzy any of this. He doesn't care about shit like this."

"Really?"

"Ozzy is hot but he doesn't have much else going on beyond what's in his pants."

"I'm a writer."

"So what?"

"Oh. Well, writers have … they, em, feel differently, you know, insight."

"You're still a man. Go on then, what's your insight?"

"Well, you shouldn't have checked the fucking phone."

With that Ozzy appeared behind Zoe, grabbing her round her waist. His goatee and 'stash were wet. His white t-shirt was stained blue around the collar. His bandana had disappeared and his dark hair was slicked back away from his forehead. He leaned down so his chin was on her shoulder and started singing along with the song that was being pumped into the air around them while pulling stupid faces and trying to lick Zoe's cheek. Zoe started laughing and turned around to him, taking his face in her hands.

Martin headed for the bar. Behind the bar there was a mirror, and he saw himself among the line of faces. He did look more scruffy than any of them, like he had walked in looking for a different bar, or got confused with what night it was. Club night? I thought it was Wild West. He bought another three bottles and when he found his way back through the dancing shouting mass of people, Ozzy took his and said, "Nice one mate. Down these and we'll head to the club. Whatcha reckon?"

Martin looked at them both. Zoe didn't make eye contact, just pushed her face into Ozzy's sweaty t-shirt. Ozzy gave a wink and a smile and took a swig from his beer bottle. When he smiled his brow creased and deep lines shot out from the corners of his eyes. Martin saw him for a moment as an old man, making lewd comments to younger men about the busty woman at the shop counter, nudging them into uneasy assent with his elbow in their ribs.

Martin drank from his bottle and looked around. Besides Ozzy and Zoe, he had no connection with anyone else in this densely packed room of revellers. And how much did he know about Ozzy? They had known each other for a few years; he was the only person besides Alison that Martin could call a good friend. And yet within a few hours of meeting Zoe he had found out more about her than he knew about Ozzy in years of friendship. Or maybe there just wasn't that much to know about Ozzy. Well, he hadn't thought that he was the kind of guy who would go a swingers club. *So, who knew? Not me*, thought Martin. *Well, he doesn't really know me. Maybe we don't know each other at all.*

"Yeah sure," he said, "might as well see what it's all about."

Outside looking for a taxi, Martin could see the tide of alcohol had come in and the city street was flooded with bunches of people clinging to each other, laughing, shouting, guys with red eyes and shirts undone, girls stumbling in heels, police standing by, and ambulances lined up at the end of the road. It was still pretty early too, only turned midnight.

"How far is it?" he asked as a taxi pulled up alongside them.

"Really not far," Ozzy said and climbed into the back seat with Zoe, leaving Martin to get in the front. Ozzy told the driver an address and they were off. Within minutes the taxi had stopped and Ozzy was telling the driver to wait, that they would be back in a minute, Martin would sit with him.

"Just gonna get changed mate," Ozzy said, as he and Zoe slipped out of the back seat.

"Am I—" Martin started, but the door shut before he could finish his question. The taxi driver sat mute, staring ahead, and Martin fished around in his head for things to say. It didn't seem natural, the two of them sitting next to each other silently, looking straight ahead at a road that wasn't moving.

Martin turned in his seat. The driver looked Indian, with tight greying hair, thin strips of grey stubble straps holding a thick straight beard, like an extension of his chin. His upper lip had no hair. The grey of his hair and beard spread into his face and his dark skin had an eerie pallor. His eyes had a yellow tinge. Maybe it was just the light, but to Martin he looked like a zombie from a Bollywood movie. He wasn't moving. It was hard to put an age on him but Martin guessed he had died some time in his early sixties.

"Hey. The chances are," Martin said, "that you and I will never meet again. I hardly ever come into the city these days, and there are thousands of taxis, right?" The driver didn't turn his head, just looked sideways at him. Martin couldn't read his expression. Besides his eyes, nothing in his face or body had changed. He continued. "Now Ozzy won't be long getting changed, he'll just throw a t-shirt on, so while it's just you and me, you can tell me. You don't have to go into detail, but what's the worst thing you've ever done? What's the thing you've done that you're most ashamed of?"

The driver shifted his gaze back to out of the windscreen. He didn't make a sound.

"There must be something, just one thing, that when you think about it, it tears you up inside, something you wish you didn't have to carry around. I won't tell a soul, it won't go beyond this moment. Tell me, go on." Besides the sound of traffic passing, Martin couldn't hear a thing, not even the sound of the driver's breathing. He straightened up in his seat, once again looking out of the windscreen.

"Okay, I won't even look at you, just go ahead and let it out. Honestly now, I won't tell a soul." The silence and stillness continued until the back door opened and Ozzy got back in the car.

"She'll be down in a second." Sure enough, Ozzy had just put another t-shirt on, but also his black leather jacket and a new red bandana. The smell of fresh aftershave circulated around the stale air of the taxi. Martin turned around in his seat.

"Are you sure this is cool, me coming with you guys?"

"It'll be fine. You should check it out if you've never been. I mean, once we're in, you won't hang out with us, you can do your own thing. We usually split up anyway."

"Really? How does that, em, well, don't you get jealous?"

"She was the one who introduced me to it. She was a free spirit from the start, so who am I to try and change her? But the first few times, yeah, I thought I should, you know, hang around with her, but it soon became obvious I'd be better off finding my own fuck. That way there's no jealousy, because I'm too busy to think about her. Thing is, when we get back afterwards we always have a crazy time ourselves. It's like fuel; the feeling lasts for days."

Martin glanced at the driver. He still hadn't moved a muscle or shown any sign that he was hearing what was being said. Zoe was approaching the car. She had changed into a short skirt and heels, with the same netted top. Her legs were pale and rather shapeless, her calves were stocky, and her knees and ankles were thick. She carried a little backpack over her shoulder. She had put more eye make-up on, black lines around her eyes and her lips were a bright red. As she opened the door Ozzy gave another address to the driver who nodded, pressed his fare button and pulled out onto the road. In the back Zoe leaned into Ozzy, working her hands under his jacket and hugging him, and he kissed the top of her head. Martin watched the numbers of the fare go up and up, and the street lights approach and pass like the same frame of film repeated.

CHAPTER TEN

H enry's phone rings. It wakes him. The sun is shining a line down the bed through the curtains and it blinds him as he sits up. The sheets cling to his skin, the thin material rising with him off the mattress then peeling slowly away from his sweaty back as he leans forward and reaches down to the end of the bed. He can hear the phone vibrate somewhere on the ground, rattling on the bare boards. His head throbs and he closes his eyes as his hands feel around in the tangle of clothes at the end of the bed. Pockets, loose change, crushed cigarette packet, wallet, phone. He opens his eyes to look at the display. Unknown number. He answers.

"Hello? Hello, is this Mr. Bloomburg?"

"Speaking."

It's a woman's voice. In her mid- to late forties, Henry reckons. There is something dark and cracked about its tone, like a dry river bed.

"Mr. Bloomburg the detective?"

"Speaking."

"I'd like to hire you."

Henry closes his eyes again. *Well, she doesn't sound upset, this isn't spur of the moment, she's thought about it. I bet it's a follow job. She sounds tired, like it's the end of the day.*

"Okay, well, what does it involve?"

"I want you to follow my husband."

"Do you think he's having an affair?"

"I know he is."

"Well Mrs. …."

"Call me Maya."

Maya, not a common name. Maya, the illusion. Henry has an image of her. Dark complexion, thick black hair, brown eyes.

"Well, Maya, I will be in my office in, eh, fifteen minutes if you want to call back then and well, I can take some details and tell you what I do."

"Fifteen minutes? Did I disturb you, Mr. Bloomburg?"

"Is that okay for you, or do you want to call later?"

"I'll call in fifteen minutes, thank you."

"Okay, talk then."

Henry flops back onto his bed with his phone still in his hand and pulls the cover over his head. Ten minutes. Ten minutes more.

The pounding of the digger on the road outside starts. A hydraulic arm, arched like a steel insect on the skin of the city, jabbing the street. Henry counts the impacts. Fifteen. Then a rest. Other sounds drift into focus, and symphonise the dull drone of the city, before the machine attacks again, and they scatter. Over and over again. The digger has been outside his apartment for what seems like weeks. It's moved a few feet. No, he's not going to be able to rest. He gets out of the bed and pulls off the sweat-covered sheets.

In the small dingy kitchen the window looks out to a brick wall opposite. Henry pulls up the window, letting the humid air of the alley into his narrow kitchen. He pulls out sheets from the washer/dryer and puts the others in. He goes back into the dark bedroom with the one solid bar of daylight cutting across the bed and puts the clean sheets on. The mattress is still damp with sweat.

Back in the kitchen he lights a cigarette from the gas ring and puts the kettle on to boil. On the counter is a map and he leans over it. The city. Red dots and blue dots. Blue is where the girls lived. Red is where they were when they disappeared. He calls Kramer.

"Anything today?"

Kramer sounds flustered. Henry can picture him, empty coffee cups sitting on case files and print outs, crumbs on the keyboard, an officer standing at the desk, waiting for him to finish the conversation.

"Yes. One. Here it is, Bloomburg, but then I gotta go. It's em, it's ... Hollie Mandell, been missing for three days, reported late last night. Age twenty-two, last seen at the Brunel Centre on Jackson, never got home."

Henry puts a red dot on the map.

"Home is?"

"Home is 44 Alderton, West Brunel. Bloomburg, you getting anywhere? Still chasing your ghost?"

"Kramer this is why I don't work for you anymore. You would've pulled me off this a long time ago."

"You bet your ass I would've. You're looking for connections that don't exist, Bloomburg, I work in the real world." Kramer hangs up.

Henry sticks a blue dot on Alderton. There are golden stickers for where bodies are found, but he hasn't used any yet.

Henry puts the cigarette to his lips and leans out the window. The wall opposite doesn't have any windows, just dirty brick right down to the alley below. He exhales and watches the smoke. The sky above the roofs is low and grey, like a lid pulled tight.

The kettle boils. The phone rings.

"Hello, yes, I'm in my office now."

He pours the water from the kettle into the mug as Maya starts to explain. She's been married to this guy for six years. During the last two years he has been doing a lot of business which he won't tell her about. He doesn't pay attention to her the way he used to, and when he does it is through big overblown gestures—masses of flowers, expensive gifts, bought, she is sure, out of guilt. They had often talked about how once Kayleigh, her daughter from another marriage, was gone to University, they would have so much more time for each other, and the house would be theirs for the first time.

As she talks, Henry opens the fridge and takes out the remains of last night's take away. The sauce has solidified and the noodles are clinging together in a tense cluster. He pokes the formation with a fork. But it hasn't worked out that way, they spend less time together now than they ever did.

"... And I know, I just know he's having an affair."

"Has he had an affair before?"

"No. Mr. Bloomburg, I have a question for you."

"What's that?"

"Are you good at your job?"

"Maya, I've been doing it a long time. I always find out what people want to know. Sometimes the client wishes they hadn't asked the question, but that's not my job. My job is to find answers. What does your husband do for a living?"

"Security."

"For who?"

"For a chemicals firm."

"Which chemical firm?"

"I don't know."

"Okay, well, I can follow him and report what I see to you. Have you asked him straight out is he having an affair?"

"No."

"Well, that might just save you a lot of money."

"No, I don't want him to know I know."

"Okay."

He throws the noodle box into the sink followed by his cigarette butt, which sits smoking on the sticky mound.

"Okay, it all sounds pretty straightforward."

As soon as he hears the words he knows he'll regret saying them.

CHAPTER ELEVEN

When the taxi stopped they got out near an old pub whose windows were boarded up and whose door was covered in graffiti. They walked down a dark side street to a double door which had a small logo above; the outline of a five-pointed star with "The Sugar Club" written across it.

Ozzy knocked on the door and it was opened by a burly bouncer dressed in long black coat with a scrunched-up face like a long eared bat who gave a nod of recognition to Zoe and Ozzy and squinted his eyes at Martin, looking him up and down before standing aside and letting him pass.

They stepped inside to a brightly lit but short corridor where there was a ticket booth. It looked like an old cinema booking office. A woman in her fifties behind the glass with her hair tied up in a bun greeted Zoe and Ozzy with a smile and took their money and then asked of Martin, "Single male? Is he with you two? Now normally love, we don't admit single males after 11:30, but seeing as you're with these two, I'll let you in." She pointed to the laminated entrance fee card stuck against the glass of her booth, and as Martin paid asked him did he have a locker. Martin shook his head and looked confused, she put her head to the side and said, "Ah, it's your first time." She smiled and leaned forward, raising her eyebrows and speaking slowly as if addressing a child, "Do you want me to show you around love?"

Ozzy said, "It's alright, I'll give him the grand tour, show him the ropes," winked and steered Martin away from the booth and toward the door at the end of the corridor.

Through the door the light changed. It was much darker. There was a slow pulse of music, not loud enough for Martin to hear what song was playing, more of an ambient background noise, a dull thudding with a slow swampy movement of music around it. As his eyes adjusted to the dimly lit room, he saw the dance floor and low couches, and a bar on the far side. There were some people on the dance floor, gathered around in little circles. Rising from the centre of each little cluster was the top of a shiny pole going up to the ceiling. There was movement on some of the couches, and Martin could see a few people standing at the bar.

Ozzy leaned into him. "So this is the bar. No alcohol, but they do some good cocktails, just won't get you drunk. This is like the get-to-know-you room, if that's what you're after. Through there—" he pointed to a doorway on the other side of the bar, "—are the separate rooms. Each one has got a different thing going on. Come on, I'll show you." Zoe was already walking toward the bar. They walked after her and Ozzy said, "Baby, I'm just going to show Marty what's what. I'll do a cocktail." She didn't turn around.

Martin tried not to stare at the people who were fondling each other on the couches. There was kissing and groping, buttons undone and straps eased off shoulders. In the dim light it was hard to see any faces.

The doorway had a thick curtain hanging over it and Ozzy held it back as Martin walked through its musty smell and into a hallway. The hallway was painted black, with two red neon light strips on either side, running along the join of the wall and the ceiling and the wall and the floor. At the entrance of three rooms the line broke and framed the doorway. Large windows looked into each room.

Martin followed Ozzy down the corridor. Through the first window was a room with a table. On it, a man with a black eyeless mask lay on his back. Black straps pulled tight over his white soft bulging torso as a woman squashed into a PVC bodice whipped his trembling goose-bumped skin. Her dyed red hair stood up from its roots with every strand held in place by sticky hairspray, and her skin was a yellowed tan like smoke-damaged leather. The flesh of her arms and shoulders wobbled with every stroke of the whip. Through the glass Martin could hear the man calling out in muffled exaltation through the closed zip of his mask. On a bench against the wall another man sat huddled over, skinny and balding, his hand furiously pumping in his lap as he watched the woman from behind, concentrating on the movement of the rolls of flesh trapped in the PVC skin, on how the hem rose above her drooping cheeks when she delivered each blow.

The next window showed about five or six people, stripped naked in a room with two desks and a few office chairs, all writhing and pushing against each other, men with sweaty foreheads and beer bellies and women with closed eyes and faces scrunched up. On the walls there were maps of the world and posters of cityscapes and a flow chart with the line rising steadily then ending in a peak. The lights in this room were much brighter than in the hallway and gave skin a pale and almost transparent tone, emphasizing even more the red flushes and marks and stripes where the skin had been slapped or grabbed or scratched. Martin could see ribs and shoulder bones, fleshy thighs and fatty necks. Right in front of him a man whose bum cheeks were covered in black and grey downy fur was getting up from a kneeling position between the legs of a woman lying on one of the desks, wiping his lips with the back of his hand. As he stood he turned slightly and his penis stuck out at a low angle beneath the overhang of his belly, performing a tired salute. The woman's legs were spread, and without the man's shoulders to rest upon, they hung down, not touching the floor and Martin saw her puffy lips frame a loose drooling vagina, breathing like an unconscious bearded mouth. The man moved to the side of her and leaned over to kiss her, while kneading the big breasts which lay spread over her chest, spilling down onto her side.

Martin took his gaze away from the room and looked to either side of him. There were other people in the hallway, looking through the windows, safe in the knowledge that they couldn't be seen. Martin asked Ozzy, "Where do you usually end up?"

Ozzy motioned toward the end of the hallway. "I'll show you." He went ahead, walking quickly, and Martin followed.

The last window showed an empty room, just a bed with a bare mattress and bare walls, like a jail cell. Through the curtained door at the other end of the hallway and they were in what looked like another bar, but this one had bamboo furniture and brightly coloured tie-dye sheets on the walls with TV screens between, showing a woman in her early twenties rubbing oil over her tanned and toned naked body, her lips inflated into a pillowy pout, her eyes encouraging the camera to come closer, come closer. There were some figures sitting around one of the tables, Martin could make out two heavily built guys with broad shoulders and big arms. The others there were girls, it seemed, but the bulky frames of the men were blocking his view.

"Back there is all a bit fat and over fifty. Upstairs you got some private rooms. Usually, like if a couple hooks up, a guy or a girl or another couple or whatever, they can go in to one of the private rooms and not be disturbed. Policy there is you can't go in unless invited. There is one big open room upstairs too, a kind of free-for-all, doesn't always happen, but when it does, well … And downstairs, that's something else."

"Cellars and dungeons?"

"You got it. Cages, chains, proper whips, weights—"

"Weights?"

"For hanging off piercings."

"Ah! Shit!"

"Wipe-clean areas too, it's worth checking out just for the sound effects."

A wave of laughter came from the table and Martin saw one of the women lean to the side to look at Ozzy and him. Her eyes flicked off him in a second and lingered on Ozzy, scanning up and down, before she sat back into the group and joined in the laughter. He said to Ozzy, "Hey, I feel like I should at least have a drink in my hand, let's go back to the bar."

When they got back to the darkness of the bar room, Martin scanned the room for Zoe. He ordered two cocktails and the guy behind the bar asked did he need rubbers or booster. Ozzy said rubbers, yeah, and bought a handful of flat foil pouches. He gave Martin two and they clinked glasses.

"I'm gonna leave you to it," Ozzy said and walked back through the thick curtains.

Martin leaned against the bar and sipped his drink. The smell of the sweet syrupy cordial hit the back of his throat and his stomach turned. As he put his hand to his mouth and wondered whether he was going to vomit, a black man in a red cowboy hat and no shirt approached him. He was tall, easily a head over Martin and he smiled and said, "Hey, you lookin' for some banging? Wanna make a fast fuck? That's why you're here right? I got a lady in the play-room lookin' for some deep connection man. You come up, yeah?" The hat cast a shadow over his eyes and his wide smile gleamed in the dim light.

Martin straightened up. "I've just got to find a friend, then yeah, I'll be there."

"You don't need no friends, man."

"Ha, yeah, sounds good, I will come up in a minute."

"You better, man, you don't wanna miss this pussy." He brought his hand down on Martin's shoulder and held it there for a second as his smile got even wider, then turned and went through the door.

There was moaning coming from a huddled shape on one of the couches, a rounded back like someone burrowing. People were finding what they were looking for, finding the places to do it, and the people to do it with.

Another man approached the bar. He was shorter than Martin. The dim yellow lights of the bar reflected on his bald crown, giving the skin on his head a sickly iridescence. He was suited in grey, and his fingers were short and stubby as he tapped on the bar. He moved his head from side to side, whistling tunelessly as he decided what to drink. He nodded to Martin and Martin returned the nod. After he decided and the barman was pouring, he said to Martin, "You all right?"

"Yeah, all right," Martin replied.

"That guy's a bit full on, isn't he?" inclining his head toward the door the black man had just walked through.

"He is, he is."

As he paid for his drink and sipped from the glass, Martin saw that his hands were much smaller than his own, like the hands of a child. Martin wondered for a moment if there was something in the lighting of the room that was skewing his sense of proportion, whether the shadows were playing tricks on his eyes. The man whistled again, then smiled.

"Ashley," he said, "Ashley Morris is my name."

"Martin."

"Nice to meet you Martin. You here with someone or—"

"Well, yes, but they've, em …" He looked around again, hoping to catch sight of Zoe. There was no-one dancing around any of the poles now, and the shadows held figures he couldn't make out.

"I'm here with my wife and another couple we know. Over there." He pointed to a sofa on the far side of the room. Martin had to focus for a moment before he saw two ladies and a man laughing. They were all fully clothed, they could have been in any bar in town.

"You're welcome to join us if you want. That's Ted and Rosie, they're lovely. We met them here a while back. Ted's got a print shop, doing quite well for himself, and Rosie's got a lovely set of jugs." He sipped at his drink and checked Martin's left hand. "Not married, eh? Not found the one yet? Well you know, you never know when you're going to meet her, the trick is knowing that she's the one. I knew the second I saw Ellie. She got onto the ski lift and I knew she was the one for me. She even had her goggles down, I still knew. We hardly said a word. All she said was how amazing it was to be above the trees and what a beautiful view it was, and I knew. Explain that. Now I own a company manufacturing ski lifts. Explain that."

Martin thought of Lucy. She'd laugh at him for being in a place like this. She'd want to hear the details. She'd tease him for being perverted, but say she liked it, really.

"If you ever fancy skiing then I can recommend some real quality resorts. Here you go. You never know. Stranger things have happened." Ashley Morris offered Martin his card. Martin took the card and when Ashley invited him again to join the table, he declined, saying thanks but he should track down his friends.

"Well, mate, we'll be around. Lovely to meet you, really lovely to meet you," said Ashley and walked back to the couch where his wife was now kissing Ted who was doing well for himself in printing. Martin took out his mobile phone to check if Alison had texted or called. It was 00:46. There was a message waiting. *Good night x.* The barman was standing behind him.

"You can't use your phone here. You have to turn it off. No calls or pictures."

Martin held down the Off button and the message disappeared. The moaning from the burrowing back on the sofa near him was getting louder. A snorting and gasping had started, too. Martin put his phone in his pocket, took his drink from the bar, and walked through the thick musty curtains. As he passed the windowed room in the black hallway he saw the woman still whipping the pale lumpy red-striped skin of the faceless man, him still tied in the same position, her hand raised above her head exactly as she was when he first saw her, the skinny balding man still hunched over his jerking fist. The bodies had moved in the other room. There were more in there now; legs straddled the office chairs, flesh was flattened against the tables, the bright light sinking into the pale skin, exposing sinews and veins and rolls of fat. In the last room two women in their sixties were kissing, mouths open and tongues waggling, both with lacy knickers and breasts which hung loosely. Around them, three men were tearing open condom wrappers and squeezing and tugging at their flaccid penises. Martin opened the next set of curtains.

In the room with the bamboo chairs, the two big guys were standing and kissing, grabbing at each others' crotches roughly with their pants around their thighs, and the girl who had checked Ozzy out was crouched behind one of them with a finger wedged between his cheeks and the other hand in her pants. There were two other women at the table, and as Martin passed he saw their eyes look up then slide right off him. On the flat TV screens the woman was still rubbing oil and gesturing, on a loop. *Suck me, Terry,* said one of the guys to the other, and Martin walked through the next door to a stairwell. He went up.

On the next floor was a series of closed doors behind which Martin could hear thumping and moaning, clattering and random shouts and groans. And then on his right was an open doorway. He walked through.

He was in a big room with a high ceiling, like a warehouse. There were wooden pallets leaning against the walls, the air was cool, and the ground was hard and dusty. There was a cluster of about ten men all facing the centre of the circle. The towering black man, now naked except for his red cowboy hat and a pair of mustard socks, saw him and enthusiastically came over, a massive penis jutting out straight in front of him, waving and nodding like a thick dowsing rod.

"Yeah, man, I knew you would come, come on, come on."

Martin put his drink down on the cold floor with a hard clink and joined the edge of the group. Some of the men were naked, some still had their pants on and had just undone their flies, some had their shirts on, some still had a drink in one hand, all were concentrating on one girl on the ground. A pair of high heels were on the ground beside her and her skirt was rolled up around her waist. A guy was between her legs, pushing into her with short quick thrusts. As Martin moved closer, he saw beyond the pale back whose skin was stretched tight over a bony spine and sharp shoulders, and saw the netted top and bleached hair.

It was Zoe.

He was seized with an urge to run to her, push the men away. He would gather her up as one would a fallen child and take her away from here.

Her make-up had run, and her black eyeliner looked smeared down one of her cheeks. Her face was in a grimace, her eyes squinted, and she panted and gasped as the big black guy moved around the circle and knelt beside her face and took her by the hair. She looked up at him and spat at him before he pushed his penis between her lips. Beneath the brim of his red hat his white smile was stretched across his face. She started to make choking sounds and lines of spit dripped from the edges of her mouth. Martin found himself getting hard.

The guy between her legs shouted and groaned and spasmed before backing away on his knees as another man took his place. The heavy breathing of the group was getting more and more intense. There was a fire burning in the men around him and now it was in him. In his head first, like a slow motion violent hypnosis. First he felt it behind his eyes, and then it spread throughout his whole body, a fiery intensity.

He joined with the group. Their intent was totally focused and direct, like one organism with no thought, a beast with only white blind heat within. He had become one of them, or they were all different versions of him. One of the men in the group moved over her and ejaculated, spilling gloopy sperm onto her stomach. She moaned louder, and that encouraged another to do the same, his knees buckling as he squeezed a tiny penis with two fingers and a thumb, farted, and released a string of white drops onto Zoe's chest.

Martin moved behind the guy who was between her legs and undid his pants. He let them drop and took his penis in his hand, feeling it thicken as he waited for the middle-aged overweight balding man with the hairy back in front of him to be finished. He crouched down to get a condom from the pocket of his trousers which were crumpled around his feet. He was hit by a thick sickly smell. He saw the feet of the pack. No-one was barefoot, not even the naked ones. The beast had pairs of socks, trainers, slip on shoes, scuffed heels, shined toes. His fingers found the foil packet in among the coins and keys and his phone, then he straightened up, brushed his hair behind his ear, and concentrated again. In seconds he was stiff. He started to unwrap a condom as the guy cried out a name then rested his head on Zoe's sticky breasts before rolling aside.

Martin went to step forward, but pants around his ankles stopped him mid stride, so he took two half steps. He was starting to unroll the condom over the tip of his penis while keeping an eye on Zoe's now exposed crotch. Her thighs were thick and pale and greasy. There was nothing underneath her, no blanket or cushion between her bum and back and the hard floor.

Zoe looked up. Zoe and Martin's eyes met. She whipped her head to the side dislodging the penis from her mouth and hissed at him, "Fuck off."

The other men all turned as one to Martin, all of them with their cocks in hand. He felt light-headed. They all had wavy hair and beards. He saw all of their faces as his own. His own eyes looking back at him, ten pairs of his grey eyes, red rimmed and tired, focused on him.

"Fuck off," Zoe said again, louder this time. "You fucking creep. Have you any idea what a fucking creep you are?"

The black guy said, "Getta fuck away, you prick."

One of the men pushed him. Someone grabbed his shoulder and pulled him back. His pants around his ankles caused him to shuffle back, his arms outstretched and rotating as he tried to keep his balance and then failed, falling onto his bum on the cold hard floor. The circle closed, immediately disregarding him and focused again on Zoe on the ground. He could see that she was turning on to her front. As he watched, his penis shrank and shrivelled. The condom hung from it like an old snake skin. Through legs and buttocks he saw another man kneeling behind her, thrusting, red faced, as the circle of men ejaculated onto her back, her shoulders, her hair. She had her face pressed to the cold ground of the warehouse floor.

Martin pulled up his trousers and stood up. He turned and went back through the door into the hallway.

The noises around him now sounded threatening. Each connection being made was hurting, and the long wordless groans and thumping grunts were not of pleasure but of agony. Martin walked quickly back down the stairs and through the doors and curtains and the black corridor with the red neon strips and the big windows. Back through the thick musty red curtains to the dark shadowy bar where a woman carrying drinks, wearing Ozzy's red bandana, passed him, out through the ticket booth and past the bat-faced bouncer and onto the deserted street.

Without stopping or slowing down, he walked away from the club down a street he did not know. He caught sight of his reflection in a car window. Check shirt, faded at the elbows, belly straining at the buttons, an unkempt beard, and thick wavy hair. His reflection slid off the glass as he kept going. He passed a take-away, greasy clumps of meat revolving around a spinning pole and a thick-set man in a dirty white apron standing bored behind the counter.

He had to find a taxi that would take him home, back to the carefully measured streets of his clean new estate. He wanted to look out his window at the familiar identical houses, see the cars pulled up safely in the driveways, watch as the televisions were switched off, and see the lights in the windows go out before midnight.

He was getting further away from the Sugar Club. The streets were terraced, rows and rows and rows of front doors. The next turn led him down another street of houses and shop fronts, parked cars on one side of him and closed doors and metal shutters on the other. He kept walking.

The scenes from the club kept running through his mind and he picked up his pace, to put as much distance between him and what had happened as he could. The warmth that was in the air earlier in the night was gone, and a gust of cold wind rolled with him down the street, pushing past him, through him, as he hunched his shoulders.

At the next junction he saw a gap in the houses across the road. It was a wire fence with a playground inside. The steel of the slide and the iron frame of the swings reflected the street lights and glowed in the dark silence of the street. Martin crossed the road and went through the gate. Behind the wire fence the ground was softer than the footpath, softer than the floor of the Sugar Club, softer than the floor that Zoe's face was pressed against.

The cold breeze blew again, pushing the swings. A false telescope on top of the climbing frame started to spin slowly. Martin sat on one of the swings and pushed himself forward. As he swung back, his feet dragged along the ground and he came to a stop. He heard the sound of rain hitting the steel of the slide. The iron fence started to rattle. He knew that it was going to rain hard. He wanted to stay at the playground longer. He remembered that feeling as a child, not wanting to go home. But he always had to leave. Now the rain was bouncing all around him; all he could hear was the sound of the water falling against metal and stone.

Headlights of a car approached and Martin saw the taxi light on its roof. He stood out on the road and waved. Already there were puddles for the wheels to splash through. It stopped. Martin's clothes were wet and the rain poured down his brow and into his eyes. He opened the door and sat in. It was the same one, the zombie that had dropped them to the club. His skin was even paler than before.

"It's you. Hello, again," Martin said.

The driver turned his yellowed eyes and said, "Excuse me?"

"It's me, from earlier, you know, the question?"

"Where to please?"

"Oh. New Acre."

The rain on the roof of the car and the splashing of the water on the road were the only sounds washing around the car on the journey home.

CHAPTER TWELVE

L ucy's hair is cut short, ragged, and spiky, and is dyed bleach blonde. Her beautiful pale neck is exposed, smooth and delicate with the symmetry of a classical statue. The white of her hair has brought out the sparkling of silver in her eyes.

Gregor is standing in the hallway dressed in a black tuxedo, looking up the stairs, waiting to take her out. When she appears, she is wearing an elegant floor-length dress, an opulent blue shimmering material. There is a single embroidered strap running over her shoulder, leaving her other shoulder bare. The embroidery runs across her chest, following the contours of her breasts and curving in a wave down to the side and finishes in a point at her hip.

As she walks down the stairs to him, Gregor tells her how magnificent she looks. From his suit pocket he takes a black velvet-covered box and steps to her with it in his hands.

"I want you to wear this," he says. Inside is a diamond encrusted collar, sparkling. She turns around and watches in the hallway mirror as he fixes it around her neck. She shudders slightly as he clips the clasp in place. He looks in the mirror too, and they stand for a moment regarding each other's reflection, his so dark and hers so pale. Then he says, "Let's go."

When they go out together, he tells her it's business first.

They sit in the corner of an exclusive restaurant at a table with six seats. The owner comes and greets them. Gregor introduces her, and the owner bows low, saying how lucky he is to have such a beautiful woman in his restaurant. Expensive wines and dishes of food are brought to them. Plates of freshly-steamed mussels and oysters, bowls of baby eels, a platter of sardines and whole shrimp, and the main dish is octopus paella, cooked in its own black ink.

Three men in suits come and join them. They all make a fuss of Lucy when they first meet her, and then within minutes she is forgotten. Soon the table is full of half-empty dishes, shells sucked dry and piled, discarded eel, fish and shrimp heads, baskets of broken bread, full glasses, and talk. The octopus oil has stained everything, and the men's lips and teeth are black and grey, their fingertips inky and they continually dab around their mouths with white napkins which become more crumpled and soiled as the night goes on. Lucy just sits and listens.

When Gregor talks his hands stay still. He leans into the table, his hands on the table in front of him, but does not raise them. He talks of shipments and purity ratios, about setting up kitchens and moving cooks.

"So we've got it now. There's nothing from outside the country, it's all in-house. How many kitchens are ready?"

One of the men is overweight and wears glasses. His hands are chubby, his fingers are short. He speaks now. "We have three ready to go, all with cooks in place. The Ashfield site is already in production, we should have a batch by the end of next week."

"Who's the cook at Ashfield?" Gregor asks.

"It's the ex-teacher."

"Well, we need to keep an eye on him. If he was dipping his dick in his students, he might be tempted to have some sleep-overs. They were under-age too, weren't they?"

"Under-age boys," says another of the men. He is big and brawny with dark skin and a gold tooth. He has long thin dark hair on the backs of his hands. He squints his eyes when he talks and waves his hands around, as if he's trying to push the words away from himself as he speaks. "But it never went past the school authorities, so he's not on a register or anything. He'd be a fool to fuck this up with the money involved, he's broke. He won't fuck it up."

"It's obviously his dick that makes the decisions. Spike, you need to talk to him, tell him anyone else in the house and we'll break his back."

Spike is sitting with his back straight on his chair. He nods. He's the biggest of the men, shaved head with huge broad shoulders and a thick neck, on which is a tattoo of a scorpion with its tail running up behind his ear. His face is hard and unforgiving. He glances at Lucy; she looks away. She can imagine this huge man picking up a skinny teacher and breaking his back over his knee, snapping him in half like a branch. Gregor keeps talking.

"The compounds are in place, ready to move, we just have to get the ingredients to the kitchens this week. The main thing is, once they're up and running, can they be dismantled quickly? I want to know how fast it can all come down, it needs to be mobile. Quick, quick, you know what I mean? How about the drop-off for the ingredients? Is everything set up?"

"We've got the drop-off in place." The dark skinned man talks again. "We could have picked up ingredients cheaper abroad you know, Gregor. There's a whole raft of contacts out there we could've called in."

"In-house. Right from the start, I've said it, everything in-house. If it's picked up that this shit is being moved around in bulk outside pharmacy companies they're going to legislate against it in a heartbeat. At the moment, they don't know it exists, let's keep it that way for as long as we can. Once it's on the streets it's a countdown to a crackdown, so this time is precious to us. Get your mind off how you would have got your European bum chums involved. We need a protocol for taking down a kitchen. If there's heat, then the first thing out are the ingredients. We got to keep them ahead of legislation as long as we can. If they can't be moved in time, then they need to be destroyed. The cooks need to know the drill; they need to have something ready twenty-four seven that can burn those ingredients quickly and safely without burning the whole place down."

"We gonna have to fit a wood-burning stove in each kitchen? How else are they safely gonna get rid of compounds quickly?"

"We don't have to have it inside. Put it out back. All of our kitchens have a back yard or a garden, right?"

They continue talking.

Lucy sips from her glass. Spike hasn't said anything yet, just nods assent. She looks at his face again. He's attentive, his eyes follow who is talking, and every now and then his eyes flick over to her. She gets the feeling that he's on the outside too, as if he ended up here by chance and is now having to concentrate to keep in position. She waits until he glances at her again, then smiles gently when their eyes meet. He does not, but she sees that his eyes soften, just for a second, before switching back to a steely hard set.

The way his eyes change remind her of her father. Late at night, she would wait up for him, trying to stay awake until she heard the back door latch click and the sound of him putting his saxophone case in the space beneath the stairs. Then she would creep downstairs and put her face around the kitchen door. It was like this, late at night, after he had been singing and playing all night, that his eyes were different, softer. He always looked happy to see her, and he would beckon her into the kitchen and make her a hot chocolate and pour himself something dark and strong-smelling.

They'd sit at the table in the low light and she'd ask him about where he had been playing and about the people dancing and he'd smoke and tell her stories about what the music did to people, or about his drummer or bass player, or his beloved saxophone, or about his homeland and how different it was to here. How he wouldn't be able to earn any money doing this job back home.

Once, when she said to him how much she loved their late night chats, and how he seemed more relaxed than during the day, he said, *That's the music. That's swing and rhythm and blues. You can't play that all night and still be uptight.*

There were times when her mummy was out for the day and when the rain was coming down hard, leaking through the window frames and coming in under the back door, and he would pull out some records and put them on the old battered turntable. They'd move the chairs aside and take each others' hands and dance around the kitchen to the sound of scratchy big band swing.

He showed her the basic dance moves, spun her around, passing hands around his back, counting time with her and showing her when to kick her feet. *It's good to dance together, but you don't need someone if you want to dance.* He would pour himself a glass and tell her that music was a place you could lose yourself, leave the world behind. *That's what I use it for,* he said. *So if you really want to dance, it doesn't matter about the moves. Let yourself go, let the music move you. There's not many places in this life, this tough life, that you can totally lose yourself, so when you get the opportunity, then do it.* They would dance on the creaky floor, changing records, while the rain threw itself against their crumbling walls and crept further and further under the back door. They would dance until her mother came back and his eyes hardened up again.

Lucy takes another sip from her glass and empties it. Spike sees this and picks up the bottle and holds it out with a raise of his eyebrows. She nods and he stands and leans over the table. He pours, emptying the bottle. His shirt is tight across his chest. His hand holding the bottle is clean and his fingers are long and slim with clean nails. The fat man's nails are bitten to the nub and the dark man's nails are long, not far off claws at the end of his hairy hands.

Gregor is talking about the market for Spiral. He wants to find the hands of the middle class, the money, not the street kids selling themselves for the next pathetic rocky hit or whatever else they can get their trembling hands on. When he speaks about addicts the edges of his mouth turn down. "This is a party drug, for people who can afford to party. Really strong, the rush feels like it never ends, goes on for hours and hours, a good six hours of thinking you've hit the top only to find yourself higher again. Once the word gets out, this will be the most demanded party drug. The street kids and prostitutes can stick to crack and smack."

The fat man drinks some wine and wants to talk again about what happens when a kitchen gets busted. "Detection risk," he says, "we've got to break the line back to us."

Gregor says, "That means getting stooges in place. Who have we got?"

The dark man with the hairy hands says that he knows a guy who should be in the ring.

"Rocky, black guy, he's got connections up north. He runs out of—"

"No," says Gregor, "not him."

"He's worth considering if we want to move stuff fast. And once we use his connections, he's disposable. He's not that bright. Young, ethnic, they'd pick him up in a flash."

"No," Gregor says again, "no, don't touch him, and if you have any contact with him now, break it."

"Why? What do you know about him?"

"He does runs for Stranstec."

For the first time Gregor moves his hands up to his face. They are clasped as if he is about to say a prayer. The air has suddenly tightened, there is a tension. The others round the table are fixed on him, motionless.

"Stranstec will pounce if he knows about Spiral. And when Stranstec is on your back, you're never going to get up again. No. If we are going to put stooges in place it's got to be someone who's already in the ring. Someone who's already in the ring but doesn't know it."

The fat man says, "Stranstec runs girls, doesn't he? Why should he be?—"

"I said no, and that's it, damn it!" Gregor slams his hands down on the table. There is a shocked silence, which is broken by Gregor waving a waiter over and ordering another bottle of wine.

The talk goes on and on and Spike keeps topping up Lucy's glass. Another plate of food arrives. Gregor's hands are back on the table now, relaxed, and he talks about purity ratios again and distribution channels. The other men answer deferentially, look to one another, listen and chew, drain their glasses and agree.

She wonders why he has brought her. She looks around at the men at the table. They all carry the confidence of men who are used to telling others what to do and how to do it. They have expensive watches on their wrists, large rings on their fingers. Gregor is not the strongest, nor the biggest, and certainly not the most threatening, but he is the leader.

She thinks of her time with Archie, of the lines and lines and lines of cocaine, the constant flow of speed, meth, and poppers for the ups, the roofies and ketamine for the come-downs. Long stretches where days and nights lost their meaning, when the traffic of people through the flat was so much that she would keep herself locked up in the bedroom, not because she was afraid of anyone coming in, but because she was confused by the changing faces, the friends of friends and hangers-on, the revolving conversations, and the swell of hysteria which some would bring with them. When Gregor had come along she had been on roofies for days, feeling momentum drain from every moment, like heavy time being pushed uphill. Since she's been at Gregor's she's experienced more silence than she can remember.

When the talk's over the fat man stands and brushes himself down. He smiles at Lucy and says how lovely it was to meet her. His teeth are still stained from the octopus ink and there are still bits of food in the folds of his shirt as he turns and walks away.

The dark man is next to go. He does not acknowledge Lucy at all as he stands and says to Gregor, "This shit is taking its time. I want to see some return. I want to see it soon."

Gregor doesn't stand. He extends his hand across the table.

"Ali, you know it's got to be right before it goes. We all have a lot riding on it. When it hits it's going to hit big. Don't get nervous now." They shake. Then he goes and there are just the three of them.

Gregor finishes his wine and beckons to the waiter for the bill. After he signs for it, he says to Spike that he needs him to keep an eye on Ali. Spike nods and leans forward. Spike speaks, and for the first time Lucy hears his voice. It's not what she expected. It's got a high tone and the words land lightly in the air between him and Gregor.

"He's changed?"

"Something about him has changed, I just don't know yet what it is," Gregor replies.

The waiter comes back with their jackets. Gregor takes Lucy's, saying as he puts it on her shoulders, "That must have been boring for you. Let's go to church."

O O O

The club is an old church, restored and renovated. The DJ is in the pulpit. They pass a full dance floor and go to a table on an upper level. Gregor watches as Lucy, who has been drinking quietly all night, comes alive.

"Well, how about that? Isn't this black and white music? Is it?" he asks her.

Lucy tries to drag him to the dance floor.

"It's remixes, come on dance, dance!"

He stays in his seat, shaking his head. "You go, you go. I can't. I can't dance. You go," he says.

She downs her glass of wine and walks away from him. Gregor sees her step out of her inhibitions, sliding them off with a shrug of her shoulder. She moves away from the shadows of the club tables as Frank Sinatra starts to croon. *All of me, why not take all of me, can't you see I'm no good without you.* A heavy dub drum beat kicks in and throbs throughout the club.

Lucy's hips swing as she walks down the steps, away from the saints on the stained glass windows of the upper floor, down to where lights are spinning and bodies moving. Her diamond collar sparkles. *You took the part that once was my heart so why not take all of me.* The beat gets into her and she surrenders control. She dances wildly, twisting and grinding, pushing herself against the stone pillars of the club, running her hands over her breasts and twisting her hips, as she slides her back down the pillar and throws her head from side to side. Then she pushes herself back up, and her hips find the beat again. She holds her dress and whirls it like a flamenco dancer while the thud of the bass drum propels her across the dance floor. She knocks against couples and dancers, bouncing off them, her momentum unbroken.

The DJ in the pulpit mixes in another old classic with a drum and bass backbeat. *Now you say you're lonely, you cried the whole night through.*

Gregor watches as men try to dance and flirt with her. Some of them try to keep pace with her, try to dance alongside her, but it is like trying to hold a whirlwind, like trying to catch lightning. Man after man approaches her, and each one resigns in a matter of minutes. Every now and then she glances back up the steps at where Gregor is sitting; she can see him in the shadows, sitting at the table with Spike, his drink in his hand watching her. Spike is talking to him.

"You're still uptight. Everything okay?"

"I don't think that Ali mentioning Rocky was a coincidence."

"You think he's in with Stranstec?"

"Stranstec is going to get as close as he can and Ali has been around for years. He's bound to have dealt with him. Who's to say they haven't kept a connection? Stranstec knows how to work people. That's how he works, he manipulates. He's got people working for him that don't even know it. He's a clever bastard. Spike, I need you on Ali. It's a critical time."

"You got it. Ali doesn't know the process though, does he?"

"No, but he did all the sourcing and the distribution channels. If he spills to Stranstec, there's no need for him to know the process, he'll just wait and bandit the distribution line. We'll have done it all for him. Is that bag still safe?"

"Yes."

"Good."

Gregor hasn't taken his eyes off Lucy all this time. She looks up at him now. She starts to crawl back up the stairs toward him, keeping her eyes locked with his, before she stands again and turns, running one hand through her hair and the other over her hip, going back down to the dance floor, giving herself back to the music. *Well you can cry me a river.* Gregor sips from his drink. Spike leans into his ear.

"She's crazy man."

Gregor nods.

"Yes. Beautiful and crazy."

"If she's like this now, imagine her on Spiral."

CHAPTER THIRTEEN

I t rained for weeks. From the window of the writing room Martin watched the puddles gather and grow. When she had got back from her parents' boat house, Alison told Martin that she had been standing in front of the big glass wall when the clouds came over the horizon and the rain started to fall on the lake. She had never seen clouds like them, it was straight out of a painting or a CGI scene in a movie and then when the rain hit the big glass windows, it was like someone had suddenly thrown a bucket, and she knew that it was going to stay. The wind that followed seconds later shook the boat house and pushed waves across the lake. *The floor was moving*, she said, *the whole house was moving*. It was the first time that she really felt like she was in a boat. She realised there were no foundations beneath her.

Her parents were glad that she visited, and they both sent their love back to Martin. That was what she said to him, but Martin imagined her mother topping up her wine glass and her father refilling his pipe as she told them both how useless he was, how he still wasn't earning any money.

That evening they had curled up together on the sofa and promised that they would pay more attention to each other. Alison suggested making goals that they would try to achieve before the end of the year. Martin agreed that this was a good idea. When she suggested that there might be areas of life he was not fulfilling by concentrating on his writing, he became defensive. *Until I get this, I don't want anything else from life*, he said. *Well*, she replied, *there's no harm in thinking what else there might be for you, but if you stay where you are, life can't offer you anything. You're not giving life a chance,* she said.

That talk was weeks ago and it still burned in his mind, through the days of rain, those words, *you're not giving life a chance,* always there like the constant *tap-tap-tapping* on the window behind him as he sat at his desk.

When he wrote, all he wanted to write about was Lucy. Each paragraph made her more real, in each line she revealed more of herself for him. He would sit back in his chair and picture her just doing something mundane, perhaps eating, absentmindedly brushing crumbs over the edge of the table and looking out the double doors at the back garden. She would stare at the statue, the two bodies embracing and twisting together into the earth, before finishing her mouthful and getting the cloth and brush. He wanted to appear behind her now as she rubbed the cloth over the table and put his arms around her, press his lips to the curve of where her neck and shoulder meet, and feel her exhale slowly and then match his breathing to hers.

As the rain continued to fall, Martin rewrote and rewrote chapter after chapter. The walls of the room began to crowd with sketches in black pen, boxes with sentences and arrows pointing to circles with words inside. When he was not writing he would close his eyes and look on Lucy, watching her wander aimlessly and beautifully around Gregor's house, being careful to not leave a mark, wiping any trace she left away.

He watched her take the books down from the shelves one at a time and read, the way she tucked her legs underneath her when she was on the couch, the way she licked the tips of her fingers before she turned the pages. She'd sit there for hours, in that curled up position on the big couch reading books about terrible and noble men.

Martin felt sometimes that he was losing sensation in his body, all he was using was his fingers and eyes. Occasionally he would rise from his seat to stamp his feet and walk around the small room, just to regain feeling in his legs.

One night as he stamped his feet, Alison said as she came up the stairs, "I'm going to the gym. Do you want to come?"

"No."

"You could go in the pool while I'm in the gym."

"No, I've got to keep going on this. Next time."

Alison sighed "Okay," and went into the bedroom. The door was not closed. Through the thin gap he saw her pull tight leggings up to her waist to where folds of flesh bulged and hung over the top. She put a t-shirt on, covering her pale plain body and then went downstairs. The door closed.

Each time Martin looked from the window of his writing room to the fields beyond the red brick estate, they were more flooded with brown water. One day he saw that two plastic bags had got into the thin rectangle of grass that was the back garden. He went outside to gather them up. The ground was soft and the mud moved beneath his feet as he walked. Getting to the end of the garden, his feet slid beneath him twice, and twice he ended up on his back. The mud stuck to him. The second bag had blown against the trunk of one of the trees against the back fence. Martin, soaking wet with his back and legs covered in mud, bent low and ducked under the branches to get the bag. Under the trees, the ground was dry and hard. In fact, this low space between the trees with the fence behind had been sheltered from the constant rain and stayed dry.

Crouched over, he turned around to face the house and sat down on this piece of dry earth, wondering how this one space had escaped the creeping water that was spreading everywhere he looked. With his knees against his chin, he looked back at the house. The branches from the trees dropped low in front of him and crossed over each other. He looked through the branches up to the window of his writing room. He imagined himself standing up there, looking out on the fields beyond the estate. I can't be seen here, he thought. He stayed there for a while, holding the two plastic bags, watching the rain throw itself against the back of the house.

CHAPTER FOURTEEN

In the back of the private car on the way back to Gregor's house that night, Gregor leans over and kisses Lucy. She kisses him back. His heavy breath rushes out as if he has been keeping it in since he first saw her. She puts her hands to his face and their mouths open wider. They grope each other as they kiss. She pulls at his belt and he says, *Not here, inside.* She whispers in his ear, *No, now* and takes his hand and pulls it under her skirt. He gets two, then three fingers inside her. Her mouth opens more and more and he sucks on her tongue. When the car stops outside the gates of the house, Gregor fumbles in his pocket for the remote control to unlock it, then thanks the driver as Lucy climbs out of the back seat with her skirt around her hips.

Inside she pulls him into the first room, sits on the dark wood table, and grabs his shirt, pulling him to her and kissing him. Then she puts her hands on his shoulders and pushes him down so that he is between her legs. She pulls the fabric of her panties to the side and then with two hands tears them from herself, moving herself right to the edge of the table. She takes his hair and pulls his face to her groin, stretching her legs out as she does. He puts his arms beneath her legs and lifts her up from her hips, her thighs are on his shoulders and he is holding her. She throws her head back and arches her spine as if in the grip of a seizure, and she sees behind her, upside down, the canvas of moving colour.

O O O

She wakes in Gregor's bed. The room is bare; the walls are flat and have no decoration or pictures. The wardrobes are set into the walls and are a pale wood. There is one mirror, a single pane which doesn't go as high as the ceiling or as low as the floor. Lucy and Gregor are underneath a light blanket. He has his back to her. She feels the collar still around her neck.

She leans upon one elbow and looks around the room. There is no bedside table, no chest of drawers, no sign of life other than the bunch of twisted and entwined clothes on the floor and the two of them in the bed. He turns over so that he is facing her. He rests his head on his arm. His chest is broad and covered in hair. She smiles at him. He is neither smiling nor frowning, his face is neutral. She moves closer to him. He lies flat and she moves down in the bed so that her head is resting on his shoulder, her cheek at his chest. She expects to be able to hear his heart, but cannot. They lie there awake together in silence until he suggests breakfast.

"Yes, I'd eat something," she says. "Although I did eat a lot last night."

"You danced a lot, too."

"That was a fancy place we went to, before the club."

"That's one of my favourites."

"It's nice eating out."

"Mmmm."

"That club was good, too."

"The Church. Yes."

"Do you go there a lot?"

"No. I don't usually go to clubs."

"Why not?"

"It's all decadent. The short skirts and high heels, women showing themselves off. It's not the women that turn me off, it's the groups of men looking for something to stick their dicks into. I bet you went to a lot of clubs with Archie."

"Why did we go last night?"

"For you. You had to listen to us talking about business all night. I thought you might enjoy it."

"Well I did. Thank you."

"Did you know the songs the DJ played?"

"Of course. I mean, they were remixes, but I know the originals. Did you?"

"No."

"Well, I guess if you don't listen to music …"

"Hey, I hear music all the time, I just didn't recognise those songs. I've never seen anyone dance like you."

She smiles and leans up on her elbow to look down at him. "That's that swing thing, baby."

He turns over onto his front and folds his arms on his pillow, resting his head. She lies back down facing him. They smile.

"Tell me about that swing thing."

"Well it's a dance, you know. The music was for dancing. Not formal dancing, just a few steps and then a lot of shaking."

"A lot of shaking? Not a very specific dance."

"That's just it. A dance where you can let go and do what you want. And when people get to do what they want, they dance crazy dancing."

"Who danced it?"

"It started with the slaves bringing their rhythms. The rhythm, the dance, shaking it all up, letting it all out, that came from underneath, from the poor, from the ghettos, the shacks."

He smiles. "Is that why you like it? It's ghetto music? You a ghetto girl?"

She pushes him gently. "Don't tease. I like it because it makes me dance. And that makes me feel … Do you ever dance?"

"No."

"You don't know how it feels. It sets you free. And you never hear swing music in clubs. How did you find that one?"

Gregor turns over again, onto his back and pulls her close.

"Spike. He knows where stuff happens. He's always got his ear to the ground. I've never seen him dance though."

They laugh. "That would be quite something, to see him rip up the dance floor."

"It'd have to be some big dance floor."

They laugh again. She gives him a squeeze and a kiss on the chest. She listens for any sounds from the road, or birds outside. There is nothing. She puts her head on his chest. Nothing. This must be the quietest place she's been.

"Did Archie ever take you out?" he asks.

"Yeah there were some clubs we went to. None as nice as that one though. All house music, and everyone popping pills. We'd go out to eat sometimes. He took me to the Kasamet a few times."

"The Kasamet? The curry house on Richmond?"

"Yeah, it was good, big portions I remember."

"That place was closed down about six months ago."

"I knew it had closed. Do you know why?"

"It was run by a family I used to have dealings with. They had issues with their meat."

Lucy pushes herself away from him and looks in his face.

"What do you mean?"

"They didn't want to go through the usual channels. Finding ways to cut corners, I guess it was a business decision. A bad one."

"So where did their meat come from?"

"Well, probably *abattoir* scraps, but it was the gangs running the meat, that's what stopped the business."

Gregor leans to her and strokes her hair gently then kisses her. Then he breaks off and looks into her eyes.

"How did we end up talking business again?" He kisses her again then rolls over, pulls the cover back and stands up.

"I'm going to get some coffee on the go."

He walks to the wardrobe door and steps into a walk-in closet, disappearing.

She gets a sudden flash in her mind. An image of a scene that Archie once described to her after the Kasamet had closed. The owner, an Indian man, had been found tied to chair, his head bent back so that his eyes were focused on the ceiling, with a huge saucepan sticking out of his mouth, its handle rammed down his throat. Archie had said that he had been like that for days before they found him. It is as if he is in the room now, in front of her, swollen neck, flies buzzing over his face, feeding on his open eyes, crawling down the sticky handle and disappearing into his mouth. Lucy lets him sit there, lifting her head from the pillow, as the image gets more solid she takes in every detail.

She asks, "How long have you known Spike?"

The question rings round the room for second before Gregor steps back out. He is wearing a white dressing gown. He looks at

Lucy lying in the bed, half covered with the sheet, her bleach blonde hair tussled, one of her breasts exposed, her pale arm reaching to the edge. As he walks past the bed toward the door he stops in front of the mirror. His torso is lean and muscular, his hair is sticking up at angles, ruffled.

"Why?" he asks.

"Do you trust him?"

"Why?"

"There's something about him. Maybe it's just the way he was looking at me."

He turns to face Lucy.

"The way he was looking at you?"

"I don't know, it's probably nothing."

"I've known him a while. You've just met him. He's a big guy, not always easy to read. Yes, I trust him. Unless there's something else you're not telling me?"

"No, no. It's nothing, just me. It's probably nothing."

"It's nothing."

He leans down to kiss her again. She sits up and puts her arms around his neck.

"Hey there's no rush is there? Come back to bed."

"Business."

Gregor leaves the room. Lucy gets up and takes her clothes, untangling them from his, and goes to the bathroom. She steps into the shower. The warm water against her face feels good and she stays there for a long time. When she comes out, she wraps a towel around herself and opens the door. The steam dissipates in the landing and she tries Gregor's bedroom door. It's locked again. She can hear him talking downstairs. She moves quietly halfway down the stairs until she can hear what he's saying.

"Who have you got covering him? I'll send you a recent photograph. Well, if Ali meets him at all, I have to know immediately. And then … yes. Yes, that'll be the end of Ali."

Gregor listens to whoever is on the other end, Lucy takes another step, then freezes as she hears Gregor shout into the phone. It is the first time she has heard him angry and the intensity of it sends tremors of fear through her. "I DON'T CARE WHAT CARDS ALI IS HOLDING, IF HE'S WITH STRANSTEC, I'M

HITTING HIM!" She moves quickly back upstairs and into her room. She closes the door and leans against it. The girl on the edge of tears looks at her from the canvas.

CHAPTER FIFTEEN

Alison stopped taking the train into the city because she was getting so wet. Once in the car she very quickly began to relish having that personal space. Even if she was sitting in traffic, at least she was comfortable. At the end of the day she didn't have to rush to the station, she could stay late, she could go home whenever wanted to.

In the office, she was the manager's first choice. He chose her to be the one who dealt with important or tricky contracts. One contract was representing a very wealthy vendor who was picky about who he sold his property to and what they were going to use it for. He wanted the property, which was a listed building, to retain the design features he had installed as well as the official heritage architectural features. She met with him several times and let him talk and talk, asked him about his business and interests. She secured a sale for above the price he was expecting, and she also showed him around some exclusive properties she knew of, on the pretext of showing him examples of what some of the most sought after architects were designing for the city centre. *What you are interested in is a very specialised area,* she told him as they took in the view of the city from a high rise studio space, *and the passion you have is truly a vocation. Converting old to new. I think that you will love Park Road. Not many properties like this come along at this kind of price,* she said. They visited the Park Road property together and he went for it. The feeling of achievement as she watched the elegant loops of the vendor's signature appear on the contract was like nothing she had experienced before. Inside she was excited like a child, she wanted to jump up and down and clap her hands, hug everyone in the room. Instead she smiled broadly and congratulated the millionaire on making an astute purchase. When she reported to her manager he was astounded.

"They bought? Hang on, weren't they selling?"

"Yes, they sold and they bought Park Road."

"You sold theirs? And they bought another? Park Road? They bought Park Road?" He scanned the papers she had put on his desk, open mouthed.

"Good grief, Alison, I really don't know how you did that. I put you onto them because I thought they were a pain in the ass. Alison, you're a treasure. Here, there are some other interesting inquiries coming up you might want to handle. The Phoenix development, do you know about it? You should take a look." He took some files from his drawer.

"I know it, that's not due for acquisition for months."

"We've got a heads up. Take a look at what they're doing." He handed her a file. She promised to give it a look over and walked out of his office, leaving him looking at the paperwork and shaking his head.

As she walked through the main office she could feel the eyes of the others on her. She felt energised, like she had just been linked to a chain of electricity.

Back home, she was sitting on the couch with her laptop open, reading from the screen and turning a pen slowly between her teeth as Martin flicked from one news channel to another.

"You are getting later and later," he said.

"Later and later?"

"Home. After work."

She continued to read from the screen, scrolling down.

"That's because I'm working later and later."

"And who are you working with?"

She looked up. "Martin, I'm working alright? It's not like I'm missing out, when I get back you're stuck up in your room anyway. I'm not working with anyone."

"Do you have to work when you get home?"

She closed the laptop and put down her pen.

"Okay. Sorry, I'm here now." She leaned back and lay across the sofa, so that her feet were in Martin's lap. "Can you do my feet babe?"

"Sure," he said and put his hands around a foot.

"Where's the remote?" she asked, and he handed it to her.

While she pressed the buttons to skim through the channels, he watched the changing images on the screen and massaged the sole of her foot with his thumb. She went through channel after channel, occasionally stopping for longer than a few seconds, but never long enough for Martin to get a grip of what the images were saying.

"There's nothing ever on," she said.

That night they went to bed together and lay side by side. They didn't turn the light off and lay facing each other.

Martin saw the rounded contours of Alison's face and the lines around her eyes and mouth. Her eyes closed slowly as she put her hand to his face and moved her head so that her lips met his. They kissed tenderly and she slowly rolled on top of him. This was the first time in weeks they had been this close.

Martin tried to think, had they made love since the rain started? Since the Sugar Club? He was willing himself to get aroused. He felt no sensation in his groin, he knew that they were making contact, but he felt nothing. They caressed each other, Martin running his fingers up and down her back, Alison gently holding his head and neck as their mouths opened wider and their breathing got heavier. Alison eased her hand down his chest, over his stomach and down. Martin felt she may as well have put her hand into a black hole, into a vacuum.

"I'm sorry," he said, "it's not … sorry."

"Martin," Alison replied, "don't apologise, I like kissing, let's just kiss." They did, but all Martin could think of was why his body was not responding to what his mind was telling it to do. He tried to concentrate. The sickly thick smell of the pack of men jerking their cocks in the cold storage room of the Club came to him, and his stomach heaved. He dry retched into Alison's kissing mouth. She straightened up, straddling him. "What was that? Are you okay?"

"I'm just not feeling great, let's just …"

Alison looked down at him and said, "Yeah, you look a bit yellow." She moved off him. Martin turned away from her, curling his knees up to his chest, pulling the duvet over his shoulder.

"I'll be fine, I'm just not feeling right. Can you turn off the light?"

Alison leaned from the bed and turned the lamp off. Immediately Martin felt himself relax. The darkness of the room gave him some distance from her, from himself. He didn't feel like he had to say anything when the light was off.

"Oh yeah," she said through the dark, "I meant to say, I've got that office thing tomorrow night, it would be great if you could give me a lift in."

"No problem."

"It shouldn't be a late one."

The rain continued to fall.

CHAPTER SIXTEEN

Maya's husband drives a big black four-by-four with tinted windows. There is someone in the passenger seat, another man.

The car is easy to track. Henry has tracked so many lives over the years, followed so many people's personal maps of the city streets. Each time it is like a combination lock; a simple reordering of the familiar and each person has their own code to unlock the city. Henry has an imprint of the city in his mind. The pathways he has tracked crisscross and connect like synapses. The patterns are embedded, they can never be undone. Henry's mind is a mesh of the tracks left by others people's lives, secrets, and crimes.

All the time he passes through the city like a ghost, unattached and unseen, making no marks of his own. His thin frame and sunken eyes do not encourage a second glance. One look is enough to see right through him. His small, thin-lipped mouth does not demand any attention, his inquiries are innocuous enough never to be called to mind again, and his paper-thin presence is instantly forgettable. When people do speak to him, they often empty out their souls, tell him what they could never tell anyone else. Maybe it's because they sense that he will disappear. Maybe it's because, in his expressionless face, his unjudging, unflinching demeanour, they see that he will never have anyone to tell, and if he does tell, no-one will listen to him anyway.

O O O

Maya has sent some family pictures to his phone. She is as Henry pictured her, but younger. Her voice carries a weight of years her face does not. She has attractive exotic features, like a Caribbean queen. Her husband is broad and muscular and very tall, shockingly pale in comparison, with a bald head and a thick neck, on the side of which is the tattoo of a scorpion. Her daughter looks like her, or how she would have looked as an awkward teenager. There is a palm tree behind them and sand at their feet. The picture must be a few years old because the girl looks young, about fifteen, skinny, straight hair, and braces. He stands behind the two of them towering like a smiling colonial giant who is about to snatch them off their tropical island.

Within an hour of trailing, Henry sees it's clear that the Scorpion man doesn't work for a chemicals firm. First he goes to a run-down area in the north part of the city, to a cluster of high-rise flats constructed generations ago, rising like rotten teeth from the skyline.

Henry sees the black four by four pull up in a car park. Henry parks up and watches the children roam in gangs and the broken and elderly shuffle past. The Scorpion man, dressed in a black suit, gets out of the four by four and it pulls away. He enters the block of flats. These layers of concrete were designed to be used, not admired, and are now abused and feared, even by those who live there.

The clouds behind the grimy flat roofs pass quickly until the Scorpion man comes back out from the foot of the tower dressed in stained white overalls and walks to a white van. He puts a hold-all, which is weighted so that the straps are straining, into the back of the van and then gets in the driver's seat. Henry notes the number plate and lets the van get to the end of the street before starting up and following.

He follows the van east, around the city ring road to a wealthy suburb. The white van turns off the main street and down a leafy estate road. Halfway down, in the shadow of an old elm, Scorpion gets out and carries the hold-all to the side door of a semi-detached, where he knocks three times. The door is opened by a man in glasses and they disappear inside.

Henry unties his shoelace and gets out of his car and walks down the street. Beside the van he kneels to tie his lace and slips a tracker on the underside of the van. He walks a bit further, and crosses the road. He lights a cigarette and looks at the house Scorpion has disappeared into. All of the curtains in the house are pulled across. The garden is tended, the grass no longer than next door. The face of the house is giving nothing away.

Henry walks back to his car. While he waits he looks again at the family picture and checks the tracker receiver on his phone. Twenty-four minutes later Scorpion emerges with an empty hold-all and gets back in the van. Henry lets him pull away, then opens up his glove box and rummages through some laminated cards till he finds the one he is looking for.

He goes to the house, to the front door, and rings the bell. No answer. He rings again. Still no answer. Henry takes the card from his wallet. It is dark blue laminate with gold writing and a lightning bolt across the top. It says *Sorry we missed you, Don't miss out on our outstanding power offers—the Power Fix team.* He bends down to peek through the letter box as he puts the card in the door. He can't see anything, but a smell of chlorine mixed with ammonia comes to his nose, like cat piss in a swimming pool. Henry gets back in his car and switches the tracker on his phone on. The van is moving toward the centre of the city. He could wait here until the glasses guy leaves the house and then get in and check it out, or he could follow Scorpion. It's still early in the day; 12:50. Henry gets the feeling that the glasses guy doesn't leave that house very often. He starts the car and follows the van into the city.

The city in the day is noisy and hot. The traffic moves slowly and Henry cuts across some streets to come out within sight of the white van. The van parks in a car park near the central train station, in a long-term bay. Scorpion emerges from it without his white overalls, back in his dark suit and with a briefcase and a shoulder bag, looking like a businessman on an overnight trip. Henry watches him walk out of the car park and disappear into the throng, people all moving with purpose, all with somewhere to go, all dressed in dark city clothes, crisscrossing shades of grey and blue and black. Henry undoes his shoelace again and goes to the white van, detaching the magnetic tracker.

Back in his car, he calls Maya.

"When he takes his calls, where does he go, in your house I mean? Does he have an office?"

"In the garden usually. We have a gazebo, he stands there and talks and smokes."

O O O

Within an hour Henry is at Maya's house, finding suitable locations for tiny microphones in the timber gazebo in the garden. The house is a well-kept detached, with a walled garden at the back. Under the circular gazebo roof sit two wicker armchairs and a glass table with a full ashtray in the middle. Maya sits on one of the chairs. She looks more tired than the Maya in the photograph, her nose more bulbous, her eyes smaller. There are string lights tied up to the eaves of the gazebo. Henry unscrews one and attaches the microphone in its place.

"You don't have a wife do you, Mr. Bloomburg?" Maya's voice rises lazily from the wicker chair. Henry finds the power switch for the string lights and turns them on and off and on again.

"Some people are never meant to share themselves. Some are never meant to keep anything of their own. I try to tell my daughter this, but it's not something you can teach, you have to live it to learn it don't you think, Mr. Bloomburg?"

Henry checks the signal on the transmitter, then turns around.

"That's done."

Maya leads him back to the front door.

"Maybe it's something you don't understand, Mr. Bloomburg, trying to come to terms with someone who has turned it all around. What you thought was the best idea turns around and it the worst thing you could have done?"

She opens the door.

"Mrs.—"

"Maya."

"Maya, everything is turning all the time. It's hard to make sense of something that won't stay still. I'll be in contact."

Henry goes and gets some food from a drive-thru before settling down in his car just a house away from the Scorpion man's home. He finishes each of his chicken wings and his French fries.

Into the cola he pours some rum and drinks and smokes and dozes.

His phone rings. It's Kramer.

"Kramer. It's late."

"I'm on stake out. I got something for your ghost hunt, Bloomburg. An artefact to add. A hand."

"A hand."

"Severed at the wrist. Lab says maybe eighteen months since separation and likely female."

"Where?"

"It was from the beat. Some small time dealers were busted on the street—kids selling weed and pills. They tried to get rid of their stash in a small alley behind where they were dealing. When the boys went to clean up, they found the hand. Lomax road. Right in the middle. It's sealed off, but nothing else so far."

"Lomax. Okay, thanks Kramer. I owe you."

"If it comes to anything, you can owe me. You on a case?"

"Same as you. I got chicken wings."

"Ah. Bucket or basket?"

"Basket."

"I'm on bucket. It's gonna be a long night."

Henry sees the black four-by-four approach and pull in to the drive.

"My man has just arrived. I got to go. Thanks, Kramer."

Henry hangs up and sits up straight. Scorpion is still in his formal suit. He sees Maya welcome him home with a kiss. She reaches her lips up to him like a deer feeding from the branches of a tree.

Soon Henry picks up his voice from the bug in the gazebo. He speaks with a tone that surprises Henry. There is a softness to it, a rise at the end of each sentence.

"Yeah, sure," he is saying, "I can do that. I got somewhere safe. When do you want me to get her? Okay. Well, if there's heat, yes, of course, best keep her out of it. No problem. Let me know if there's any change, I'll let you know when I've picked her up."

CHAPTER SEVENTEEN

Alison was supposed to be there at nine, but by the time Martin pulled up outside the restaurant it was twelve minutes past.

"Blame me," he said as she stood from the car.

"I will," she said and closed the door.

Martin watched her walk quickly with her handbag above her head to the door of the restaurant. The vibration of their argument was still in the car.

They had sat in silence till they got to the first roundabout, Alison with both hands on her handbag in her lap and Martin in his loose jeans and grey sweater top, and then, as the car veered onto the slip road and her head lolled to the side so that her hair touched the glass of the passenger window, he pushed down the accelerator and they were speeding down into the rush and spray of the motorway. Alison said, *Jesus, slow down!* The motorway was moving fast, the surface water was thrown up into a constant cloud around the cars, so that tyres disappeared, and the steel and glass shells were agitated, their outlines unreliable. It was the lights, the pairs of red lights ahead of the pumping wiper blades that gave any sense to the road. *I thought we were in a rush,* said Martin. Alison slammed her handbag in her lap. As she started to shout a truck overtook their car, splashing water against the door, and blinding them with a flash of water as it passed. Everything was noisy and distorted.

"I would like to get there alive! Slow down! How can you have nothing to do all day and still manage not to be ready when we need to go? This is the only thing I asked you to do, to get me there on time, and you can't even do that."

"You're such a drama queen. We're only a bit behind. How come this is such a big deal anyway? You never get this dressed up if we go out."

"We never go out—Watch out! You're too close! Slow down!"

The rushing traffic on the wet road and the constant whipping of the blades across the window was loud in Martin's head and Alison's voice sounded shrill and anxious on top of it. His fingers gripped the wheel and he clenched his teeth. His muscles tensed and he pushed down on the accelerator even more, swerving out of his lane and overtaking cars in front, then swerving back into the lane.

Alison started really shouting now. "Martin! Martin! Stop, it's too fast!"

Martin pulled out of his lane again, just as a car came speeding up behind them. There was a loud beep and flashing headlights. Martin pushed his foot to the ground. Ahead he could see there was a queue and cars ahead were slowing. He took his foot off the accelerator and pressed the brake. He felt the tyres slide and control of the car leave his hands. The feeling was like being electrocuted—all of a sudden every cell in his body was vibrating at a different speed and the car lost all of its weight as if the steering wheel had come off in his hands—and then he caught control of the car again and the moment was over. The motorway traffic slowed as it started to bottleneck into the city roads. Martin and Alison were soon part of a long wet metal chain, as the water on the city roads squeezed the traffic even tighter together. The pools against the footpaths had spread into the streets. The urge to rip the steering wheel from its mount and crash the car had passed, but Martin still seethed. He couldn't bring himself to look at Alison.

"You didn't even think to invite me," he spat. "I bet the others there are bringing their partners."

"You've always said how much you hate this kind of thing."

"I've never been to this kind of thing."

"Well if you wanted to go, you should have said, and then I would have made you buy some clothes and get a haircut. You haven't been out of the house in weeks. When was the last time you even had a shave? Just let me out here, I'll walk the rest of the way."

"No, you won't. If there was something for me to shave for, or get dressed up for, then I would. You have no idea how fucking hurtful that is, you know."

"Well do something about it. Do something about something for once, and just trying to drive like a moron does not count as doing something. Right at these lights. Ten minutes late now."

"Alright, stop going on about the time! I'm sorry okay? I'm sorry I caused you to be late."

"It's up here on the right. Anywhere here."

"I'll drop you right outside."

"You don't have to, anywhere here is fine."

"I'm dropping you right outside."

"You can't stop right outside."

"I'm stopping right outside."

After she had walked through the door of the restaurant without looking back, he pulled away and was back in the traffic. *My God*, he thought, *I need a drink, I need to get out of this car. I need to change this. I need to do something.*

He drove aimlessly through the waterlogged streets of the city. His mind was like a piece of short elastic, he tried to stretch it but it kept snapping back to his angry desperation, and every time it did, it hurt him more. Before long he was driving alongside the great wide river, swollen and fast flowing, the massive weight of water rolling and muscular, moving with blind unfulfillable purpose.

There was an old bar in the docks that he had not been to in years. He used to meet a girlfriend there, years before he met Alison. It was the only place she felt they could go where she could be absolutely sure no-one she knew would see them together. The promise he kept was to never mention her husband or family when they were together. She would talk about her teaching job and the people she worked with. The bar would gradually fill up with old men, talking about racing results and football scores. The seats smelled, and on the yellowed walls were old pictures of the shipping yards as they had been, of men standing proudly in the past, surrounded by cranes and boats and full storage yards.

The streets were quieter the closer he got to the old dockyards, the lights were further apart, there was more space for darkness in between. He turned down a side street and pulled over. As he turned the lights of the car off and took his keys from the ignition, his phone beeped. It was a text message. From Alison. In the shadows of the car, the phone screen illuminated Martin's face as he read. *Sorry about earlier. I feel terrible. I don't like us fighting x.* He read the message again, and was just about to press reply when somebody fell against the bonnet of the car. He snapped up in his seat. The window had steamed up and he couldn't see.

There was a shape on the bonnet that was sliding off as if it had been hit. Martin's heart seemed to double in size and he felt it fill his chest. He opened his door and stood out, his big heart now pounding as he peered around the door of the car. The person was standing up again, unsteadily. It was a woman.

It was Zoe.

Her hair was wet, pushed down onto her head and her white jacket was stained with grime from the wet street. She held a handbag in one hand and with the other leaned against the car to steady herself.

"Zoe. Zoe, are you alright?"

She looked up at Martin. He could see the effort in her face as she tried to focus on him.

"It's Martin, Ozzy's friend. Are you okay?"

"Ozzy, that cunt," she slurred. "You know him? Well you can tell him from me that he's a cunt. From me. Cunt."

"I will, I will. What are you doing out here? Who are you with?"

Zoe looked around her, and then at Martin. Her face changed. Her eyes opened wide and her mouth downturned, and she said, "I don't know. Ozzy, cunt … but I don't know …" Her voice broke and she started to cry, "… I don't know where I am."

Martin stepped to her and put his hand on her arm, rubbing it, tilting his head and bending his knees a little, so that his face was level with hers. "Don't worry. Hey, I can give you a lift home. Don't worry, we'll get you home safe and sound." She looked into his eyes and wiped her hand across her nose. The rain was beating down, running down her face. His face was getting wet, too, he could feel drips running down his collar.

"Really?" she said. "Really? Home?"

"Of course. Come on, you're soaked."

"What's wrong with your eyes? What's your name again?"

"Come on, I'll get you home."

"I want to go home."

"I'll get you there, Zoe. Come on. Who were you with?" He walked her round to the passenger side and opened the door. "Who were you with?"

"I don't want to go back to Ozzy's, I want to go home."

"Sure, we'll get you home now."

She stumbled into the car and Martin closed the door. As he walked around to his side, he looked up and down the street. There was no-one around, no traffic had passed, nothing except the rain falling through the lights and into the shadows. At the end of the road he could see the distant yellowed light from the windows of the bar, the Bucket O' Blood, though its outline was lost through the dark and the rain. He sat into the car. The sound against the roof was a frantic metallic Morse.

Zoe looked a mess. He could see her bra through her netted top which looked like it had been ripped at the collar. She was soaked through and seemed to be just about holding her head above a rising tide of unconsciousness. In one hand she held her handbag, and in the other she was clutching a broken necklace, a cheap string of badly coloured amber glass beads. She turned to look at Martin, her eyes straining with the effort of focusing.

"I recognise you, I know you. What's wrong with your eyes?" she asked. "What was your name again? Matty?"

He turned the key in the ignition. The engine started and he looked again in his mirrors. Deserted. The only movement was the water falling from above, dappling the street lights, and the water of the great broad river behind him, pushing all the waste, the sediment, the unwanted excess, beyond the city.

"Max," he said. "Max is my name."

CHAPTER EIGHTEEN

L ucy takes the joint being handed to her. She holds her breath in and passes the joint around the table. Then she laughs and a cloud of smoke comes from her mouth and she coughs. She is with Franz and two friends of his.

Martin has never seen her laugh before.

One of Franz's friends is doing an impression of a dancer, posing and moving around the kitchen table. Franz had delivered some clothes for Lucy. He had been back and to the house a few times, each time bringing more clothes for Lucy and helping her try them on. Gregor had seen they were getting on well. This time Gregor had spoken quietly and evenly to Franz in another room while Lucy pulled a new dress over her head and turned to see her side profile in the mirror. Then Franz came through the door and told Lucy to get her shoes on if she wanted to come to his place for a party.

Now the long curtains are drawn across Franz's balcony door and a breeze is pushing them gently, softly billowing into the room. Lucy's laughter bounces gleefully around the apartment. Franz comments on how lovely it is to hear her laugh. She says it does feel good, like she hasn't laughed in the longest time. *Gregor, he takes care of me,* she says, *but he's not exactly a bottle of laughs.* They all laugh again, and their laughter rolls itself out of the balcony door, bouncing off the opposite building, down onto the narrow street below, reverberating with a life of its own.

Martin sees the voices, clasped together turning one over the other like a ball of colours lighting up the street. He turns his attention back to the apartment.

It's later. Lucy is lying back on the sofa, dozing off as Franz and one of his friends continue to chat and laugh at the little table. The night is still warm, the balcony door is still open, the orange curtains are still billowing gently. She knows that soon Gregor will be there to collect her and bring her back to his immaculately clean house, and so she wants to enjoy this feeling of unadorned comfort. She smiles as she drifts off. She can hear Franz explain that the reason he won't ever ask the guy out is because he enjoys the feeling of having a crush, and fulfilling the wish might totally change the feeling. It's better to stick with what you have if you're happy than risk it and end up heartbroken. That's happened too many times.

Lucy feels herself slowly sinking into the old battered couch, she senses the warm embrace of unconsciousness. Gregor will be here soon to pick her up.

Lucy wakes in the quiet of the front room. The sofa has become uncomfortable. The balcony door is closed and Franz and his friend have gone to bed. She sits up. There on the table is Franz's phone. She picks it up and pushes the keys to write: *I'm in. First chance to contact. Not my number. G address 406 Alderway south. Do not reply.* She types in the number and presses send. On the phone display a letter grows wings and ascends like an angel. She clears the message history and deletes the text log. On the table is the box with tobacco and weed in it. She sits at the table and rolls herself a joint. She puts it in her pocket and rolls another.

CHAPTER NINETEEN

The next day the rain stopped. In the morning Alison was making coffee and looked out the window to see a patch of blue in the sky. She went to the front door and stepped outside. The clouds had whitened and broken up. The sun shining through was a gentle balm on the young skin of the estate, and there was a freshness, a rejuvenation in the air that she breathed in deeply. The front door of the house opposite opened and a tall man dressed in shorts and t-shirt, carrying a gym bag, walked to his car door. He waved across at Alison. *It's stopped,* he said with a beaming smile. That was the first time Alison had ever heard him speak. *I know, at last, isn't it great,* she replied. *I was going to build an ark,* he said and they laughed as he got in his car. Alison stayed on the doorstep and as he pulled away he gave a salute and she waved. Her car was not in the driveway. Martin must have had an early night and would be getting some shopping in before the Saturday afternoon rush.

This is the kind of day that we should go walking, she thought, and we can get over that stupid row last night. *Walking is always good for getting perspective on what seems like a big deal. They could go somewhere nice for lunch, a country pub, or make lunch and bring it. I wonder what Martin will bring back from the shop, if he's thinking the same thing.* Alison was idly thinking these things and enjoying the warmth of the sun on her face when her car pulled in to the driveway. *Not a very thorough shop then,* she thought, but that thought stopped as she saw Martin emerge from the car.

He had had his hair cut. Right back. And his beard was gone. A rush of joy passed through her and she clapped her hands together and squealed. He stood by the car with a sheepish smile, rubbing his now shaven scalp.

"Oh, my God, Martin, you look totally different!"

"You like it?"

"Yes, yes!" she ran toward him "I love it! Oh wow! You look a lot younger! And I can see your chin, your lovely, lovely chin! Martin, you didn't say anything!" She ran her fingers over the thin film of hair from his forehead over his crown and onto the back of his head. "Oh I like the feel of this. It's like having a new man. Who's just been released from jail."

"Good, I'm glad you like it. Wait till you see my tattoos."

"You didn't."

"No, I didn't."

"Do you? Do you like it?"

"I'll get used to it I think. It's nice not having a beard. Weird. Feels odd you know? But I like it. And you're right, it is a damn fine chin. Hey, you're still in your dressing gown. Come on, get inside. First though …" he opened the car door and took out a plastic bag. Inside was a shoe box.

"What's this? For me?"

"No, for me," Martin said and pulled back the lid. Inside was a pair of running shoes, with black and red stripes down the side.

"What? You're going to start …"

"Well, just around the estate you know."

"Martin, I don't believe it."

"I'm not going to do a marathon or anything, don't get your hopes up. It's not like I'm suddenly going to be an athlete. Just a bit of running."

Alison looked again at the running shoes and stood on her toes and kissed his cheek.

"I think you're great," she said.

"I haven't done it yet, I haven't done anything yet."

"Yeah, but most people don't bother even trying. Are you going to start today? It's not raining. Can we go out? I would love a walk, wouldn't that be nice? Have you smelt the air?"

"I can smell coffee. Let's get you inside, you're not dressed, come on." He put his arm around her and they walked together away from the car and through the front door. They didn't mention the argument the night before. Martin didn't ask how the dinner had gone. Alison didn't ask what he had done for the night. The clouds drifted further apart, thinning as they spread, letting the blue and the sun pour through, rolling its way over the streets of the new estate and to the hills beyond.

O O O

Martin started to jog around New Acre estate every morning. As Alison pulled out of the driveway he would wave her goodbye and tie the laces of his running shoes. He would close the door and put the key in the zip pocket of his shorts and set off.

It took him a while to get used to moving the weight of his own body at more than a walking pace. At first he pushed himself too hard too quickly and by the time he was at the second turning he was bent over double, hands on his knees, with his heart thudding in his chest. Only on the third day did he find his natural pace. He started to take different routes around the estate, exploring every road and cul-de-sac, until by the end of the week he had found a good circuit.

The tarmac beneath his feet was not as tough as he had thought it would be, there was a slight give, a sponginess, not like the streets of the city. His route took him out of his driveway and right, straight down Paxton Drive, past the turning for Scott Close and Barry Close, then across the road and left down Wyatt Way.

The houses on Wyatt Way changed. The driveways were wider and the gaps between the houses were more pronounced. There was an extra window in the upstairs although the houses didn't seem any wider than the ones on Paxton Drive. As Martin jogged down the slight incline of Wyatt Way he would glance up at the extra upstairs windows of the houses, hoping to see evidence of elaborate lives, imagining the extra room stretching the possibilities of the lives lived within, but never saw anything behind the glass.

Once he reached the end of Wyatt Way, Martin turned right along Macintosh Close, and here a wooden fence ran straight along beside him while across the road the houses nudged back closer together and the driveways squeezed back to their regular size. Sometimes a cat, thin and grey, would leap up from the path in front of him, balancing on the thin slats of wood and eyeing him, watching him coming closer, out of breath and sweating, before lithely disappearing into the greenery on the other side.

Martin didn't encounter many people while running. New Acre didn't have a local shop or any kind of commercial centre within it, so there was no reason for people to walk. He did pass the occasional woman walking a dog or pushing a pram, and there was a cursory exchange of nods, but that was it. Only at the edges of the estate did he have to consider moving aside for anything. That was where the bushes and trees had started to stretch their branches over the wooden fence, making a slow effort to reclaim the space as their own, and Martin ducked a bit or ran on the road until another house stood between him and the countryside.

When he reached the end of Macintosh Close, Foster Road curved back up the hill again and joined to Scott Road Martin steeled himself for the climb back up to his house. Here he didn't look at the houses, he had his head down, focusing on lifting his knees and his feet, one after the other, feeling the strain in his calves and the sweat on the back of his neck and the burn in his lungs as he pushed himself up the hill.

The first time Martin took this route, all the way around New Acre and back up the hill, he got through his front door and went straight for the sink. He poured himself a pint of water and held himself up on the sink edge, gulping it down before slumping to the floor and listening to his heart race, feeling his neck tighten with every breath. His chest ached with every breath like an iron plate compressing his lungs and his thighs ached and burned. This is what change feels like, he thought. Like it wants to kill me.

CHAPTER TWENTY

Lucy is submerged in a dark dreamless sleep when the knock on Franz's door comes. She hears it dimly, as if it is a memory she is trying to recall but keeps slipping away. Franz is at the door, just in his underwear.

Lucy opens her eyes and leans over the arm of the sofa to see the shape of a huge man in the hallway. It's not Gregor. Her throat constricts and her stomach drops. Why is Gregor not here? Who has come for her?

Franz is asking the same questions to the man at the door. The replies come in a soft lilting accent. It is a voice which offers words rather than putting them down. She relaxes immediately. It's Spike.

Franz lets him in, turning around and calling, "Lucy, wake up sweetie, your chaperone is here, and it's Spike, you lucky girl." Spike squeezes down the narrow hallway and through the door. Lucy lies back on the couch and pulls the blanket over her.

"Lucy, I've come to get you. Gregor's been delayed," he says, "and won't make it home tonight. He sent me to get you."

"You're taking me home?"

"Well, no. Gregor doesn't want you at his house alone tonight."

Spike is too big for the flat, his head nearly touches the ceiling and the table and chairs next to him look small and fragile.

Franz steps from behind his huge frame and looks up to him.

"Well, she can just stay here."

"No, she has to come with me."

"Is that okay with you, babes?"

Lucy nods.

"Okay, just close the door on your way out. Goodnight, sweetheart."

Franz leans down and gives her a kiss on the cheek. As he squeezes past Spike he runs his hand across his chest and says, "Nice to see you big boy." Spike is eyeing everything in the room, the phone and the box of weed on the table, the cheap prints of old cigarette advertising on the wall, the bookshelf stuffed full with fashion magazines.

When Lucy sits up and asks why Gregor can't come and get her like he said he would, he looks surprised and says, "I thought you might know by now that with Gregor, it's really best not to ask, it's always complicated. Don't worry," he says, "where we are going is safe. Trust me."

In the car she says, "Spike, you would tell me if anything had happened to Gregor, wouldn't you?"

"Don't worry," Spike says, "he's fine, this is just a precaution. You know how protective he can be."

Lucy looks out the window at the passing streets, so quiet at this time, so many shadows which now hide so much, but in a few hours in the daylight will have lost their mystery. She tells herself that there hasn't been enough time since the message for anything to have happened. Anyway, she thinks, Stranstec always likes things thoroughly prepared. He will move in on Gregor, but when he is ready, and not until he is sure it will work.

Lucy says, "Can you put on some music?"

Spike turns the radio on and the car is filled with the sounds of tinny electric guitars and drum beats which sound like a fly in a can. Lucy remembers the first time she saw Stranstec.

O O O

He was sitting obscured by a cloud of cigarette smoke. The desk in front of him was piled high with forged documents: passports, birth certificates, and work permits. She had heard the men in the truck talk about him, call him the captain. She put her papers on the table. He took them, scanning. Through the fogged-up window she could see the lights of waiting vans. The two girls who went before her were getting into one of them.

She said, "I'm not going to be a prostitute."

He looked up at her, the cigarette dangling from his lip.

"Listen," he checked the papers for her name, "Marketa, is that your name?" She nodded. "Marketa, sweetie, when you see the difference between what your sisters get paid for sucking a cock good and what the poor bitches who clean and serve and slave all week get, you'll be on your knees asking me to give you a letter of recommendation."

"They're not my sisters. Let them do it."

Stranstec leaned back in his chair and put the cigarette out in the full ashtray. "Whatever, but if you came to this country to make good money, then …"

"That's why I came. And I will be rich. I will not have to spread myself for ten men a night to do it when I can do it for one. One who counts. Like you, I like you."

Stranstec sat back in his chair. "You don't know me."

"And you don't know me. But you do like me, don't you?" she said.

"Your English is very good, Marketa. What age are you?"

"Seventeen."

"And why are you here?"

"To make myself."

"To make yourself?"

"To make me who I want to be."

A shout came from behind the door. "Boss! Another coming in!"

She said, "Can we come to some arrangement? You and me?"

He shouted back, "Wait!" He stood up and walked around to her, taking her by the arm, and led her back through the door she had just come through. There was a line of girls, all looking scared and unsure, and she passed their eyes without meeting them. Stranstec led her into a small narrow kitchen and said, "You will have to wait here. This will take a while. There is tea and coffee. Nothing to eat, or, wait …" He reached up into one of the door-less cupboards and pulled down a packet of biscuits. Then he left her and closed the door.

She turned the tap on and held a cup beneath the flow of water, but her hand was shaking too much to hold it steady. She leaned against the worktop and tried to calm herself. It had worked. He was going to take her.

Since she was a young teenager she had known she had a power that she could use. When she was fourteen she saw a phantom appear in the eyes of the principal of her school as she stood in front of him and played with the hem of her skirt. She learned that she could summon that black spirit into the eyes of men, and now when she had needed it most, she had done it again.

That was how she got together with Stranstec. He had put her in an apartment and gave her money once a week. At first he used her only for short, almost apologetic, sexual visits, but as the weeks passed, he began to stay for longer, talking, making food for them both, bringing movies for them to watch together. He would bring marijuana for them to smoke or cocaine for them to snort, occasionally he'd arrive with a new outfit for her and a handful of speed tablets.

She used the money he gave her to go to English lessons and attend computer classes. She bought a laptop and downloaded all of the '30s swing jazz music she could. She would dance around her city apartment in her pyjamas, spinning around with her eyes closed following the deep loose sound of the double bass.

She started to know the city. She had her favourite café, her favourite bar, her favourite cinema. Stranstec spoke of his plans to get rich. She wanted to go to university. She had seen her mother work two jobs, cleaning and stitching in a garment factory, and still have to come home every day to a cold leaking shell of a house without enough for the three of them. She had seen her father, rich with a thousand melodies, sicken and starve. She wanted to be comfortable, educated, always have enough.

One day Stranstec told her he was going to leave his wife. The movie they had been watching had just finished. It was an evil spirit that moved from person to person who was responsible for the murders, which was why every time the detective caught a new suspect, they could never remember what they had done, and another sickening sadistic murder occurred somewhere else. It could never be stopped. She was lying across his lap in the darkness of the front room of her little flat as the credits rolled on a shot of the detective walking away into the city when he told her.

"There's something new coming to the street. It's going to be big. One of my contacts gave me a sample and will be able to get me a bag. It's going to make somebody a lot of money, and I can be that somebody. But I'll need your help."

She sat up and faced him. He brushed her hair back away from her face, over her ears, and leaned close to her.

"You're the only one who can do this, but once it's done, I can leave Julie, and we will have enough to go wherever we want and do whatever we want to do."

"What about the girls?"

"I've been tired of running girls for a while now, you know that. Ever since I found you I'm tired of sending scared sweet faces to vans waiting in the cold. Since I've been with you I don't want to do that anymore, and here's my chance, our chance, to get out. At least with drugs, people have a choice. They choose to take or not to take, and this stuff, Spiral, a lot of people are going to want to take it. I'm serious, this is going to hit big."

"What is it you want me to do?" she said and he took her hands and told her.

He told her all about Gregor, and how he could get her to him. Gregor is a powerful man, and dangerous, but he knew how to play him. First there was Archie, but he would be no problem for her, that would be the easy part. He would set Archie up for Gregor to come. He wouldn't be able to resist her. She would have to stick exactly to the plan, right to the end. It might take some time, and during that time Gregor could not suspect a thing. When he did come and get her, Spiral would be his and they could do whatever they wanted.

"And you promise you'll leave Julie? It will be just you and me?"

"I promise. Just you and me."

"Ok, I will do it. But I will have to not be me. I will have another name. Lucy."

"Lucy?"

"Lucy. It was what my daddy called his saxophone. Lucy."

"When you go to Archie, you will have nothing, like you just came from the van. Okay? Like you never met me. You've got to forget that you met me."

The last time she had seen Stranstec, he had kissed her and held her close.

"You've changed my life," he said, "and now you can change both our lives forever. Be careful. Just stick to the plan, and I will come and get you. Remember who you are. Lucy. Lucy. Remember, you have nothing, you are nobody. You are nobody. Lucy."

O   O   O

She tells herself this again as she sits in the passenger seat and watches the empty shadowy city pass by. Remember who you are. Nobody. Now she's glad it was Spike and not Gregor who picked her up. She would not even allow herself to think of Stranstec when Gregor is with her, for fear that Gregor can see straight through her, straight to the images that now run through her mind. Just the thought of being in his car now makes her feel suddenly uncomfortable and vulnerable, as if she has just realised she is naked.

She looks at Spike, his massive bulk, his big arms extending to the steering wheel, his head nearly touching the roof of the car. She can see why Gregor entrusts him with so much. He doesn't ask him to deceive, though. It's hard to imagine Spike lying. Lucy looks at the scorpion running from his collar bone, up the side of his neck, its tail curling around behind his ear. She imagines it carries messages from his body straight to his brain. The messages don't get corrupted. There is a directness, an uncomplicated physicality that Spike possesses.

But if Gregor wanted to hurt her, he wouldn't send Spike to do it. When she heard Gregor talking on the phone to Spike he didn't say, *You'll have to take him out*, he said, *I'll have to take him out*. She had seen Gregor's eyes as he cut into Archie's ear and the blood erupted over his blade. She recognised that excitement, that flash of pleasure in him when Archie screamed, because she felt it too. It was a rush of adrenaline, like an electrical current activating every molecule in her being. Gregor had seen it in her. She wonders where Gregor is now. She imagines him leaning over a cowering figure, pulling the knife away, blood on the blade.

The car passes shop fronts, shutters pulled down, lights off, homeless asleep in doorways. What she has to do now is forget about the message and re-inhabit the frail, helpless inconsequential Lucy; the nobody he took from the squalid flat that night. As the buildings get higher, she asks, "Where are we going?"

Spike replies, "You'll stay with someone I know. She's nice, you'll like her."

CHAPTER TWENTY-ONE

The running got easier. The steady rhythm of his feet and the quickening of his breath liberated his mind. He knew exactly where he was going—Paxton, past Scott and Barry, to Wyatt, Macintosh, Foster, and back to Paxton. He knew exactly what he would see—the new dark tarmac streets, the thin squashed red brick houses topped with grey tiles, the green of the small patch of grass, the brown fence holding the countryside at bay.

By the time he got back to the house, often running the route twice, passing the same woman and her dog or pram, he would shower and shave. After his showers he had started spending time looking at himself in the long bedroom mirror. He noticed his waist was slimmer, his legs were toned. He spent time looking at his face from different angles, lifting his chin, turning his head, to see if the double chin which he had noticed once his beard was gone was receding. He thought it was. *If I keep this up,* he thought, *I might change completely.*

After drying off he would sit down and type. He tried now to move the story forward, tried to remember what it was he had done in those short stories for *Noire* which had started this process, and sat down in his upstairs back room, *Ready now,* he thought, *ready now to get to grips with this story.* His breathing as he sat in front of the glowing screen was fuller than before, he thought, as if before he started running he hadn't been doing it right. His note-taking was more elaborate now. He tried to write every idea that ran through his head. The walls were becoming crowded, pages with diagrams, words underlined, and timelines with red marker points for crucial plot interventions.

Alison was still late getting back from the city. There were always meetings or extra paperwork which kept her at the office. Martin promised her he would take her out somewhere, *They needed a night out together,* he said. On this day, as he stood in the shower, watching the white soap slither down his slimmer, toned legs, he thought of a night at the opera. He stepped out of the shower and put a towel around himself, and went straight into his writing room. He had just booked two seats at the opera for them when his phone rang. His hair was still wet and as he looked at the call display drops fell and obscured the name.

It was Ozzy.

"It's safe to go back in the water," Ozzy said. "Billy's gone."

"Billy's left ICE?"

"Not left, he was fired."

"That's fantastic news! Rob finally saw sense or what?"

"No, well, Billy was off duty and drinking in the bar and he came on to Sophie a bit heavy."

"Like how?"

"Nothing he hasn't done before—commenting on her tits, standing way too close—that kind of thing."

"Yeah, so? He's been doing that to staff since I was there."

"Yeah, but Sophie has got together with Rob, so now it's not just harassing a member of staff, it's coming on to the boss's piece."

"Ha! So Rob got rid of him!"

"He's gone."

"Great! That's cheered me up. Billy never was much good at following what was going on around him. Did he not know they were together?"

"Apparently not. And get this, he cried when Rob fired him."

"Ha! Even better!" Martin unwrapped the towel from his waist and started drying his hair with one hand while talking. "So let's hope whoever takes his place in the chain isn't such an idiot, although I do think you'd have to look pretty hard."

"Well, not quite as bad, but no angel either."

"Who? Do I know them?"

"Me."

"You? Rob's put you on duty manager?"

"Yup. Watch out ICE, there's a new boy at the helm."

"Well, you have done your time. That's great, man. So do you get to boss people around now then? Has the power gone to your head yet? Have you shaved the pirate 'stash into something a bit neater and more central?"

"Not yet. Marty, come back to the club, man, even for a few shifts, I'll sort it for you. You should come back. How do you manage it, not working? I mean, don't you get bored?"

"We should hook up again, it's been a while, just let's not go back to the Sugar Club. Let's find somewhere else to go."

"Oh, yeah, that was the last time wasn't it? I haven't been back since, although I did hook up with a cracking brunette that time if I remember right. Pity her husband was there, too. Yeah, there's a thing, Zoe's off the scene."

Martin's breath froze. He stood up and half sat down for a second, pausing there with his legs bent then sat slowly down, his bare damp skin slowly sticking again to the seat.

"What, you stopped seeing her then?"

"Everybody stopped seeing her."

"What d'you mean?"

"Nobody's seen her for weeks, she's gone right off the radar. Her family have been putting photos of her all over the place, in the city, on the Internet. Missing."

Martin stood up again. He had the towel over his head and he pressed the towel to his hair, slowly rubbing from his neck to his forehead.

"How long ago?"

"Eh, weeks ago, I guess just after all that shitty weather, yeah, just when the sun came out, she was gone. I had the police at my place."

"The police?"

"Yeah, but it was just routine, I mean, the girl that she whacked in the Alabama ended up pressing charges, so they were looking for her in relation to that, assault charges. That's why everyone reckons she's gone to ground."

"Are you worried?"

"Worried?"

"Yeah, worried, I mean, she was pretty stuck on you, wasn't she? Isn't it odd that she hasn't contacted you?" He was walking around the room, dry now, naked but for the towel which he moved from over his head to his shoulder.

"She's probably stuck on someone else. She was getting a bit clingy anyway. It's only her family who have made a big deal with the missing persons thing, and she didn't give much of a shit about them anyway. People come and people go, man, it's not always a big dramatic thing."

"You don't think anything's happened to her then?"

"I think anything could have happened to that chick. She was nuts, yeah?"

"Yeah. She was." Martin was facing away from the door, with his back to the computer screen, with the towel over his shoulder, looking out the back window. The trees were coming on, their lower branches spreading and their tips reaching higher. Martin thought of the space beneath them, the unseen hollow. *There could be someone sitting, hunched there, looking straight at me right now,* he thought, *and I wouldn't see them.*

CHAPTER TWENTY-TWO

Night has had the city for hours and all of the lights in the house are off when Scorpion gets back in the big black car and reverses out of his drive. The red rear lights are high and bright, and Henry follows them at a distance. He lets them go out of sight and turns on his tracker. Scorpion goes toward the river then swings east, through the quiet night-time streets of the suburbs, past business parks and retail outlets, empty and huge, still illuminated by giant lamps shining on the brand symbols.

It's nearly three by the time the Scorpion's car stops outside a row of apartments. By the time Henry pulls up to where he can see the car, Scorpion has gone into the building. About ten minutes later he's walking out with a thin blonde, her bleached hair cut short in a bob style, who looks like she's just woken up. She's rubbing her eyes, and he's talking to her, leaning his head down to her as they cross the road. Her features are straight and symmetrical, as if she has been cast from a prototype. There's something in her, the way she holds her jacket around her shoulders, the way she neither acknowledges nor ignores Scorpion that draws Henry in. There is an energy, a strength in her that eclipses Scorpion's intimidating bulk.

One thing he is sure of is that this is not the Scorpion's lover. They know each other, Henry thinks, but are not friends. Still, there is nothing to suggest she doesn't want to go with him, there's no hesitation as she climbs into the passenger seat. Scorpion looks around before getting in the other side, scanning the road. His eyes slide over Henry's car and he closes the door.

The engine starts and he pulls out onto the road. Henry follows him back toward the heart of the city, through the empty streets, the dark shell waiting for life to crawl back into it. They turn east and drive to the university. Near the university are roads and roads of identical student flats. He sees the black four by four turn right onto what he knows is a cul-de-sac. Henry pulls up and walks around the corner, staying in the shadows.

The night is cool and still, and the sound of the engine is the only noise on these quiet streets. Scorpion drives to the end of the road, to the last block of flats on the right. Beyond that there is a big iron fence blocking the campus. Henry watches as Scorpion gets out of his car and goes around to open the door for the blonde. They walk together to the foot of the apartment block and buzz on the door.

He looks around as they wait, straight down the road to where Henry is standing. His face is hard and serious, like a statue on a city main street, a monument to a triumphant warrior. Henry is sure that he is far away and covered in shadow enough not to be seen, but he feels a chill run through him as if Scorpion has just looked straight into his eyes. He is being much more watchful now than he was early in the day.

The blonde is looking around too, taking in the detail of the dark street. Henry sees Scorpion speak into the com button and push open the door. The two of them disappear inside.

Henry walks to the foot of the building and then across the road to the apartment block opposite. He thinks about pushing some com buttons to get the door open, and then sees that it is off the latch. He goes up the stairs and finds a spot on a dark corridor with a window out to the road. The buildings are identical so he can see into the corridor opposite. He scans the windows of the building. There are some with lights on, but most curtains are drawn. He looks for silhouettes, for movement, but can see none. He waits a long time in the darkness.

He is used to this, watching from the shadows, observing and recording the actions of strangers, people obeying motivations which he does not have to justify. When he was on the force every case drew him in, he became part of it all, tangled in the messy lives of people hurting and deceiving each other. Now his job was to be detached. To observe and report.

Through the window to his left he can see over the big iron fence to the buildings and lawns of the university. Everything is so measured and neat when there are no people to blur the lines. The apartment block is new. Henry can sense there is a tightness in the fixtures, that the walls haven't been lived in for long. The lives within the building haven't worked their way into the walls yet.

He has a cigarette in his mouth but doesn't light it, just rolls it back and forth over his lower lip.

A door opens on the corridor opposite and the big Scorpion steps out. He is talking to someone who is much smaller than him and standing just inside the door. The light from inside the apartment shines on him and Henry can see that he is smiling. His face has turned gentle, his eyes have softened. He walks away down the corridor and the door closes.

Henry stays until he sees Scorpion leave from the front door of the block of flats. He watches him from above as he gets in his big black car and pulls away. Then he walks down the stairs to the door. He steps outside and lets the door close gently, leaving it balanced on the latch without closing. He takes a lighter from his pocket and lights the cigarette. He can hear birds singing from the university compound. The notes reverberate around the buildings. The darkness is slowly dissolving. Daylight is finding its way back into the city.

It's ten to five.

O   O   O

Henry drives back to the house on the elm-lined road. The curtains are still drawn and all the lights are off. The sky is more blue than black now and in the eerie half-light he climbs over the gate at the side of the house and goes into the back garden.

The back of the house is not like the freshly-mowed clean front. The patch of grass in the back yard is long and unkempt and smells of cat faeces. Dead leaves and debris from the trees lie scattered on the concrete. The back door is a glass sliding door and has a thick curtain on the other side. There are layers of spider webs around the door. The kitchen windows have blinds all the way down on the inside. They are blocked off too. There is a build-up of grime and dust and webs around their edges. They have not been opened in a long time.

He steps back and looks at the upper windows. None of them are open. The only way in is going to be through the front door, or forcing the latch on the sliding door at the back. It's getting too light now. He's going to need to wait until the glasses man leaves the house before he can get in.

He looks again at the back sliding door, and sees his shadowy reflection in the dusty grimy glass, a distorted shape in the pre-morning light. In one cold moment the shadows around him solidify and tense up, as if ready to pounce, and he sees his reflection as that dark misshapen figure he followed to the docklands.

Henry's heart stops and he freezes. The reflection does not, it slides jerkily off the glass and disappears into the shadows. The moment is gone.

Henry climbs back over the fence and out onto the road. He sees the first lights come on in a bedroom across the road. People's days are beginning. He walks back to his car. It's time for him to get home.

In his kitchen he leans over the map. Lomax Road. He takes a gold dot and carefully tears it in half. It tears unevenly, like a waning half-moon. He sticks it in the middle of Lomax. The red dots make a jumbled uneven pattern. The golden moon is right in the middle.

He climbs into bed, feeling the clean white sheets against his skin. He reaches up to close the gap in the curtains, to keep the band of daylight out, then flops onto his back. Within minutes he is in a deep sleep. An hour later, the mechanical digger starts its daily task of breaking up the road outside.

CHAPTER TWENTY-THREE

Alison was late again. When she got home, Martin told her that she should get out her best dress because he had booked them seats at the opera. She threw her arms around him and squealed.

"Tonight?"

"Yes, straight after dinner we'll go into the city."

They had never been to the opera before, but it was something that Alison had talked about. This production was Strauss's *Salome*. Martin had at least heard of it before, so thought it was something they could follow, and the tickets were *buy today, half-price*.

After dinner Alison disappeared upstairs while he tidied up the kitchen and front room. He took the vacuum from under the stairs and unwound the lead, the high-pitched vibrating drone getting even higher as he pushed it into the corners and along the side of the couch. He ran over the carpet again and again and again until Alison came back downstairs. She looked elegant in a close fitted black dress with her hair falling generously over her shoulders.

"You look beautiful, really classy," Martin said.

"It's not too tight is it? I think I've put on weight," she said as she patted her stomach, pulling it in then relaxing again, watching her stomach move in and out.

"You look fantastic." He kissed her cheek as he passed her and went upstairs. He put on a clean white shirt and a suit jacket and came straight downstairs again.

"Off we go?" he said.

"This is exciting," Alison said as they stepped outside the door. Martin hoped that the neighbours would glance out their windows and see this glamorous couple emerge, see that they had somewhere special to go. Alison walked around to the passenger's side of the car and stood as Martin said, "Allow me madam," and opened it for her.

As she sat into the passenger seat Martin saw a necklace he didn't recognise in the space between the seat and the door. He was just about to mention it when he saw next to the amber string of beads were two laminated cards and some pieces of crumpled paper. A cold fist formed in Martin's stomach as he caught sight of a face on one of the laminated cards. It was Zoe.

"Oh this will be nice," Alison said as she pulled the seat belt over her shoulder. "The opera, how grand." She smiled up at Martin as he closed the door and walked around to the driver's side with a tense panic rising through this body. His mouth went totally dry, his tongue seemed to grow. He stopped for a second before he opened his door. He slowed down his breathing and opened the door, and sat into the car.

"Yeah, it's about time we did something like this. Do you know the story? The story of Salome?" He turned the key in the ignition.

"Are you okay babe?" Alison said. "You look all pale." Martin started to reverse the car.

"I'm feeling a bit off, maybe something I ate earlier, but I'll be fine, don't worry, we're going to have a great night."

"Well, I'll drive if you aren't feeling right."

"No, it's nothing." He straightened the car on the road and put it into gear. "I'll be fine."

As Martin watched for traffic at each junction and eased the car from the slip road to join the motorway he was thinking how he could get rid of the debris from Zoe's bag. It had been there, unnoticed for weeks now, her unblinking eyes looking out from the laminated card at the grimy grey carpet at the bottom of the door, and now all it would take was one glance from Alison, one movement of her hand down to side of the seat, and their worlds would crash together. He would have to go back to the car once they had parked up, on the pretence of having forgotten something. What could he forget? What could he empty from his pocket now without Alison noticing?

"So what's this whole thing about then?" Alison asked. "Salome? Is it classical Greek stuff?"

"It's biblical I think. John the Baptist is involved, and Herod, but I don't know the details. Best to come at it blind, I'd say," Martin replied.

"But will we understand it? Operas aren't in English are they?"

"There will be notes on the programme we can follow."

"I'm very excited," Alison said, and reached her hand across, putting it on Martin's lap and squeezing his thigh. "It's a lovely surprise."

"Well, we are due a night out." Martin smiled at her.

She did look beautiful. Her hair framed her face and her eyes shone in the dull light of the car. As Alison looked at him now, every muscle in his body ached and it felt like his lungs had contracted. He would have to get parked as close as possible to the theatre and run out during the intermission to gather Zoe's necklace and cards from the car and dump them somewhere. For a second he saw Zoe sitting where Alison was, her bleached blonde hair wet, her white jacket still spattered with rain, her short skirt riding up to the tops of her thighs and her legs slightly apart and her eyes half closed, her mouth opening and closing as if fighting for breath, slipping in and out of consciousness.

Martin turned away, looking back at the road. A cold sweat was creeping from his lower back upwards toward his neck, like flood waters rising on a dam. The road was narrowing as the motorway ended and he slowed to let a car slip in between him and the car in front. The driver gave a flash of his indicators as thanks and eased into the lane. Martin felt light-headed, then realised he had been holding his breath. He inhaled suddenly and deeply. The cold sweat had reached his neck and was spreading down his arms. His shirt was sticking to his skin. He glanced at the passenger seat again. It was Alison, looking at him with a worried frown.

"Are you sure you're okay, babe? We don't have to go. You don't look right."

"Hey, I said I'm fine. We'll be there in a minute, I'll feel better once I'm out of the car."

When they reached the theatre multi-storey car park, Martin went as close as he could to the entrance and slowed right down, scouring the lines and lines of cars for a gap. There was nothing anywhere near the entrance and they went up and up looking for a space. Around and around they drove following the spiral higher and higher until they ended up parking one level from the rooftop. Martin jumped out of his seat and rushed around to open the door for Alison, making a big show of extending his hand and keeping her eye contact as she stepped over the amber bead necklace and laminated cards.

As they took the lift down to the ground level, Martin tried to calculate how long it would take him to get back up. He could throw the necklace and cards over the edge of the car park. The necklace would fall and smash on the street and the cards would be scattered by the winds. They would flip and turn down the street, be stepped upon and swept into the gutter, wet cracked and bent.

As they entered the foyer of the theatre, Alison tightened her grip around Martin's waist. It was teeming with people in fine clothing, fitted suits and flowing dresses, women with sparkling jewellery and men with bow ties and shined shoes. Those who were not in suits or tuxedos, flowing dresses and furs still carried an elegant cool chic as they sipped European beers or rich wines. The carpets were a royal red, the ceiling high and illuminated by a magni-ficent chandelier. Martin could hear beyond the hubbub of the crowd the sweet sound of a string quartet gently pushing the swell of harmonies and luxurious melody through the rich air. He wished he had a suit he could have worn, instead of his old suit jacket and jeans. He felt like a shabby cousin, invited to an occasion because of family loyalty, not because any one really wanted him there.

"I'd like to pop to the ladies before we go in," Alison said into his ear.

"I'll get the tickets then," he replied, and she kissed him on the cheek. As she turned and walked away Martin felt the tension being drawn from him like a wave going out.

He queued and was just having the tickets put in his hand when Alison was by his side again, saying, "You won't believe who I just bumped into."

Martin turned and there behind Alison was a man in his mid-fifties, with a receding hairline and a dusting of silver stubble over a strong defined chin, wearing a black tuxedo with a white rose pinned to the lapel. Next to him was a tanned and slim blonde, younger than him by at least ten years, probably more. She was wearing a deep blue dress which swept to the ground in an elegant wave from her hip to her heel. They were both smiling at him, expectantly. Martin saw the man's eyes flick over him, taking in his suit jacket and jeans, right down to his scuffed shoes, but the action was so quick as to be almost imperceptible. The smile didn't change. Alison stood slightly in front of Martin as she spoke.

"Martin, this is my boss, Andre Exor, and, sorry what was your name again, I'm terrible with names at first."

"It's Cassandra," said Andre, extending his hand. "And it's a pleasure to meet you, Martin. I've heard so much about you."

"Really?" Martin replied as he shook it. "There's not much to hear I would have thought."

Andre Exor turned his smile on Alison. "You're right, he is the picture of modesty. No wonder you've got your feet on the ground. Martin, you've got a fantastic woman here you know. She is causing quite a stir in the company. Her ideas are turning heads."

"Oh that's great," Martin said. "Well, she does love her work."

"And you, a writer! How wonderful to be able to create intellectual property. It is, after all, the intangible immeasurable resource. Creativity! You two are rich with it! Creativity! That's what Alison brings, that's why we love her! Whatever you're doing—" Andre winked conspiratorially "—keep doing it."

Martin shook hands again, and Andre suggested that they meet up for a drink after the show. Alison said that would be a lovely idea, and Andre said that he would call her. *There is a lovely spot nearby,* he said, and with an enthusiastic "Enjoy the show!" Andre Exor and Cassandra turned away and headed toward the auditorium.

"Well I didn't expect that," Alison said. "Do you want to have a drink with them after?"

"I guess so, I mean, if you want to."

"I think we should."

"Okay."

Martin checked his ticket and they made their way up the carpeted stairs to the stalls. Their seats were right up at the back of the auditorium. The scale of the room was intimidating. Beneath the great vaulted ceiling and the drapes which fronted the stage, the seats seemed tiny. When he sat down Martin felt as if he was perched on an unstable peak of an elaborate canyon, and should he lean forward he would precipitate an avalanche of the wealthy middle aged, a debris of corsets and bow ties. Alison started to read the programme and he tried to calculate how long it would take him to get to the car and back again.

"Do you want me to read the translation as we go? There is quite a lot, oh wait, there's a scene synopsis, that'll do won't it? Martin?"

"You can just pass it to me when you've read it, or maybe not, we'll see. I was kind of expecting not to understand anyway."

The auditorium was filling up. Heads moved into place, the low hubbub of indeterminable conversation vibrating up through the air to where they sat. Martin could hear the random brief musical exclamations as the orchestra settled into place. *How long,* he thought, *how long before I can throw Zoe from the car? Throw her to the streets, where she will be dissipated and forgotten.*

"Oh, it's exciting," Alison said. "Look, let's go down there, it's closer, a better view, come on." She pointed to seats at the edge of the balcony, several rows in front, which were empty.

He protested, "We can't switch seats, what if the people are just late? Look, it's about to start, everyone is sitting down now."

"If they turn up, then we'll move back, come on, quick." She stood and he stood with her, and they excused themselves from the row right against the back wall, and disregarding the *tuts* and disapproving noises made by those around them and those who swivelled their legs to let them past, got to the seats on the edge of the balcony just as the lights began to fade. As the lights dimmed and the murmur of conversation died, Alison leaned into his ear, put her hand on his and said, "See, this is better isn't it?"

The orchestra started up and the curtains opened. A giant moon dominated the backdrop. The size of the actors took Martin by surprise. How small they were! They were like figurines, toys in the distance. At first he felt disappointed, and then he felt foolish for being surprised. They were actors on a stage after all, not on a screen. They did not move about the stage with grace, but rather seemed to blunder about, heavy footed and over-conscious of their positions.

When the singing began he glanced at Alison. She was transfixed. Sound filled the auditorium. The voices rose from the stage toward the golden arc of the ceiling, full of power and dramatic intent. The voices were so much more than the figures in the spotlights, they filled the theatre. It seemed absurd that such powerful streams of sound could be created and controlled by the shapes onstage. They were like fists of noise. They flew around and against each other, battling and crunching in the eaves of the great auditorium. There was not harmony, there was tension and the air was in turmoil. Martin leaned forward and looked over the balcony. He could see all of the heads beneath him, all of the rows and rows of people in the balconies opposite, all focused on one point.

As the performance unfolded Martin found himself caring less and less about what was on stage and staring instead at the heads below him. The power of the voices and the drama of the stage had hypnotised them, and the tension in the room built and built until, by the time the actress was dancing the dance of the seven veils, Martin saw the auditorium as a room full of decapitated heads on platters, severed from reality, served at the orgy of performance art.

O   O   O

When the performance finished Martin and Alison stood in the foyer while the theatre emptied.

"I thought there was going to be a break," said Martin. "An intermission."

"Do you want to meet up with Andre? I think it would be good, I've never seen him outside work before."

"Where do you think we'll go?"

"Somewhere fancy I bet," Alison said as she absentmindedly brushed the front of Martin's suit jacket. From her handbag, her phone started to ring.

"Right on cue," said Martin as she took it out and answered. As she spoke she turned away from Martin. *Yes, we'd love to,* she was saying and then she started talking about where the car was parked. Martin watched people's backs go through the glass doors in couples and groups as the last of the audience left the theatre. It was so quick, the transition from full to empty, *But I guess that's what happens when the show is over,* he thought. The bar staff closed the shutters and after the rattle and the click there was a thick silence, broken only by Alison's voice. *Okay,* she said, then she turned to him.

"He's outside now, we can take a lift with him."

"What about the car?"

"We'll just leave it here and come back for it later. Andre says it's 24-hours."

"I think I left my phone in the car."

"Really?" said Alison and started to dial his number.

"Oh, actually, it's in my inside pocket."

"Let's go then." Alison held her arm, he took it, and they walked to the exit. Outside was a long black car. The back door opened as they approached. Andre Exor's balding head appeared and he beamed at them.

"Hey, you guys, come on get in!" The back of the car had sets of seats facing each other. Alison and Martin sat in with their backs to the driver. Andre sat facing them, with Cassandra next to him, her body angled away from him, so she had to turn her head to smile at them.

"Very good of you to invite us," Martin said, as the car pulled away from the front of the theatre. "Where is it we are going?"

"It's a lovely little place, great drinks, some food if you want it. Run by a lovely Greek guy, Savas. It's members only, so you'll have to sign up to be a member on your way in, but it's nothing really. What did you guys think of the opera?"

"Oh I loved it," Alison said. "So intense, it really drew me in."

"And you, Martin?"

"Yes, it was quite something. Maybe a bit serious." They all laughed. "A bit of slap-stick might have been good." There was more laughter.

"We're here," Andre announced, and the car stopped.

"Wow, that was quick," said Alison. They all got out of the car. Martin looked back up the road the way they had come. The theatre was just a few hundred metres away. When he turned back Andre was walking across the pavement with Cassandra on one arm and Alison on the other. They were walking toward an elaborately designed door with a golden plaque above it. As he walked closer to the door he could make out the detail of the carved motifs. There were waves and spirals, and in the centre a circular sun sending out straight lines to the edges of the door.

Andre waited for him to join them before pressing the bell which was in the centre of a cast of a flower on the wall. Martin could see that Alison was nervous with excitement. The door opened and Andre stepped confidently through, taking the women with him. Martin followed. There was a smartly dressed man at a counter, who smiled broadly and said, "Mr. Exor, good to see you, sir, and Madame Cassandra. You look stunning as always."

"Thank you," said Andre, "I have with me two special guests who need to enlist."

"Certainly, sir, shall I put you down as their advocate?"

"Yes."

"Well then, sir and madam, if you would step forward and fill out these membership forms." His eyes slipped from Alison to Martin and lingered on him for a moment. Andre saw this and said, "This is Martin Tripp, the author," as if the gentleman at the door would then recognise his name. "They didn't know I was bringing them here tonight."

"Very good," said the man, "It is a pleasure to welcome you both."

Alison filled in her form in a matter of seconds, confidently and efficiently. Martin stepped to the counter and started to fill in his. Under occupation he hesitated before writing *Author*. At the end of the form there was what seemed to be a confidentiality clause, the breach of which would mean expulsion from the club. Martin scanned the thick paragraph of legal speak before signing the end, with a queasy feeling that he had put his signature to something without understanding fully what it was.

The man thanked them again and stepped aside, extending his arm and revealing the staircase. Andre took the lead. Alison linked her arm with Martin. He leaned into her and said, "You okay?"

She nodded and said, "It's all very exciting."

When they reached the top of the staircase the room opened up in front of them. It was a large lounge bar, with plush sofas around small glass tables, wooden panelling on the walls, and vibrantly coloured prints with lights embedded behind them, so that they glowed. There was a long bar with mirrors behind it which stretched to the ceiling. The room was populated with smartly dressed men and women in expensive dresses, their wrists and ears laden with sparkling jewellery. Andre took Cassandra and Alison by the arm again and strode to the bar. Martin followed.

"I'm buying, what do you want?" Alison and Cassandra chose their drinks, then Cassandra said she was going to freshen up. Alison said that she would, too, and they walked off together. Andre watched them go, then whistled an intake of breath, looking at Martin.

"Hey?" he said, "Hey? You got a great woman there, Martin."

"I know, I know," Martin replied. Andre turned back to the bar and ordered their drinks then turned back to Martin. "Some interesting people in here, let me show you."

He started pointing people out to Martin and naming what they did. There was the deputy chief planning advisor for the city, drinking with the transport secretary. Over there was the editor of the city's biggest selling daily paper, laughing with the manager of the city's largest investment trust. Just sitting down near the back of the room was one of the judges from the big television talent show with a bunch of hangers-on, and that guy there with the purple shirt was one of the producers of the show. Coming out from the restaurant room was the furniture designer who set up the Make a House a Home chain. Martin asked, "Do you come here a lot?"

"Enough. I've been a member since the start, so it feels comfortable. It's a good place to network. But hey, you, Alison says you're working on something big."

Martin dug his hands in his pockets and winced. "Em, it's, well to be honest, I don't like talking about it until it's done if you know what I mean."

Andre took his elbow and leaned into him. "I know. I know exactly what you mean." He squeezed then let go. He picked up his drink from the bar and handed Martin his. "You've got to guard your intellectual property, I know. I'm not going to ask you about it. Believe me, I know. You start talking about it, next thing you know there's a TV show all about that idea that's taken you years to craft. And a bad TV show, too! One that turns what should have been a genius idea into something mediocre and run of the goddam mill. One that uses a half a dozen mediocre writers to patch together a bad script acted by the same old TV faces. Then all the impact of your idea has been taken away and you're left with something no-one wants to touch. I know, I know, and it's the best thing, not to talk about it. What it does tell me though is that it's gonna be great, eh? Am I right? Am I? Go on, tell me I'm wrong."

Martin zipped his lips shut. Andre slapped him on the back. "Haha! I like you, Martin. I wish I had that creative gene. Just a little bit of it. I can see it in your eyes. Those eyes. You see things differently. I spend all my time dealing with concrete and steel and numbers. Once a building is up, then it's a numbers game. The numbers can move, but the building never does. But ideas ... ideas can grow and move, they can change things, change the way people see things and if a person sees things differently, well, it can change that person, and you! You are the change. You are the idea that made that change.

"You know, a building, ah the building only starts fulfilling its potential when the numbers hit a certain point, and most people who work for me only see the numbers. Your Alison, on the other hand, she sees the people behind the numbers, and that makes her different. Because she does that, she sees options that others who are chasing numbers just don't see! Then next thing, the numbers come back rearranged in an order that no-one who was chasing the numbers could have put them in! You know what I mean?"

"I know what you mean."

"Of course, you do, because you're an artist! You see beyond the ordinary stuff, beyond the money machinery, the profit margins, the dividend yield, the QMV, and IPUs, you see past all that, and I envy that, I wish I could. All I seem to do is make money, money, but is there any learning in that? Is it filling anything other than my pockets? I honestly don't know."

He looked into the middle distance, as if for dramatic effect. Martin sipped his drink, at a loss for anything to say. He saw Alison and Cassandra coming back.

"Cassandra seems lovely, how long have you been together?"

Andre put down his drink, looked past Martin, opened out his arms, and with a beaming smile said loudly, "Well, what a picture! Really I feel like I am in the presence of royalty with you two beautiful ladies." He handed them their drinks while saying to Alison, "There are some people I must introduce you to, come with me." Then he turned to Martin and Cassandra, "Excuse us."

Martin watched as he manoeuvred Alison across the room toward where the transport secretary and the deputy chief planning advisor were sitting. Cassandra was looking at them too.

There was a silence before Cassandra said, "Do you smoke?"

Martin shook his head. "No, no I don't."

"I want a cigarette. Shall we go up?"

"Up?"

"Outside."

"Okay."

Martin followed as Cassandra walked across the room and up another set of stairs. The stairs wound around and around until they were in the open air, on a rooftop terrace, where bunches of people stood around the tables and chairs, and Chinese lanterns glowed from behind a little bar. The rooftop was dwarfed by the buildings around; they rose up into the night sky on either side. Martin thought of the stage he had just seen, and the size of the actors compared to the theatre.

Cassandra walked to the edge of the terrace, and leaned against a barrier. Martin followed her. He could feel the thick hum of traffic in the air, as if he could reach out over the barrier and take a handful. He could see the car park from here. He could guess where his car was, where Zoe was still trapped. Cassandra put a cigarette to her lips and lit it.

"Well it's nice to meet Alison's boss at last," Martin said. "He does know how to talk, doesn't he?"

"He likes the sound of his own voice." She exhaled. The smoke stayed as a little cloud before drifting and then being swept into the night, upwards toward the buildings beside them. She was older than Martin had first thought. Her face was smooth but she had a hardness around the edges which could only come with age. Her nose turned up at the end and her lower jaw protruded, making her bottom lip stick out and giving her a look of self-disgust. "He always knows what to say, no matter who he's talking to."

"That's quite a talent. He seems like a very successful man."

"There are different measures for success. As you gain it, the measures change." When she drew in on the cigarette, the end glowed and her cheeks hollowed. Martin thought he saw the edges of her eyes pull down into her face. He felt her looking at him.

"One is how you dress, I guess. I wish had known we were coming here. These are my comfy pants, you know, for sitting in theatres."

She didn't say anything, just continued to look straight at him.

"So how long have you guys been together?" Martin asked.

She exhaled another cloud of smoke. "So you're a writer. Do you make a good living from that?"

Martin felt his face go red. "No," he said, "not yet. Am I wrong then? About you two being together?"

"Yes and no."

"Ah, it's complicated."

"No. It's very straightforward."

"So you're with him. Or you're not with him."

"Anything else you want to ask?"

"Just making conversation."

"Then talk about the weather or that god-awful drag of a show we saw," she said, flicking her cigarette over the edge. "Tell me how beautiful I look in this dress and ask who the designer is, talk about how what you're writing is going to start a new literary trend, tell me the growth predictions for the company you're associated with or something; that's making conversation."

Martin didn't say anything for a moment, just sipped his drink.

She stared at him then said, "I'm going to get another drink." She turned and walked away. Martin saw the dark patches of liver spots on her shoulders, and the creased and bunched skin around her shoulder blades, and where her dress cut into her back. At the top of the staircase she turned and said loudly, "Are you coming then?" Martin saw faces on the terrace turn to him, and he shrugged and followed her.

Once down in the main room again he looked around for Alison and Andre. Cassandra said to him, "A dry Martini," before giving an elaborate and enthusiastic greeting to a fat man in a sweaty suit, smiling and letting him kiss her cheek as if a switch had just been flicked inside her.

Martin didn't go to the bar, but wandered around the room, slipping unnoticed between the lush dresses and dripping jewellery and the dark suits, whose heads and hands could be severed and swapped and still look the same.

He saw Alison and Andre in a huddle with two other couples. Andre was holding court, engaging them in a story which, Martin could tell as he approached, was building to a punchline. The two couples and Alison were rapt with attention, and Martin held back. Andre's arms were bent at the elbow, his hands facing upwards, moving in repetitive circles as he spoke, as if lifting the air around him again and again. Alison's eyes were growing wider as she watched him, and when the climax of the story came, his hands made fists and shot up, and Alison erupted with laughter, as did the other two couples.

As the laughter subsided, Martin stepped in beside her, putting his arm around her waist. Andre opened his hands again and put his arms out wide. "Martin! Hey Martin, let me introduce you! Brian and Casey, this is Martin. Brian and Casey run Venus Models, and this is Ted and Rosie. Ted is in printing, snapping up all the contracts that used to be sourced outside the city. *The Tube Times*, and *Night Out*, the freebies, you know the ones, they're all coming out of the Crown Estate now. I've tried to get him to tell me his secret, but he's not giving anything away, are you, Ted?"

They all laughed, and Ted said, "Got to keep something under my hat, and you know most of everything else, Andre. A man's got to have some secrets." They laughed some more.

"Well, it's just a matter of time before you're printing the works of this man here. Martin is a writer, a hot tip by all accounts." Martin smiled and shook his head as the group turned to him.

"No, no, it's all a front, I'm really just a daydreaming house-husband."

There was more laughter, and Alison said, "No, that's not fair, you've been part of *Noire* for a while," and then to the others she said, "It's an online magazine, very popular. He's their top writer." The others nodded and enthused, and as Alison spoke about fan mail and interest from publishers, Martin didn't know where to look.

She was talking a good pitch, but Martin just saw clusters of words stuck in bundles of paper and a slow hard drive in the spare room. They were going nowhere. They had no weight, no consequence. They could be deleted and thrown away in a moment and nothing would change. Even if they did move beyond his room, he was sure they would never mean anything to these people, that he'd never contribute anything to this room, this exclusive club.

Casey started to talk about some hot young talent that she had just signed, some actor who should just shut up and pose, because that's what he is best at. If he just concentrates on the pictures and stops being distracted by trying to act he could be everywhere this time next year, but what can you do when people won't listen to you? Martin angled himself to talk into Alison's ear.

"I'm not feeling so hot. I think I might have to go." She looked at him with disappointment. "You can stay and get a cab home if you want, but I think I should try and get home."

"No, I'll come back with you, it's getting late now."

"Listen, I really don't mind if you want to stay out with Andre. You know, if you think it'll do you good, work wise. I understand."

"No," she said, "it's good. Something's already happened, so it might be a good time to leave."

"Something's already happened?"

"I'll tell you on the way home."

"You work fast." Martin gave her a kiss on the cheek. "I'll get the car. Be outside in ten minutes, yeah?"

"I'll just come with you now."

"No, you stay and finish your drink, say your goodbyes." He turned to Andre and the others. "Well, lovely to meet you, but I'm afraid we are going to go. I'm off to fetch the car."

He extended his hand and Andre gripped it. "Martin, it's been a pleasure to meet you at last. So enlightening. We must meet again, maybe some of your creativity will rub off on me."

Martin promised they would indeed see each other soon and nodded to the others. Ted shook his hand and handed him a card as did Brian who said, "When you need a publicity shot, give me a call, we'll sort something out for you."

"Like sending through a shot of one of your best-looking models for the author shot?" Andre said. "It can't hurt can it? I mean, no-one should really know what the author looks like." They all laughed.

"Only prerequisite is that he's got a six-pack and he's not smiling," Martin said, before saying goodnight again to their smiling faces and turning and walking out of the private members' club.

The night air was warm and moist, and the lights of the cars passing on the busy road showed a curtain of tiny raindrops hanging in the air. It took him minutes to walk to the car park. The lift up to the level was brightly lit and stank of old urine. It rose slowly, and Martin thought that this was like a steel solitary confinement cell. The light would never be turned off, and the outside world would disappear. As he watched the numbers change, Martin's nervousness grew.

When the lift door opened and he saw the car across the empty grey concrete parking bays, his gut tightened as if he had seen Zoe herself standing by the car, looking straight at him. By the time he got to the car, his stomach was churning and his back was sweating. He opened it and went to the passenger side.

There were the amber string of beads, some crumpled paper, and two laminated cards, with Zoe's pale face looking up at him from behind the plastic. He picked them up. The card with her picture was an out of date student ID, and the other one was a loyalty card for ICE with which you could get discount drinks. He sat in the passenger seat and opened up the bits of paper. Two receipts, just looked like grocery stuff, and a voucher for discount beauty products. The beads were cheap, they had no weight to them. Martin went to the edge of the parking lot and threw them over. He didn't hear them hit the ground. He threw the receipts and the voucher over too and the loyalty card.

Something stopped him from throwing the student ID. On one side was a barcode, on the other her name and a photo. He looked at Zoe's face through the plastic. She looked happy. It must have been enrolment day. There would have been excitement in the air, an anticipation of beginnings. The enrolment halls would have been full of new students, brimming with a wealth of latent potentialities. This day would have marked the beginning of so many exciting futures, and as Zoe Hollander sat in front of the camera, she knew that this would be the picture that would be presenting her for the next three years. She smiled. *Click.*

Martin walked to the other side of the car park. The city lights blinked and blurred through the thin veil of rain and he threw the card over the edge. Like a leaf, it flipped and turned in the night air, face, barcode, face, barcode, face, and disappeared into the dark.

Martin walked back to the car and turned on the inside light. He checked underneath the seats, in the foot wells and the dashboard drawers, again and again until he was sure that there was no trace of Zoe left.

As he stood by the passenger door, scanning around the seat, he glanced up and noticed the glowing red tip of a cigarette in the shadows of a car parked a few spaces down. He heard the lift doors behind him open, and Martin felt panic grab his neck and squeeze. He closed the passenger door and walked around to the driver side without looking around. In the car his hand shook as the key found the ignition. In his rearview mirror he saw a thin dark-suited figure pass, tossing a cigarette aside and heading for the ticket machine.

It was Henry. Martin froze. His hand stopped shaking. Henry took the ticket from the machine, and Martin saw his face clearly as he hurried back to his car. There was no doubt. It was Henry Bloomburg. The car pulled off and Martin looked again at this familiar face, focused and set in deep concentration, as it passed behind him. Then he was gone, and the car park was still. Slowly, Martin pulled out and followed the winding route down to the street.

By the time he pulled up outside the private members' club and Alison got into the car and clicked her seat belt into place, his head was feeling clearer and in control, but separate from his body, as if he was looking calmly at himself from the outside, watching through the windscreen as Alison leaned over and kissed him on the cheek.

They drove out of the city, and Martin asked what had happened. Alison leaned her head back against the head rest and took a deep breath. When Andre had introduced her to the deputy chief planning advisor, the talk had turned to the docklands.

On the motorway, the dusting of rain disappeared and Martin switched off the wipers. The sky beyond the hills was clear and stars were rising over the horizon.

The docklands was going to get a renewal, and only certain companies were going to be able to bid. So far it was looking like business and leisure contracts and some private high-end residencies. When they moved away from the deputy chief planning advisor, Andre had said that he wanted to be in on the residencies, and he wanted Alison to head up a team to make sure they secured the contracts. *What that meant,* she said, *was getting clients interested at the planning stages, even the pre-planning stages, creating perceived interest. Finding what they wanted and telling them it would be there for them, and keeping in contact with the authorities and keeping up with what the other companies were planning.*

They turned off the motorway, around the roundabout, and started the slow incline to New Acre. The silhouettes of the houses behind the fence didn't have any lights on. Martin looked at the digital clock on the dashboard. It was 0:47.

As they turned into the estate, Alison said, "You look a bit better than you did earlier"

"I feel a bit better, just tired now. It's a late night for you, are you going to have a lie-in tomorrow? I'm sure Andre will understand."

"No, I'm going to be first in the office tomorrow, researching potential clients."

"Really?" Martin pulled the car into the drive and turned the engine off.

"Well, you're going to be up for your morning run aren't you?"

"Yes, I suppose." They sat for a moment in the silence of the car. Through the windscreen a full moon looked down on them.

Alison said, "It's nice to be out of the city, isn't it? Where it's quiet." Martin agreed and they sat there together, just out of reach of the shadow of the house, quiet for a while.

CHAPTER TWENTY-FOUR

When Henry dreams, he goes back to where he has been. He dreams of the reflection, the shadows, the back garden, the windows with the cobwebs, the gate. He retraces his steps, moves back along the streets he has driven down, etching the route deeper into his mind, following it back, back to the tree-lined estates, the university apartments, to Maya's house, back to the city, and ending up at the filthy high-rise flats.

Then it starts again. Every corner he turned, every car he passed, every doorway and shop front, the cracks in the streets at every junction, all of the details of the face of city push themselves into his brain, making an imprint, and every time he dreams it, it's pushed deeper like fossils under the weight of thousands of years of rock.

The same dream, over and over again. And every time he travels the route there is a heat he feels from the buildings, from the road. It's the body heat of the city and he sweats in the bed, until the sheets are damp.

O O O

In the morning Henry takes the sheets from his bed and balls them up. He takes out the sheets from the washer/dryer and shoves the damp ones in. He pulls the clean sheets tight over the mattress, smoothing them out. He puts on an old set of overalls, faded at the knees and elbows. He combs his hair into a side parting, takes a tool bag from the cupboard, and goes to the car.

At the edge of the university he finds the building the Scorpion brought the woman to. From his glove compartment he selects a laminated card and puts it around his neck. He puts on a thin pair of glasses. Walking into the building and up the stairs he looks across at where he was sitting last night. He finds the door, and gives a knock. It's answered by a beautiful young woman. It's Maya's daughter, Kayleigh.

She's older than she was in the photograph; her dark hair cascades around her face and her eyes are deep and dark, just like her mother's. She is dressed in a thick jumper and pyjama bottoms, with slippers that have bunny ears. Henry smiles and shows his card. As she looks at it, he looks beyond her into the room. There is the jacket that the blonde girl was wearing last night hanging on the back of a chair.

"It's just a problem next door with the wireless Internet server, need to check if it's affected the rest of this floor or not. Would you mind checking your computer for me, see if it's online?"

"Okay," says Kayleigh, and as she turns, Henry puts his hand into his tool bag and flicks a switch on a thick black box. It's a signal jammer and a minute later Kayleigh comes back to the door carrying her laptop with a confused look on her face.

"It was working a minute ago," she says, "but now it's not."

"Same thing was happening next door, the signal coming and going. It's just a fault in the connection to the phone line, that's all. It only takes a minute. Will I sort it out for you?"

"Oh, yes, please, come in," she says, and Henry follows her into the apartment. It's small, a few steps in and they are in the kitchen. It's clean and on the table in the next room there is a pile of books, then a low sofa in front of a TV. Besides the jacket over the chair, there's no sign of the blonde. The door to the bedroom is closed. She puts the laptop on the work surface in the kitchen.

"Do you know where the Wi-Fi adaptor is?" Henry asks.

"I think it's over there on the other side of the sofa," she says.

Henry looks and there is the Wi-Fi adaptor, going into the same port as the phone. Right above it at head height is a square mirror with the words "reality is overrated" in red cartoon italics at the bottom. To his left is another door, slightly open, to the small shower and toilet.

"Yeah, this is it, I've just got to replace the adaptor." He bends down and keeps talking over his shoulder. "It looks like the whole building might need attention. Hopefully it's just you and your neighbours."

"Okay," she says, and wanders back into the kitchen.

Henry takes the adaptor out of the wall and plugs it back in again. He flicks the switch on his signal blocker. He takes out a bug from his tool bag and undoes the adhesive from the back. He holds it in his hand as he sees she has her back to him, then straightens up and in one quick movement sticks the listening bug to the back of the mirror. He turns around.

"All done," he says.

"Wow, that was quick." She turns to her laptop and peers at the screen. "It seems fine now. Thanks."

"You shouldn't have any more problems," Henry says as he walks to the door.

She walks him out, saying thanks again before closing the door. Henry walks a few steps before taking his earpiece from his pocket and fitting it in his right ear. He puts the receiver in his pocket and presses the call button. He can hear a tap running, someone filling something.

"Who was that?" It's not Kayleigh's voice. It's the blonde. She must have been in the bedroom. Her accent is thick, Eastern European

"Just some guy to fix the Wi-Fi."

"Oh. Have you heard from Spike?"

"No, do you want some coffee?"

"Oh yes, thanks."

Henry starts to walk down the corridor, the two voices in his head.

"It's an Italian roast. I'll do some steamed milk, too. My mum got me this coffee maker and it's been the most used thing since I moved in. It's amazing."

"I know, I know, good coffee is so important. Have you tried the flavoured range? The vanilla is addictive."

"Oh, I know. I did have it, but I'm out. I went through it so quickly. I do have the hazelnut in here somewhere." There is the sound of cupboards opening and things being moved about.

Henry wonders if last night was their first time meeting. If so, then they really have hit it off, the conversation is comfortable and familiar. He flicks the off switch and takes his ear piece out. It's time to find Scorpion.

O   O   O

Maya sounds like she's woken up from a deep sleep. Her voice is cracked and the words are coming out slow.

"She's studying history and modern politics. But she hates him. What has she got to do with anything?"

Henry put a cigarette to his lips and lights it as he says, "Most likely nothing, I just need to know as much as I can about everyone, it makes it easier that way. Has he been home?"

"He was, but not for long."

"Did he sleep?"

"I think so. He had been in bed."

"Do you sleep in the same bed?"

"Yes, but I was asleep when he came in and then when I woke up he was gone, but I think I remember him being there in the middle of the night. I don't know."

"You're a heavy sleeper. Do you take anything to help you sleep?"

"Mr. Bloomburg, you are in my employ to investigate my husband. I'm paying you to find out what I don't know. I already know all about me."

She's talking like she's leaning over. Her words are falling upon each other. Henry has reached his car. He stands next to it, smoking.

"Are you drunk now?"

"No, I'm not, but it's a good idea."

Her voice fluctuates in volume, like she's swaying in and out of focus. Henry thinks, maybe benzodiazepine. If she's got something like that, she would've had to get it on prescription at some stage. Anxiety or a panic disorder. He can imagine her spending money on seeing a counsellor, weekly outpourings of memories she's not happy with, hoping that talking about them will change them. Picking apart memories, reliving them again and again, hoping for different outcomes, encounters and episodes that she just can't let go of and have been forgotten by everyone else.

He reaches the end of his cigarette, the red tip burnt right down to the filter. He flicks it on to the road. Maybe Maya is paranoid and there's no affair. Scorpion is just a dumb errand boy for some rich crime family, and Maya is a paranoid addict.

"Oh wait, no, he was in bed last night, for a while anyway I remember now. Or was that ..."

"Okay, well I'll let you know." Henry hangs up, gets in the car, takes off his glasses, and unclips his ID card, putting it back in the glove compartment.

He turns on the tracker. Scorpion's car is in the centre of the city. It's stationary. By the time he gets to it, an hour later, it still hasn't moved. It's in a car park near the business sector, and the crowd of tall curved banking buildings looking in on each other in a conspiratorial cluster. Henry drives around and around up and down and back up the levels until a space appears on the same level as Scorpion's car. From where he is he has a clean line of sight to the car. He leans his seat back and adjusts the rear view mirror so that he can see the pay station. He waits.

CHAPTER TWENTY-FIVE

Since the opera, Alison was at home less and less. Her working hours stretched into the evening and she would often go for a dinner with Andre and clients.

Martin's time at the house was more and more undisturbed. When he got up in the morning she would be gone, and he would take his time with breakfast, listening to the radio and taking the clothes from the washer and hanging them on radiators or outside, cleaning the dishes left over from the previous evening, before he would get changed and go for his run.

When Martin was running around the estate his thoughts travelled through his head with an ease he was not used to. It was as if his body was a machine, and the cogs and pistons were working together to pump out thoughts on a production line, and he didn't have time to inspect each one, just glance at each as they just passed him on a conveyor belt, odd misshapen products of his body and mind. As he got faster and stronger and started running the circuit twice every time, he gradually stopped being surprised at the shape of his thoughts. Whatever he was thinking by the time he got to Foster Road for the second time would be cast aside as the struggle of the hill rose up in front of him.

He was writing more. The story had a momentum which he was trying to keep up with. At this rate his book would be finished in a month. He looked forward to the day when he could send it away. When he could press send and get rid of Gregor for good. No more redrafts, he'd say, either take it or not. That's that. He could always go back to writing short stories for *Noire* again. Those stories felt like they were written a lifetime ago.

It was Saturday and Martin was running past the big houses on Wyatt Way. He saw a scaffold being erected on the side of one of the houses and he stopped for a moment, running on the spot, to try to see what was going on. A voice came from behind him.

"Martin? It is Martin, isn't it?"

He turned to see a worker in a fluorescent hard hat with an open folder standing next to an overweight guy in a white shirt and braces who was squinting at him, scrunching up his face. Martin recognised him, but couldn't place from where.

Then the man said, "It is Martin! I wasn't sure. It's Ted, Ted from the club." He walked across the road, extending his hand. Martin stopped running on the spot. The first person that Martin thought of was the small fellow he met in the Sugar Club, the guy with the ski lift company, but this wasn't him. That guy was Ashley. This Ted must be from the club he went to with Alison. He recalled the group he was talking to before he left, remembered Alison trying to make it sound like he was a successful writer.

Ted, Ted.

He remembered the dark suits and red faces, the iridescent purple of one of the women's dresses, ringed fingers clutching glass stems, a bulging neck and sweaty rolls of fat above the collar of one of the men as he laughed. Was that this guy? Martin scanned his face and tried to imagine him laughing.

Ted. Ted.

Then Martin saw the couple sitting on the couch in the shadows of the Sugar Club with Ashley's wife, saw Ted's red face over Ashley's wife's shoulder as he tugged at the strap of her bra through her top and pushed his thick tongue against her neck, leaving a sticky trail as Ashley handed him a business card and told him how great his friends were. For a second Martin smelled the thick sweaty air of the Sugar Club.

"You don't remember me do you?" he said to Martin, shaking his hand.

"Yes, yes I do, it's just I was introduced to a lot of people that night, I'm just trying to remember what it is you do."

"Printing. At the Crown Estate. And you're the writer." They moved onto the pavement together as a car passed. The guy on the other side was taking a pencil from behind his ear and making notes on his folder.

"Of course! You and your wife were there, em it was …"

"Rosie."

"Yes, Rosie, I'm sorry I'm so bad with names. Yes, Andre was trying to get you to reveal the secret of your success. I remember. What has you out this way, this isn't your place is it?"

"No, no, I just bought this place for my daughter, but she hasn't moved in yet, and she's got me surveying for an extension already. She's got me under her pretty little thumb. But how about you, where do you live?"

"Just up the road on Paxton Drive."

"Oh, near the top. Tell me, how's the writing going?"

"Well, you know, it keeps me out of trouble."

"And we all need something that does that."

"Ha, ha, indeed. How's the printing?"

"Busier than I can handle at the moment."

"Is it just the free papers you print?"

"Oh, no, but they are the big contracts we landed. We've been building lots of smaller contracts, too. There's a lot of small publishing houses who do special interest stuff, as well as travel agents and property brokers putting together brochures."

"Interesting stuff. I guess there's a big market there."

"It's huge. I mean anyone can post on the net but that's actually made the market for us bigger because everyone can self-publish if they want. We are the final link in the chain to make it look classy. We just keep getting bigger."

"Wow, that's great."

"Well, if Andre is taking notice then we must be going the right way, and the bigger we get the more competitive we can be. The programmes for the theatres, we do them. You know all the fliers for the clubs in town? Well we've started on those too."

"That's a lot of clients to manage."

"Tell me about it, but I knew it would be big. We can do it all, see, from the handouts for the strip clubs to the metaphysical poetry magazines. We can cover it all."

"The final link in the chain."

"You bet. Hey, listen, if you ever want a job, just let me know. At the moment I'm advertising, but seeing as you're a friend of Andre's we could skip the formal interview."

"Well, I don't know if we're friends really, my wife works for him."

"Oh, yes, you're friends all right."

"Really?"

"Oh, yes, don't look surprised. Look, I know what it's like, trying to judge where you stand with someone like Andre. He's so successful, he knows everyone worth knowing, he moves in the right circles, and he's got this big persona, so when you first meet him it's hard, you know … you're thinking, well does he really like me or is he just networking, you know, working it? But the way he was talking about you and Alison I'd say you're friends with the guy. Let me put it this way, he'd take your call."

"Okay, well you guys seemed all pretty close." The sweat had started to dry inside Martin's top and on his legs and he felt a chill run through him. He started running gently on the spot again.

"It's different when there's money involved. It's like someone's always got their eye on your missus." The worker with the fluorescent hat now had his folder tucked under his arm and was walking across the road to them.

"Something to consider though," Ted said, "if you want to get your head out of the book? I'm at the Crown Estate."

"That's very good of you. I'll keep it in mind. I'll let you get back to it. I'm going to keep going."

"You go right ahead. It's good to bump into you, Martin. Say hello to Alison for me."

"I will," said Martin, and he started to run. Just before the road curved around he crossed over and glanced back. Ted was pointing at the house, talking to the worker, who was scratching his head again.

When he reached his door, he realised he didn't have his key. The driveway was empty and he sat on the doorstep for a moment. The house across the street had a window open and there was the sound of a vacuum cleaner and music, some sixties pop tune which was being sung along to tunelessly by whoever was cleaning. Martin stood up and started to jog gently again.

He found himself back on Wyatt Way, approaching the house with the scaffolding again. Ted was there, in the driveway, now leaning against a car that wasn't there before, talking to someone on the phone. He saw Martin and saluted as he got closer. Martin slowed down and walked to the house. Ted finished on the phone, putting it back in his pocket, and resting his back against the car.

"Around again?" he said.

"Not on purpose. I forgot my keys."

"Ha, ha! Well my daughter has turned up," he slapped the roof of the car, "and is inside now measuring up the rooms. When she comes out she'll have a list of furniture for Daddy that'll be as long as my arm."

"Oh, the joys."

"Yup, she's got me, all right."

"I've been thinking about what you said and I think I'll pop into the Crown Estate to see you soon, you know, about a job."

"Great! That didn't take long! Well, I'm going to be going there in a minute myself if you want to come take a look."

"I'm not exactly dressed for—"

"Don't worry, hey it's fine, like I said we can skip the formal interview. Just come down and take a look at the place, yeah?"

Ted's daughter emerged from the front door. She slid big sunglasses down from perched high on her head to over her eyes and put her hand on her hip. She had keys in the other hand and her bulging handbag hung down from her elbow. "That's it, Daddy," she said, "I'm going to have to stay at Stacey's until the walls are done anyway. I'm going to get some hangings for the landing and some lamps. I've got a lunch at one, so I'll go now and I'll call you later, and you can sort the painter out." She walked over and Ted opened the car door for her. She climbed in and the engine started. Ted and Martin stepped back and the car reversed out of the drive and took off up Paxton Drive.

"Come on," said Ted, "let's go," and they walked to Ted's big black car.

Martin sat in and closed the door. His bare thighs stuck to the leather seat. He felt small in this car. Instinctively he felt his pockets for his phone to send a message to Alison, but his phone was in the house. The central locking clicked into place as the engine started and they were on their way.

They went south of the city, around the ring road, and on to a huge straight road with rows and rows of industrial complexes on either side. This area was totally flat as if it had been levelled by a giant roller, all of its bumps and textures flattened and pushed to the edges.

Ted explained how long he had been in business and what the growth predictions were for next year.

Martin gazed at the size of the complexes as they passed. At the entrance of each estate there was a massive billboard with a long list of the companies within it. They were lettered and numbered, so each estate had a different letter. Martin caught some as they passed. C32 Brunsteen Electrical Wholesale. E09 Arches Holdings. E61 Cooltech Ltd. J12 Albatross Fabrics.

The long straight road seemed endless. It went on for as far as Martin could see. Right off in the distance, somewhere at the end of the road, the silhouettes of high rise buildings rose into the sky. Big trucks and thick vans moved quickly along the flat straight road, and underneath them Martin could see the shadows of the fast moving clouds on the ground, rushing toward the car like the ghosts of huge mythic creatures fleeing the city. Then they turned left and they were onto Avenue M.

Martin said, "Ted, I have to admit that I've never worked anywhere like this before, and before you mentioned it, I had never thought of working somewhere like this."

"No-one does. It's actually a good place to be. There's not much beauty around here, but there is an awful lot of money. We only moved into these premises a year and a half ago, and our agreement was based upon the assumption that we'd grow. And we have. By the end of the next half-year term we expect to be filling half of this building. I'm putting different teams together for the various types of contracts we want to get. Let me show you around, tell you what I'm looking for. If it's not for you then we'll leave it there, no harm done. But I think I could use someone like you around."

"Someone like me?"

"Someone, you know, creative. Someone who can deal with the special interest side of things. Someone with experience in publishing fiction and poetry and the like. You know, arty stuff."

They pulled up outside a big building with glass doors. Martin could make out a lobby with a couch and a plant, and a desk behind which was a large plasma screen. Ted stopped the engine.

"I think you'll like it," he said, and together they got out of the car and walked into the building. As they walked toward the big reception desk, past the couch and the shiny plant with the big leaves, it occurred to Martin that he didn't know Ted's second name. Or the name of the company.

The receptionist looked up as they approached and looking over her half glasses said, "Hello, Mr. Oldman."

Ted said, "Hi, Julie," and walked past.

Martin saw Julie's eyes follow him as he walked with Ted through the reception lobby in his trainers and running shorts. He remembered that the t-shirt he was wearing said *You're still talking?* in faded letters on the back. The next door was a double door which opened as they walked through it. They walked down a long straight corridor to the lift at the end. The walls were a dull beige and the carpet was a colourless tone. The atmosphere seemed to swallow sound and the light leaked a pale wash over everything. In here Ted looked older, as if he bathed in dishwater.

Two people in suits with briefcases walked past them. Martin could feel their eyes on him. He looked at Ted. Ted shot him a smile. His teeth seemed more yellow, his tongue chalky. Martin grimaced and smiled at the same time, and gestured to his t-shirt and shorts.

"Not exactly office wear," he said.

"Ha, well. Not many people would have just said sure thing and jumped in my car, with the sweat still drying. But it shows what's important to you, and it's not dress code, that's for sure." They came to the lift door. Ted pressed the button. "Let me show you the printing rooms, and then we can talk about it all." The lift door opened and they stepped inside. Ted pressed the button. A circle of light appeared around the tip of his finger, then he stood back, next to Martin, looking ahead, side by side.

"What's the name of the company? I didn't catch it," asked Martin as they looked back out at the corridor, the two men with briefcases disappearing down the colourless perspective of the rectangular tube, the walls and carpet converging on their suited backs.

"Spiral," said Ted, and the doors closed.

CHAPTER TWENTY-SIX

H enry is just finishing the last cigarette in the pack. The car park has been quiet, a slow steady exchange of cars, a couple arguing, one guy spending a little too long looking over the edge. No-one looks over the edge of a car park for that long unless they are planning to jump. "Don't do it," Henry whispers, and then in the rearview mirror the lift doors open to reveal Scorpion. His broad shoulders fill the small rectangle of the mirror. He stoops as he steps out. He is so big that in a few steps he is at the pay station. The ticket is tiny in his hand as he looms over the machine.

Henry gets out and walks around the other side of the cars to get to the pay station as Scorpion grabs his ticket from the machine and walks quickly to his car. Henry grabs his too and gets to his car just as Scorpion is pulling out.

Out of the car park there is a one-way system making Scorpion take a left. As soon as there's a break in the traffic coming the other way he swings his big four-by-four in a wild U-turn and joins the beeping, swerving stream of traffic going the opposite way. As he passes Henry sees him leaning forward over the wheel, his face set in grim concentration. The other drivers are still cursing him, and then he's gone.

Henry puts his tracker on the seat beside him and looks for the next opportunity to turn around. He watches the red dot on the screen move erratically through the city and then, just as Henry manages to find a turning, the dot slows down and settles into a more predictable pattern. Not trying to get away then, thinks

Henry, but trying to keep someone in sight. Scorpion is following someone. By the time Henry has the car back in sight, the rush is over, he must have found who he was looking for.

Henry overtakes and gets closer to Scorpion's car. Usually Henry wouldn't track so close behind, but when you're following someone you're not inclined to check if you're being followed. As they leave the centre of the city behind and pass the turnings for the suburbs and satellite towns, Henry drops back. The traffic is less dense and Henry spots who Scorpion is following. It's a black BMW with tinted windows and it's heading straight for the docklands.

Henry follows the red dot on the GPS monitor and travels parallel. As soon as they hit the old docklands, he turns back onto the road behind the big four-by-four. He knows that when Scorpion stops he will have to be close. He knows the grid of the docklands well, and what's in it. He also knows how easily things disappear. It's a rundown landscape that has gone beyond its time. It's a place for discarded ideas, no longer useful to the rest of the city. Henry has searched these shadows and seen what they hold. Now as he follows Scorpion he feels he is going back, back to where the Fly Guy nests.

The darkness that is here in the docklands is old, it was here at the very beginning of the city, when the first boats started trading and people began building. It was pushed back, forced into the corners and to the edges. Now the city has moved on, and the old darkness that was waiting for so long has come back.

O O O

Kayleigh is in the shower. Lucy can hear the water running and Kayleigh singing some song about love to herself.

Lucy starts to search the apartment. She looks in the small wardrobe, where Kayleigh's dresses, skirts, and tops hang crammed together above her array of boots and heels and sneakers. She quickly rummages through the drawers, through bras and socks, through a drawer of belts and scarves, through cartons and tubes of body creams, packets of false nails, gels, hair rollers, fake eyelashes. Moving into the kitchen she scans through the shelves, past cereals, sauces, plastic containers of pasta and rices, sachets of flavourings.

The water stops and she hears Kayleigh sing. Her voice is weak and sweet and tuneless, like a child's. *But then you left me and now I'm blue as blue can be,* she sings. Lucy turns. There, under the window is a low table with a stack of books and fashion magazines. It's solid underneath. Lucy goes and lifts the table slightly. It comes up. The low table top is a lid. She quickly puts the books and magazines on the ground and lifts it open.

There is a dark hold-all. She recognises it. It's the hold-all from Archie's apartment. She unzips it and reaches inside. There is a plastic bag which seems to be sealed. She makes a little tear. It is packed with blue pills. Kayleigh is still in the bathroom. Lucy goes back to the bedroom and takes a tube of false nail glue from the drawer. She takes two pills from the bag then dabs a spot of glue on the plastic, sealing the little tear.

By the time Kayleigh is out of the shower, the lid is closed and the books and magazines are stacked back on top. Kayleigh is still humming the tune she was singing, rubbing her long dark hair with a towel.

Lucy asks, "Hey have you got plans for today? 'Cause I got some fun on me."

"I have a lecture later, but it's a really boring one so, well, what do you mean fun?"

"Well, I was saving them for a special occasion, but what's say we make one?"

She opens her palm and holds out two little blue pills. Kayleigh stops drying her hair and steps forward to look at what she has. Her eyes widen and she says, "Oooh," and her lips purse as if she's just tasted something surprising, something that she likes the taste of very much.

o o o

In between the crumbling buildings on a potholed street Scorpion stops. Off in the distance, Henry sees that the BMW has stopped, too, at a large fenced off area of waste land, the rubble of an old rubber processing plant, demolished decades ago.

Henry pulls over. He reaches into the glove compartment and takes out his binoculars as the door of the BMW opens. The man getting out is dark, he looks Asian; he has brown skin and thick black hair. He stretches out his hand as it is taken by another man in a dark suit, who is bald and wears glasses. They disappear through the wire fence. In the foreground the door of the four-by-four opens, blocking out everything else. Henry takes the binoculars down and watches Scorpion get out. He walks down the derelict road like a giant under the looming buildings, and looking around, pulls back the wire fence, and goes in.

Henry lights a cigarette, sits in his car, and considers. If Scorpion is tracking this Asian guy, he's not very discreet. He's bound to get seen, and then what? Henry isn't inclined to find out. This isn't an affair. Unless Scorpion is going to stick his dick in one of these guys, it's none of his business.

Henry can leave now and track the car later. He is just about to start his engine when Scorpion comes back out onto the road and breaks into a run to his car. Henry ducks down, lying across the passenger seat. He hears the four-by-four start up, and with a screech of its tyres and a revving of its engine it takes off.

Henry sits up just in time to see it turn right at the end of the road. Then he slides down in his seat with his binoculars to his eyes, looking through the arch of his steering wheel. The Asian guy and his bald friend appear, talking and shaking hands again. They go their separate ways, the Asian guy back into his BMW and the bald one across the road and away down a side street. The BMW drives away.

Henry sits back up and takes the last drag of his cigarette before opening his door and stepping out onto the footpath. He stubs the cigarette out under his shoe and walks to the wire fence. He looks at the interior of a warehouse without the exterior walls. There are some partition walls, barely standing, covered in graffiti, surrounded by rubble and debris. Flies rise from the ground as he walks, buzzing around his thin frame and the deep dark smell of rotting meat rises with them. Pipes stick up from the ground and the flies land at the mouths, swarming into the darkness. There is a broken hand wash basin and weeds growing through shattered bricks, all covered with a chalky white residue.

He pushes the wire aside and walks in, following a path through the rubble. His eyes sting and water as the smell gets thicker until he reaches a wall which is intact and a steel door. Henry pulls on the heavy handle and the door swings slowly open, revealing a pitch-black rectangle of cold air. He takes his torch from his pocket and shines its thin powerful beam into the darkness. A big empty room. A meeting place, Henry thinks, but they didn't stay very long. Henry clicks off the torch and stands there in the darkness for a moment. Here in this black space everything is still.

He turns to face the doorway. He clicks his torch on again and scans the thin beam of light around to find the edges of the room. He sees a pile of something in the far corner, it looks like a white bag. As he approaches he sees it is a set of clothes, a short white leather skirt, a ripped netted top, and a white leather jacket. A pair of white high heels lie a few feet away. There are bloodstains on the jacket and on the skirt. He moves the clothes with his foot to see if there was anything else, and sees a spread of red stain on the ground.

Henry straightens up again and clicks his torch off, letting the darkness cover what he has seen. In that moment he feels his phone vibrate and then ring and echo around the empty room. His heart jumps, his breath stops, and his brain swells, an electric wave rushing though his body, pushing against his skull. He knows who is calling. The call display reads Unknown. With breath held and chest tight he presses answer. The misshapen voice slowly rasps and scrapes its way into his ear.

"Blooooomburg. Thisss is when I tellll yooou … to ruuun." Henry flashes his torch as he spins around, the thin beam frantically searching the brutal malevolent darkness as the breathing in his ear rattles and sucks.

Henry screams as loud as he can, emptying his lungs and screeching as if his throat has caught fire, "Fuckyoufuckyou! Where are you? Fuuck you!!" but it feels like shouting at a mountain, screaming up at a cliff face about to collapse.

The voice comes again, louder, "Ruuuun Blooooombuuuuurg," and Henry, terrified, sprints back through the doorway in to the dull daylight, past the ruins and rubble, through the wire fence and to his car.

Cold with panic, he turns the key and the tyres shriek as he speeds away, his heart thumping wildly. The deserted streets of the docklands flash past, and only once he is back on the outskirts of the city, he begins to slow down and feels the sweat covering his face and neck and his hands loosen from the wheel.

He stops in traffic. Around him, he sees the faces of people safe in their cars, mouthing along with inane car music or looking vacantly out the window, waiting for their turn to move. They have no idea.

Henry puts his head in his hands. His shirt is wet on his back. He feels older, much older than before. I need to find him and finish this, he thinks. He turns on the GPS tracker again. Scorpion is headed back to Kayleigh's.

CHAPTER TWENTY-SEVEN

When Martin got home it was dark. He knocked on the door. Alison opened it and threw herself into his arms.

"Where have you been? I was so worried," she said.

"I—"

"I didn't know what to do! Why didn't you take your phone? I always tell you to take your phone out. You've been gone all day."

"Alison, let's go inside. Let me in, come on."

"I thought you'd been knocked over on your run, Martin, I thought something terrible had happened...."

Martin eased her back through the door and closed it. "I'm okay, I'm okay. I've got some news—"

"I looked at your work and oh, oh, it's all about meeting strange men for drug deals or something. Martin I was so worried...."

"Shh, Alison, listen: I've got a job. I've got a job."

She leaned back to look at him. She wiped her tears from her cheeks and said, "You've what?"

"I've got a job. At Spiral, the printers on the Crown—"

"The printers? Ted from the club?"

"Ted from the club! He's given me a job."

She looked him up and down. "You're still in your running shorts. Did you run there? What...?"

With their arms around each other, Martin told her what had happened. Alison was very excited. She insisted on running out in the car and buying some champagne.

He stood in the shower and watched the foam move over his body. His waist was slimmer than he could remember it. Maybe he just hadn't looked at himself so much before. Before she ran out the door to buy champagne Alison had said that it's all part of the change, that she knew it would happen, she's so happy that he took the job.

She hadn't asked about the book in a long time. He had stopped volunteering information. He had never once mentioned Lucy. Lucy, who is in the clean warm apartment sitting opposite her new best friend, who is asking, *Is this it? Am I up yet? How long should we wait?* For all the time he had spent behind the door of the upstairs room, Alison had stopped asking about what it was he was creating, or what he had destroyed.

After the shower he shaved his face, scraping away the tough dark stubble. He stepped back from the mirror and angled his face this way and that. He needed a haircut again, the top was starting to look scruffy. He looked at his shoulders and arms. All of this running was not doing anything for his upper body definition. Weights. Maybe that was the next thing.

He had never spent so much time looking at himself since he started running. He thought that the more he looked at himself, the less he looked like what he had always thought he looked like. His hairline was higher, his eyes were bigger. His mouth seemed smaller. Maybe it had just been hidden by the beard for so long. This mirror was much better than the old cracked and stained mirror he had looked in when he lived in the bedsit. Now maybe he was just seeing himself clearly. Or maybe it was part of the change. How long had it being happening? Change happens slowly.

By the time he got downstairs Alison was back. She had two bottles of champagne and was looking in the cupboard for the right glasses to use.

"Two bottles?"

"Well," she replied, turning around from the cupboard triumphantly with two tall champagne flutes, "things are going well at the office, too. The docklands contracts are starting to come in. Andre is very happy. We've got hold of three plots so far. Have we got that ice-cream that I like, you know the fancy one? I think it's in the bottom drawer."

In the freezer there were packets of food he had forgotten about, and a full trout, belly split, its head still on, rock hard.

Underneath was a tub of chocolate ice cream. He pulled it out. She was pouring the champagne.

Alison said, "When are you going to start?"

"Well, he said if I want to get in at the start of next week, there is a staff seminar and training for the in-house computer networks, so my timing is just right. Then he can put me with a team who can show me the ropes. It's all happened a bit fast really."

"I know, isn't it great?" Alison handed him his glass. "Ted must really like you."

They clinked glasses. Alison leaned in and kissed him. Then she took a spoonful of the ice cream. "Mmmm, chocolate ice cream and fizz. It's the simple things that make a moment special, isn't it babe?"

Martin nodded and leaned in for another kiss. She put the chocolate covered spoon on his nose. They laughed.

That night she told him that she felt this was a turning point, this was the new platform he could build upon. What a journey they had been on, it was a testament to how their relationship was so good that both of them were progressing. They kissed. She stroked his neck and kissed his shaven chin and jaw and around to his ear.

"Let's go upstairs. Give me a minute, then come up."

When Martin went up, she was lying in the bed under the duvet. As he walked toward the bed, she pulled the duvet back to show a red lacy bra and smiled, then pursed her lips in a pout, patting the bed next to her. Martin undressed and climbed into bed. They kissed and moved over one another, exploring each other's skin. Alison climbed on top of him, straddling him, grinding her pelvis against his, pushing her cleavage into his face. She reached between his legs and felt his flaccid penis. She tugged at it.

She started whispering in his ear, "Come on baby, you know what I want, come on, feel how wet I am, come on," but the more she spoke the less Martin felt any connection to what was going on. Alison said, "What can I do? What can I do for you?"

Martin couldn't even reply, he just shook his head. Alison kept trying for a while then, climbed off and lay next to him, defeated.

"Martin, it's been so long now. What is it? Is it that you don't fancy me anymore?"

"It's just a phase, just a dip. We'll come out of it."

"We? Martin I don't know what it is I should do, I haven't changed."

Martin didn't answer. He heard sounds from outside creep into the room. A car passed. A front door closed. Another engine started somewhere. Underneath, like a rumble from a deep underground river, was the dull thick sound of the motorway. It took Martin by surprise. Now that he heard it, it was loud. How could he not have heard that before? It had been there all along. Alison turned on her side, propped her head up on her hand, and looked down at him.

"At least I don't think I have. Martin? What have you got to say about it?"

"I don't really know."

"I can't remember the last time you took control. It would be nice, for that to happen. I don't want to be the one pushing all the time. Martin?"

Martin put his arm across his eyes and said, "Look, it's nothing. I mean it's not the most important thing is it? It's just a blip. I'm sorry, okay?"

Alison lay down again and put her arm and leg over Martin, getting as close as she could to him.

"We don't spend as much time together as we used to, do we? Not real time. We used to talk for hours. We did, didn't we? And you used to say all sorts of beautiful things. You don't say the kinds of things to me you used to."

Martin took his arm away from his eyes and looked at the ceiling for a moment. He wished the light was off.

"What do you mean? What kinds of things?"

"Oh, just things. Romantic things. Idealistic things."

"I can't keep repeating myself, Alison, if that's what you want me to do. Once something is said, there's not much point in saying it over and over. I mean what do you want me to do? Say everything is wonderful? The world is just what we want it to be? Our love is the most perfect, special thing that has ever been? The world can go to hell, sink under weight of its own fucking misery, but we will always live in bliss if we have each other? Will that do?"

Alison drew away from him. She turned around and crossed her arms and pulled her legs up to her chest.

"Alison, don't do that. What do you want—"

"No Martin, stop now. You've ruined it, just stop."

She was crying. He threw back the cover and got out of the bed noisily, slamming the door as he left the bedroom. He reached over and slammed the office door too, and then went down the stairs and stood in the front room, clenching and unclenching his fists.

He looked around the darkened room for something that he could break, something that would make a satisfying crash, something that wouldn't cost a lot to replace. He wanted to swing his fist and knock through the wall. He wanted to push his shoulders back, chest out, stretch his arms, to grow above the roofs and pick houses from the street, holding a home in each hand, and squash them together, crushing the bricks into dust and scatter the dust into the darkness of the fields and forests beyond the thin wooden fences, to give the darkness back that which was built to dispel it. Instead he stood in the front room between the sofa and the TV and waited for an answer to come.

CHAPTER TWENTY-EIGHT

Lucy gets close to Kayleigh, blowing on her neck, taking her shirt off. She says, *Close your eyes,* as she runs her fingers through her hair and pulls her hands up above her head. She touches her neck.

Kayleigh has never felt anything like it. She has never felt a touch so soft yet charged with electricity. She feels the touch of Lucy's fingers on her back and it draws a current of sensation which runs across her skin like a gust of wind on the barley tops in the sunshine. Lucy's touch is accessing channels of colour which run just below the surface of her skin, and until now have been dormant.

"Now you touch me," Lucy says.

Kayleigh opens her eyes. The colours in the apartment are alive, they pulse and radiate an essence which expands beyond the boundaries of the objects. The air feels alive, and when she breathes in it feels like breathing in life itself, and there in the middle of her vision is the beautiful Lucy, like a sensuous angel, peeling off her clothes as if they are layers of skin, and she is luminous, glowing from within. Kayleigh starts to touch her, gently running her fingers all over her body. Lucy's eyes close, and Kayleigh sees that they have stepped somewhere together. Lucy is the most beautiful thing Kayleigh has ever seen. Kayleigh has lost track of what time it is. She hears a noise on top of the music and realises that she has started talking. She is stringing words together, talking incessantly without pause.

"... And hasn't this song been on before? Oh, my god, look at your eyes, Lucy, are mine the same? I'm going to have to look, my god, I feel my heart racing but it's okay isn't it? It's just the drug, oh, I've got to move, come on let's dance. I've never felt so, so, I can still taste the coffee, oh shall we have some more, or make it just so that we can smell it, I've never felt so, oh I'd love to smell the coffee again...."

When Spike gets there he knocks but there is no answer. He can hear the music coming from inside. He opens the door and walks in on Lucy and Kayleigh undressed except for their panties with their arms around each other, moving slowly to the music, eyes closed, oblivious to his presence in the room.

At that moment his phone rings. Lucy and Kayleigh both turn their heads and look his way. They look like zombies, their pupils dilated so much that their eyes are black. They start to laugh and say his name, and he looks to see who the caller is. It's Gregor.

Kayleigh is saying, *Oh, my god, you've been gone for so long,* and moves toward him with her arms outstretched. Their movements are slow, as if they are underwater. He crosses the room past the two of them to turn the volume of the music down. The ringing stops.

He says, "Kayleigh, what have you taken?"

She is hugging Lucy again. Lucy has her eyes closed and a great big smile across her face.

"She had some pills."

Spike feels the vibration of the phone in his hand before the ringtone starts again. He backs out of the apartment and closes the door before answering it.

"Hey, Gregor."

"Is Lucy ready for me to pick up?"

"No, no. It's a bad time now."

"Bad time. How is it a bad time?"

"She and Kayleigh are pretty smashed. I'd leave it a few hours if you wanted to get any sense out of her."

"Drinking?"

"Yes, I think so, I just got here. Maybe some pills."

"Pills? You let Lucy take pills?"

"I didn't think Kayleigh had anything, she doesn't usually unless I get them for her. I just got here, Gregor, and they're smashed already."

"Where have you been?"

"Trailing. Trailing Ali."

"And?"

"He went to the docklands, hooked up with some guy I've never seen before, went in to the old—"

"Fishery."

"Yeah. What's that about?"

"That's the new location for the deal."

"Again? You changed again? And you had Ali check it? When you don't trust him?"

"I'm coming to get Lucy."

"Gregor, seriously you won't like what you find, give her a few hours to come round. Even wait till tomorrow. They look pretty off it."

Spike hears squeals of excitement and the music starts up again from behind the door.

"Where are you?" Gregor asks.

"I'll bring her to you."

"Where are you?"

"I'm at Kayleigh's. Please don't come here, Gregor. I'll bring her to you."

"Okay. Call me when you are going to bring her."

"Thank you."

"How about Ali? Before that meeting? Where was he then? Who was he with?"

"He was in his office, he was alone. He spent a lot of time on the phone, but that's it. When he went to the location he was with a small bald man."

"That's alright, he's a member of the development company. I arranged that. Someone's letting light in, Spike. Just make sure that Lucy is alright, and get her back to me. Don't let her take anything else."

"I don't even know what it is she's taken."

"Just take care of her."

Gregor hangs up. Spike puts the phone back in his pocket. He stands for a moment then turns and goes back into the apartment. When he opens the door the music rushes out at him, past him, and down the corridor. Lucy and Kayleigh are swaying in the kitchen.

O O O

Sitting in his car in the street below the student apartments, Henry leans his seat back and lights a cigarette as he puts the earpiece in and switches on the bug. There is music playing, music for a nightclub, big beats and throbbing bass lines. Then a door closes and the music decreases in volume. He hears Scorpion's voice.

"So what is it you've taken?"

Kayleigh and Lucy giggle and laugh. Lucy says, "They were in a bag, a bag in the cupboard."

"You've been in my bag? Kayleigh, I told you not to touch that. What the fuck were you doing going into my bag? That stuff's not even mine."

Kayleigh says, "Oh, babe, you should have one, they're amazing. C'mon take one."

Lucy joins in, "Spike, you really are so huge, I didn't see it before...."

"Do you know what it is you've taken?"

"It's fucking amazing whatever it is."

Lucy and Kayleigh start laughing again.

Henry gets out of his car and walks across the road to the apartments opposite. He passes Scorpion's big black four-by-four. The door of the apartment block is open again. He throws his cigarette down and goes in. As he walks up the stairs the conversation continues.

"That stuff isn't even on the streets yet. How many did you take?"

"One."

"Just one."

"Well I'm taking the rest out of here."

"What? You're going to go? Babe, stay and get high with us."

"No, I'm going to leave you girls to it."

"No, stay, it's amazing."

Lucy says, "We could have some fun, the three of us. Come on, just take your jacket off and ..."

When Henry reaches the same spot as he did before, he looks across into the corridor. The curtains are open and he sees Lucy's naked back, swaying. Scorpion passes her with a hold-all under his arm. Kayleigh, topless, follows him past the window toward the door.

"Stay with us," she says again. "C'mon, it'll be amazing. I've never felt anything like it. Why are you going through my bag?"

Lucy goes away from the window and toward the mirror. Scorpion is saying something about getting the keys and phone while Henry hears Lucy's voice loud as she talks into the mirror, "Holy shit my eyes. I've never seen that before. My eyes, my eyes." Scorpion is telling Kayleigh that they can't go outside, for their own safety and he's taking the keys to make sure they don't. Lucy walks away from the mirror, passing the window again, and turns the volume of the music back up, louder than it was before. Now the door opens and Scorpion is in the hallway talking to Kayleigh. He has the hold-all over his shoulder. Henry can just about hear what he's saying.

"Call me, call me if you need anything or if anything happens. Make sure Lucy knows where your phone is, I've put it on the table. Just call me. I'm locking the door so don't try and go out. You're going to be up for a few more hours yet. If you need anything call me, okay? I don't want you to go outside, so if you need anything call me, you got it?"

Kayleigh steps out of the doorway into the hallway. Henry sees her thin body, her long dark hair cascading down her naked back as she reaches up to Scorpion. He leans down and takes her in his big arms and they embrace and kiss. It's a deep passionate kiss. She says something to him and he nods and says something back to her. Henry can't hear, but it is one word and looks like, "Always." They embrace again and he cups her buttocks in his big hands and squeezes. She puts her hand on his groin and rubs.

In the apartment Lucy is at the window about to draw the curtains. She is looking straight at Henry. At that same moment, Scorpion lifts his head from Kayleigh's dark hair and looks across, too. In that moment Henry is seen, through two windows, by both of them. He turns around and walks up the next flight of stairs. When he looks again the curtains are drawn and Scorpion is locking the door. He turns around and starts down the stairs.

When he gets to the street he sees Scorpion's car and walks the opposite way. He comes to an iron fence beyond which is the university grounds. He has to turn around and walk back past the black four-by-four. He doesn't look in to see if Scorpion is in it. He gets in his car and takes off as quick as he can. He keeps an eye on his rear view mirror and switches on his tracker. Scorpion is stationary, still outside the university building.

O O O

Henry drives back into the city through the centre and to the river. At the junction at the river he goes straight across the bridge and heads down to the old docks. On one side the water pushes and rolls, on the other all of the abandoned buildings stand silently; the boarded up doorways, bare roofs with exposed beams like broken bones. He drives past dock yards with great rusting hulks of machinery standing like fossils. He passes an old church with graffiti on its walls—*God sucks my cock.*

The sky is darkening, the night coming in and the decaying silhouettes loom with an ancient malign intent. Out here in the rubble of the docklands, there is one bar which stands alone in this abandoned landscape. Its permanently drunken landlord is oblivious to the apocalypse around him. The Bucket O' Blood. It's displaced, out of time, isolated. Its yellow light shines out through dirty windows across the desolate concrete ruin beckoning souls to step across the threshold, keeping its long held promise of a place to find intoxication, a place beyond the reach of the everyday life. Henry orders a drink. He rings Maya.

"Two days' work, that's all you owe me."

"What do you mean? What did you see?"

"You're right, he's in another relationship."

The landlord, red-eyed and drunkenly licking his lips and chewing on air, puts a large whiskey in front of him.

"With who? Did you see? With who?"

"With your daughter."

"Kayleigh?"

"Your daughter, Kayleigh."

The silence he expected goes on longer than he thought it would. He has time to sit down at a table facing the door and take two mouthfuls of whiskey. He can feel the cold spreading from the phone. She must want to die.

"Are you still there?"

"Are you sure?"

"I followed him. He went to her flat, near the university, and when he came out, they, well, they kissed."

"You saw them kiss?"

"Yes. It was a lover's kiss."

Henry sees the doorway darken. A huge figure comes through. It's Scorpion.

"I've got to go."

Henry hangs up and puts the phone in his pocket. He swigs down his whiskey and goes to stand up.

Scorpion steps in front of him and puts a big hand on his shoulder and says quietly and firmly, almost politely, "Sit down." Henry sits down. Scorpion sits opposite him. This close he can see Scorpion's muscles bulging beneath his shirt, he can see just how wide his shoulders are. Henry feels light and two dimensional in front of such mass.

"Who are you working for?"

"Hey, I'm not interested in what you do."

"Then why did you follow me, who do you work for? Has Gregor sent you to keep an eye on me? You had a tracker on my car. What else have you done?"

Scorpion leans across so that his face is right next to Henry's face. Henry's heart starts to pump and he feels shivers run up his back as he feels the heat of breath on his cheek and the latent power in the huge muscular frame close to him. The giant is brimming with violence, the sinews in his neck are taut, the scorpion on his neck is pulsing.

"One last time," he says slowly, "one last time before I take you outside and rip you apart piece by fucking piece. Who do you work for?"

"Well, at the moment, I am working for your wife."

Scorpion leans back as if dodging a punch and looks at Henry in shock for a moment. He joins his hands together and puts the tips of his fingers to his lips. He knows what's going on.

"Was that her on the phone?"

"Yes."

"Did you tell her already?"

"Yes."

Scorpion lets his head slip down into his hands. His shoulders slump and he sinks lower, as if he has been punctured. Henry's heart settles down, but he can still feel adrenaline in his veins. He glances around. The only exit he can see is past Scorpion, and from where he is sitting there is not a clear view of the rest of the bar; it is obscured by a wooden panel and the massive bulk in front of him. The massive bulk which seems to be losing its form. He turns his empty glass in his hand.

"Do you want a drink? Because I'm going to have another."

"Do you know what she's going to do?"

"No, she just asked me to find out who you are sleeping with."

"And now she knows."

"And now she knows."

Henry waves his empty glass at the barman.

"Another double whiskey and…?"

"Make that two."

"Listen, I'm just an investigator. I just gather information and present it. I don't do hits, I don't do intervention. I don't care what you do, or what your job is. I had to find out one thing. Your wife wanted to know the truth, so she called me. That's it. My job's over now."

"How long were you following me?"

"Today."

"Just today?"

"Just today, and well, yesterday, too."

"Today and yesterday."

Henry can see him think, can see him run through his movements in his mind.

"Not a lot to see. One kiss."

"That's all I need."

"An easy job for you."

"Suits me fine, I don't like things complicated."

The landlord is back, putting two tumblers of whiskey in front of them with a clunk and a splash. He picks up the note Henry has left out on the table and puts it in his back pocket as he wobbles around to the front of the bar and starts to collect glasses.

"What's your name?"

"Henry. Henry Bloomburg."

"Spike, but you already knew that."

They sip from their drinks. The light in the bar feels like it is the same light that has always been there, it has never been released. It has aged and yellowed, and it infuses everything in the room with its sickly glow.

"So you're a private investigator then?"

"Uh huh."

"Aren't you going to ask?"

"Ask what?"

"About what you've seen?"

"I've just seen a situation. Now, like I said, my job is over."

"Do you know who I work for?"

"I know it's not a chemicals company."

"What about the police?"

"What about the police?"

"Don't you report to the police?"

"The police didn't employ me. Your wife employed me. She didn't want to know who you work for, what you move around, why you do what you do. She wanted to know who you're sleeping with."

"And now she knows. Have you got a wife?"

"No."

"Girlfriend?"

"No."

"So are you in love right now?"

"But we've only just met."

Spike smiles. Henry finds it odd. He wouldn't have expected the Scorpion to let down his guard, but then it happens all the time. Henry always sees that people are aching for an opportunity to rest their defences, even if it's just for a moment. They both drink.

"So are you? In love with anyone right now?"

"No."

"Aren't you going to ask me who I love?"

Henry sighs and swigs. There are others in the bar, Henry saw them when he walked in. Men in a huddle around a table, two guys drinking by themselves at the counter. A couple in the corner, a woman in her forties and a guy in his late teens. *Everyone in here has a story,* he thinks, *but it looks like most of their stories are over. They may be sensing a change, but it's the ending getting closer. This is a place where endings happen, slowly.*

"Spike, it makes no difference. If you tell me it's your wife or if you tell me it's your daughter, it makes no difference. Tomorrow I'll get a call from someone else who wants an answer to something. Some part of their lives they can't control, something under the cover. You know? They feel it in the darkness but can't pull the cover back. They'll pay me to go sneaking around and find whatever it is and then I'll start again."

Spike puts his head in his hands again. Henry considers him. He looks close to tears. He's like a child who has been awoken and found himself in the body of a warrior and seen death for the first time.

"Do you know who you love?"

"No. I was with Maya, but I don't know if it's love now. I don't know what it is with Kayleigh. I don't know."

He drinks some more and looks into Henry's eyes. Henry can see his outline tremble in the old yellow light, as if the signal is fading.

"So what have you seen? How much do you know?"

"All I care about is answering Maya's one question. My part is over."

"Is Maya at home now?"

"I don't know. I called her mobile."

"How much does Maya know?"

"I just told her about you and Kayleigh."

"And you just saw us kiss."

"That's enough. I saw the kiss."

"Fuck."

Henry swigs back his drink.

"Well, I'll leave you to it. Spike, I don't know what love is, but I've seen a whole lot of trouble it causes. It's not always a good thing, it's not always a bad thing. I'm glad I'm not in it. Love makes a mess."

Spike is shaking his head. As Henry goes to stand up, Spike rises and towers over him pulling a gun from his jacket and pushing it to Henry's temple in one swift brutal motion.

"I can't let you go." All of the rigidity has returned to Spike's muscular form, his mouth has tightened. Only his eyes betray him, they are flooded with grief.

Henry sits back down, his hands up. "Spike, your broken heart doesn't matter to me. My job is done. Don't do this. Let me go. I'll walk away and you'll never see me again."

Spike pushes the barrel harder against Henry's head.

"You're coming with me. We're going to take a drive. Get up."

They stand and Spike sticks his gun into Henry's side. He scans the bar as they walk toward the door. No-one is looking up except for the barman who gives a drunken thumbs up and pours himself another drink. The big four-by-four is parked on the street. Spike opens the passenger door, grabbing Henry's gun from the inside of his jacket before pushing him in.

"Climb across, you're driving." Spike follows him, getting into the passenger seat.

"Put the belt on," Spike says.

Henry clips the belt in place. Spike keeps the gun trained on him as he starts the engine.

"We're not going far. Go to the river."

They start to drive away from The Bucket O' Blood, down the abandoned streets of the docklands.

"Spike, you don't want to kill me. I bought you a drink."

"Don't try and fuck with me. I don't know how much you know. You're a loose end."

"Do you think I won't be missed? Spike think about—"

"Shut up or I shoot you now you piece of shit!"

Spike's head is reeling. The thought of Maya putting the phone down with his name and Keyleigh's ringing in her ear is making him feel sick. This puny fucker has brought everything tumbling down. Who knows who he is really working for. He might be playing him. He needs to be extinguished. Now.

"Turn in here, right, behind that building."

Henry swings the car off the road to the right and then pushes the accelerator to the floor. Spike shouts and Henry's heart races, his nerves set alight as he grips the wheel and braces himself back against the seat. The derelict building looms before them as Henry speeds the car toward it. He takes his hands off the wheel and pulls them back just as the passenger side of the four-by-four smashes into the corner of the building.

There is smoke and airbags. Spike is thrown toward the windscreen squashing the plastic of the airbag, bursting it with his weight. The gun is gone from his hand and Henry sees him turn with a fire in his eyes, as if his body will explode through his skin. The metal around Spike is bent and pushed in, the seat has lurched forward and Spike can't move properly. Henry unclips his belt and lunges across, grabbing Spike's neck and finding the ridge between the muscles. He presses as hard as he can, squeezing the nerve. Spike struggles and gets an arm loose, pushing it to Henry's face, but in a matter of seconds his eyes close and he is unconscious. Henry clambers out of the car and runs into the shadows of the docklands.

CHAPTER TWENTY-NINE

On Monday Alison drove Martin back to the Spiral building. When Martin indicated where to turn off and they turned off onto the main avenue of the Crown Estate, Alison said, "Oh my God, I never knew all this was here, it's huge! How long does it go on?"

"I don't know, I didn't get to the end. We're going to the M estate."

"It just goes on and on."

When they turned into the M estate and the brown brick building loomed in front of them, Alison drove right up to the glass doors at the front.

"I'm just going to let you out here. This is further out than I thought, I'm going to be a bit late. Have you got everything? Bag? Money? Phone?"

"If I hate it, I'll make my way home."

"Hey, you won't hate it, it's just daunting. Remember me on the rooftop? You helped me. Remember what you told me then? Just call me later. Good luck."

Martin got out and walked through the door. He walked down the corridors to the C wing of the building.

He got in the lift to go up to level three and guessed that the others in the lift were probably going to the same training course as he. They all had laminated cards around their necks. No-one was making eye contact.

He thought again about when he met Alison on the rooftop. What had he told her? He couldn't remember. Should he have a laminated card around his neck? Maybe you were supposed to pick them up at the main reception. When the lift stopped he followed the others to a big conference room where they all showed their cards to a woman in the doorway. She was in a suit, smiling like an air hostess holding a folder, nodding as everyone walked in and took their seats at desks with a monitor and keypad. Martin stopped when he got to the door and the woman looked at him expectantly.

"I, em, I don't have a ..."

"Ah, Mr. Tripp. Martin Tripp," she said, "I have your identity here."

Martin took the laminated card and placed it around his neck. He took a seat and waited for the seminar to begin.

o o o

Alison and Andre stood over a map of the docklands. Each plot was marked off, and where there was interest or planning either from them or another firm, it was marked on the map. The plots which they were developing were marked off in red. Alison's groundwork had reaped rewards and there was already competition for some plots. Alison told Andre what tack she had used; the grand vision of giving the city back a space which it thought it had lost to the shadows and building it back to be the shining beacon of success. Reclaiming what was originally the heart of the city, recreating the hotspot for commercial, residential, and leisure industries. This was the future and it was going to be big, bright, and profitable.

"Hell, I'm so glad I employed you," Andre gushed. "You could sell me shit for my shoes and I'd tell you to keep the change."

"We have a problem though." Alison pointed to a small square on the map bordered in black. "This guy won't sell up."

"Won't sell up? I'm surprised he can stay open."

"Well he's turned down offers and won't even have a meeting."

The door opened and Andre's wife came in. Alison took a side-step away from Andre. Andre put his arms out and said, "Just in time, we were about to break for lunch. Join us, we'll go somewhere nice."

Cassandra walked to the table and looked at the map, marked off into different coloured shapes. Some were long rectangles, some squares, some *L*-shapes. Her heels made her taller than either

Alison or Andre and she cast a thin shadow over the plots as she leaned over the table.

"Is this the docks? My god, I thought they'd built enough in this city. What else is there to build?"

Andre stepped next to her and put his arm around her, squeezing her close and talking into her neck while she grimaced, the sides of her mouth pulling the edges of her eyes down.

"They'll always think of something else. And for as long as they do, we'll keep helping them build it." He looked up at Alison. "Speaking of which, there's going to be another Acre development out where you are. Gold this time, I think, right next to yours. Now, where to for lunch?"

O O O

When Alison picked Martin up from outside Spiral, he sat into the car just as the rain began to come down.

"I'm going to need a car," he said as he put his seat belt on.

Alison smiled and clapped her hands. She had been anticipating him getting in the car and telling her how he would never go back there again. Instead all the way home he told her about the programming they were being shown. He said it wasn't complicated at all, just required common sense and the ability to read instructions properly. He had found which section he would be working in as of next week and had talked to some of the guys. They seemed alright, he said. Alison asked what he would be printing.

"The guys were talking about stuff they've been doing. Assembly instructions for furniture warehouses; no words, just pictures. Stickers for ladders. 'Not this side.' 'Danger—do not climb this side.' You know, mostly just a few words and pictures. That kind of thing. It seems like a natural place to start, I suppose, you know, to learn the ropes."

"I'm so glad. Oh, my god, I thought you were going to come out hating the place."

"I've never been in a place like that before. It's like an ant colony, lots of movement, people scurrying around, all for the greater good. I'm just taking it all in right now."

As they joined the motorway and the spray rose around them Alison said, "Well, you should take this car. I'll go back to taking the train for the moment."

By the time they got home there was water spreading over the New Acre roads. Martin held his jacket over them both as Alison unlocked the front door. They prepared dinner together and sat and ate it before going into the front room and turning the TV on.

"Aren't you going upstairs tonight?" Alison asked.

"No, put on whatever, I'll watch whatever you want to," Martin said.

Alison flicked through the channels until she got to a programme about professional catwalk models living together.

"Haven't you seen this one before?" Martin said.

"Not this one, this is series six. One of the girls in this series reminds me of Cassandra, you know, Andre's wife?"

"Oh yeah, which one?"

"That one." Alison pointed at the TV.

The model was on a shoot, near the sea. She was holding the reins of a mottled grey horse wearing a gypsy shawl and looking wistfully to the horizon. There was a photographer fluttering around her telling her how wonderful she looked and then encouraging her to move the hood of the shawl down to reveal her hair.

"For some wind dynamic," the photographer said, "that's it, beautiful, beautiful."

The model turned her head this way and that, and the wind blew her blonde hair this way and that while the camera *click-click-clicked*. The horse gave a neigh and a shake of boredom.

"I can see how she might remind you of her, yeah, but she doesn't look like her."

Alison put her head to one side. "You don't think so?"

"She looks like what Cassandra would like to look like, or maybe what she thinks she looks like."

"You don't like her, do you?"

"Cassandra? Maybe we just don't have anything in common."

"We had lunch today. She was talking about the work she does in the city. She's involved in setting up kitchens for the homeless. She was talking today about the kitchens having to be moved because of council regulations and all the trouble and bureaucracy that moving kitchens involved."

"Charity? Maybe I had her down all wrong. Maybe she just really hates opera."

"Well, she doesn't have to work, Andre's got enough for them both. I think she must be a really strong woman, if just to put up with him all the time. But that must take something, setting up and running kitchens for the homeless." Alison moved over and put her head on Martin's shoulder.

"Have you heard from *Noire*?"

Martin grunted. "They want more rewrites. They advised me to revisit the original Henry stories and draw from them. But they're going along with it, they say the writing is good."

"Oh, well no wonder you need some mindless TV time." She kissed his cheek. "Well, I'm glad you do, it's much comfier with two on the couch."

Martin kissed her back and she turned the volume up as the programme came back on. There had been no contact with *Noire* since their reaction to his first draft, since they said this is not the story we wanted. Alison shifted on the couch. The models were lining up for another shoot, all dressed in dungarees and mining hats with lamps on, their pouting chiselled faces smeared with dark make-up. Martin's mind went back upstairs into the back room, to Lucy.

He could see the door of the writing room open and Lucy walking out, down the stairs and standing in front of the TV, the glow of the screen pulsing behind her, shining through her skirt so he can follow the line of the inside of the thighs. She has her bare feet planted apart and her arms crossed. She is looking at him as if he'd promised her something and then forgotten about it. She uncrosses her arms and puts her hands on her hips, putting her weight on her right leg and cocking her hip out. She raises her eyebrows, looking straight at him, waiting for him to remember.

CHAPTER THIRTY

When Henry gets home that night he sees that money has been transferred to his account.

The following evening he is sitting at his table, naked but for a towel around his waist. His chalk skin is drawn tight over his skeleton and he is eating cold tuna from a tin, waiting for his sheets to finish drying. He picks up the phone and dials Kramer.

"Bloomburg. What have you got?"

"Nothing, Kramer. I've got nothing. I've got a memory of something horrific, beyond horrific. I've got a voice that speaks to me, but no way to trace it. I've got a nobody that lived at Lomax road. I can't find who was there. Did you get anything from Lomax?"

"Same as you probably. Just an absent landlord. The place looks like someone's been in it, but it's a mess, like a nest. There's no records. The landlord lives on the other side of the country, doesn't know a thing. Nothing traceable in the place. Some printed paper with what looks like some stories on it."

"Can I have it? What's it about?"

"It's in midtown station. Go check it out if you want. I haven't seen it but the boys say it's pretty shoddy work. Something about someone falling down a well. Bloomburg, this voice, what's it saying to you?"

"You don't wanna know Kramer."

"Well, listen, just remember why you left us. Don't let shit get under your skin, you don't want to go back there."

"I appreciate your sentiment Kramer. I gotta go."

He puts the phone down and spoons the cold fish into his mouth. His phone rattles and rings on the thin wooden counter. He doesn't recognize the number.

"Bloomburg. It's Spike."

"Spike. You didn't kill me."

"And you didn't kill me. You could have."

"So what's this?"

"She's gone. I need you to find her. Maya's gone."

"You want to employ me? You want to kill me, then you want to employ me?"

Henry looks from his window to the alley below. Some cans and plastic bags. He goes to the apartment door and looks through the peephole. The corridor is empty.

"Why are you really calling me?"

"I need you to find her."

"Usually when people go like that it's because they want to go and they don't want to be found. I don't want to help you find her if she doesn't want to be found."

"That's not how it works. Last night you said, someone calls you and you take the job. Take the job. I need you to find her."

"Spike, I'm—"

"Bloomburg, you could have killed me. You had me and you let me go. I'm not a fucking psychopath. I need her back more than I need you dead. She can cause more damage to me if she wants. And I love her. I'm going to text you an address. Come to this address tonight at ten and we'll talk about it, you have to help me."

"You think I'm going to come to you? Spike? I'm not going to be—" but Spike hangs up.

Henry sits down and keeps eating. A few minutes later his phone rings again. It's Maya. Henry picks it up.

"Hello Maya."

"Did you get the money?" Her voice is creaky.

"Yes, thank you."

"I want to give you more."

"Really."

"I want you to kill Spike. I want him dead."

"Maya, I don't do that."

"I don't care how much it costs, I want him dead."

"You'll have to do it yourself."

"I'm going to text you an address and I want you to come tonight and we'll discuss it."

"Maya, I'm not going to do it."

"Come tonight at ten, I will pay you whatever you want, just come."

"I'm not going to—" but she hangs up.

Henry puts his phone back on the table and finishes his tuna. The drone of the dryer stops and beeps. He puts the empty tuna tin in the bin. There's another rattle on the table, followed by another as the two texts come through. They are addresses on either side of the city. He could go and finish Spike and get more money. He could send Maya the address which Spike has sent, so that she can go and kill him, or send Spike Maya's address, so that he can go and find her. He doesn't want to do any of these. It's a mess. Love makes a mess. There's a story in midtown station. A story from the centre of his mystery. He takes the hot sheets out of the machine. The hot clean linen feels good against his naked body. He goes to redress the bed.

O   O   O

When Lucy wakes up she is in Kayleigh's bed. It's daylight outside. Her head hurts. Kayleigh is lying next to her, breathing deep and slow. She sits up slowly, waiting for her mind to catch up with what her body is doing. On the sheets she sees dried foam and chocolate smears. She looks down. On her breasts are chocolate smears. She remembers last night. She and Kayleigh had made a thick hot chocolate and smeared it on each other, licking it off. She remembers Spike coming in, going back out and coming in again.

She stands out of the bed and goes into the living room, where the cushions are off the sofa and Spike's huge body is taking up the floor. She has a flash of dancing in the kitchen with Kayleigh turning the lights on and off and the sound of both of them laughing. Then turning the lights off-on, off and on, off and the next time they flicked on, Spike was there, huge and angry, and she and Kayleigh started screaming.

She pours a glass of water from the tap and Spike sits up. Even sitting on the floor his huge bulk is intimidating, nearly as tall as she is.

"Is Kayleigh awake?" he asks.

Lucy shakes her head.

"Have you heard from Gregor?"

She shakes her head again. He stands up and throws the cushions back on the sofa.

"When you do let me know. And put some fucking clothes on."

He goes into Kayleigh's room, closing the door behind him. Lucy stands in the kitchen. Her short blonde hair is tussled, she has red rings under her eyes, her body and breasts are smeared with chocolate. She drinks glass after glass of water. The time is coming, she knows.

O   O   O

When Gregor arrives, she's in the shower. She stops the water as soon as she hears his voice. He is asking Spike, *Where? What happened?* Spike is saying, *It was a big truck that came straight at him. He had to swerve, hit a wall, the car is finished, but okay. A few bruises, but okay. No, the truck didn't stop. No, no police were involved, Buddy at the Workshop towed the car.*

Gregor's voice is getting more and more tense, the volume rising. *It's all still going ahead.* Spike tries to interject. A chill runs through Lucy as Gregor shouts him down; he doesn't care, *there is nothing linking Ali with Stranstec, everything is going to go ahead as planned.* Spike is saying, *you should put it off until you're sure."*

Then it will never happen, shouts Gregor.

Lucy dries herself and pulls on her clothes.

She waits for a silence and then steps out of the bathroom. The men step away from each other and Gregor smiles, but there is something in his face that grabs at her guts with a cold hand. He goes to her and she puts her arms around him and they kiss.

"You okay?" he says

"Yeah."

"Very good, let's go."

"I want to say goodbye to Kayleigh."

"Kayleigh is asleep, leave her," says Spike. To Gregor he says, "What time do you want me on point?"

"No," says Gregor, "tonight I want you right next to me, all night."

Spike's face registers surprise. Lucy is gathering her clothes from around the room.

Spike asks, "Who's on point?"

"Some boys in blue on the payroll. Get some sleep."

Then he and Lucy are out of the door and down onto the street. Lucy asks as he starts the engine, "Are we going home? Is it safe now?"

"Safe. Yes, for you it's safe now."

The traffic is heavy, the roads are full and they travel at a slow walking pace under a sky heavy with cloud. There are lines and lines of cars, vans, taxis, and trucks, all travelling so slowly, just waiting for the chance to speed off into the distance. All of those engines, all of that raw power restrained, growling and throbbing like a demon child come of age in the steel womb.

She says, "Spike said he was going to bring me back to the house. I don't think he wanted you to come to the flat."

"It was all taking too long. What did you take yesterday?"

"Are you angry?"

"I just want to know, what did you take yesterday?"

"I don't really know. Spike gave it to us, a blue pill."

"Spike gave it to you?"

"Yeah, to us both."

"A full pill?"

"Yeah. We were off it all day and most of the night."

"Do you remember everything?"

"I don't know. I've been getting flashes. I remember ... well ..."

"Was Spike there all the time?"

"Not all the time, but when he was, well he ... he ..."

"He what?"

"He fucked me and Kayleigh. I remember that."

O O O

That night Gregor and Spike drive back to the docks. The moon is full and the river is swollen, running fast and smooth out of the city, widening as it winds through this forgotten landscape. They don't speak and the shadows in the car rise and fall as they pass through the quiet streets. Spike's not used to being in the passenger seat and doesn't know what to do with his hands. He ends up sitting on them. He hasn't spoken since he got in the car.

When Gregor picked Spike up from outside his house, the lights were all off inside. Gregor can usually sense fear, but there's something in Spike which he senses but can't place, as if some great mountain has crumbled within him and Gregor is feeling the slow shockwaves. Gregor doesn't look at him. They pass a police car. Spike reflexively leans forward and touches the black sports bag between his feet on the floor of the car.

"Is that one of ours?" Gregor nods. They turn right and down a side street. Halfway down there are two cars already parked next to the big wire fence.

"This is it," says Gregor. "Are you loaded?"

Spike nods and pats the gun beneath his jacket. They get out of the car.

O   O   O

Lucy sits at the big oak table, looking at her reflection in the double glass doors. Steam rises from the cup and she curls her hands around the warm porcelain. She wears her fluffy dressing gown and her silk black negligee underneath. When they came back there were more clothes in the wardrobe and another necklace, shining from a black velvet box on the dresser.

Gregor had kissed her and said, "I'll be back with some good food later."

"It's not dangerous, is it? Is that why you want Spike there?"

"Don't worry. It's just business."

That was hours ago. She had undressed and put on her negligee, held the necklace in her hands, watched how the light bounced from it as the girl in the frame held back her tears. Then she had taken her dressing gown from the wardrobe, wrapping it around herself as she passed the closed doors to the staircase.

220

Downstairs she had switched on the television and gone through what was recorded. Reality programmes and documentaries. She had thought of the movies she watched with Stranstec in her small city flat. Gangster movies and horrors were his favourite. She had never seen the point in horror movies until she watched them with him, and then she would cling to him on the sofa, with rushes of fear and excitement running through her. She had thought about how Stranstec would laugh when she tells him about Gregor's favourite programmes. She could see him laughing. "Property programmes? Reality contests?" She had scanned through the channels, before turning it off again.

Then she went into the kitchen, and stood at the marble plinth. She looked at its alien surface and how the light reflected on it and thought how Stranstec had used that word too—business. She had made her coffee in a kind of daze.

Now she sits at the broad oak table. She wonders where Stranstec is now. She imagines him in his office. He's smoking, moving people into place, setting it all up. She's never been to his house, she doesn't know if it is smaller or more grand than Gregor's. She knows that there is life in it, not like here. Here there is evidence of life, but no beating heart. There's an unnatural stillness. She feels uncomfortable moving, as if when she is in the house she should be moved rather than move herself.

When she has stared at her reflection until she has disappeared, she gets up and turns the light off. She sits again. Now the shapes of the garden in the night appear. There is the statue. Two bodies in an embrace, holding each other like dancers, joining from the waist down and rooting into the earth as one. She sips her tea, and lets her eye follow the statue from the ground up. Now it is one body, rising up, and from it two parts splitting apart, not in love, or in an embrace but in conflict, pushing each other away. The moonlight on the stone shows what was a loving hold to be a tortured grip, and the stone faces frozen in an eternal agony.

Stranstec. He will come and get her soon. She just has to wait.

O   O   O

Inside the abandoned warehouse Gregor and Spike stand. Two long strip lights run the entire length of the long room, illuminating the room with a harsh white light, like a movie set. Between these lights is the graffiti version of God and Adam, a diseased creator giving life to a sick and feeble shell, but no-one in the room will look up to see this. There are three men on the other side of the room. One of them has a briefcase. Spike has the sports bag over his shoulder.

One of the men asks, "Just the two of you?"

Gregor replies, "No. There are more."

There is an echo in the big room, the last words ring for a second, repeating and decaying.

"Shall we do it then?"

Gregor nods, and Spike walks forward. As he does, the man with the briefcase steps forward to meet him. In the centre of the room they meet. The strip lights cast disfigured shadows on the dusty stone floor. Spike hands over the sports bag and takes the briefcase. As the two men check what has been exchanged, the dark squashed shapes beneath their feet make a monster and a disfigured child of them. But no-one is watching the shadows. The deal is done.

O O O

Driving away from the docks, Gregor and Spike are silent. The briefcase is beneath Gregor's seat. As they drive alongside the reflection of the moonlight on the river, Spike says, "Something doesn't feel right about that. Something's not right."

"Was it too easy? Is that what's bothering you?"

"I don't know, but something's not right."

Gregor keeps driving.

O O O

Lucy has moved into the front room, onto the big sofa, and has pulled a blanket over herself and turned the TV on again. She's getting flashbacks of her night with Kayleigh. She remembers the two of them with their arms around each other, feeling rushes of adrenaline surge through her body as Kayleigh cried about loving her mother's lover, cried at how cruel discovering joy can be. She remembers them filling up the bath, but can't recall getting in the water. The memories are disconnected, like headlines and glossy pictures clipped from different magazines and scattered. She feels unconsciousness start to darken her mind and she fights it. She turns the volume up as loud as she can bear it. She needs to fill this house with something, and the inane confrontative dialogue of a soap opera rolls out of the TV room and into the hallway. Arguments about discovered bigamy bounce around the kitchen and bound up the stairs and around the landing, banging against the closed doors, the patterned walls, the expensive carpets, and back down again. She should just leave now. But she has nowhere to go. She turns the volume up even more.

O O O

Gregor drives through the tree-lined estate.

"Why are we on Elm? I thought that the kitchen had been moved," says Spike.

"Yes, but there is some unfinished business we need to tend to."

They pull into the driveway. All the lights in the house are off.

"Talking about unfinished business, I've got to make a quick call if that's alright," says Spike.

"Sure," says Gregor as they get out of the car. "I'll be inside."

O O O

When Spike walks through the front door he sees the light on in the kitchen at the back of the house. As he walks past the staircase he hears Gregor's voice from somewhere above.

"Stop, Spike, stop there."

The voice is hushed and there is urgency in the command. Spike stops.

"Shhh, don't move, stay still."

Spike waits, motionless. Then he feels something sharp in his neck, followed by a dull pain. It's a needle. He whirls around to see

Gregor's hand holding a syringe retreating through the banister back into the shadows of the stairs.

"Gregor, you've—" but he's unable to finish the sentence. His legs buckle and everything goes dark.

CHAPTER THIRTY-ONE

When the lights went on in the printing room, they didn't all go on at the same time. Blocks of light flickered from the ceiling at different points, from just overhead to right off in the dark distance. For those few seconds the room seemed to go on forever, lightning flashes over a mechanical landscape. Then all the bulbs came on, and from that moment the light in the printing room was even and clear. It fell evenly on everything, there were no shadows. The machines oozed the fresh paper out with regular even sighs and cushioned clicks. The temperature was always the same, maintained by the droning machines embedded in the walls, sucking air in and pumping air out again.

Martin saw his future here. Predictable, dependable, controlled. The office spaces he had seen were busy, he hadn't liked the tangle of noises, the unevenness of the movement, the potential unpredictability of the countless sweaty shirt backs in position at their desks. But here, here he felt a sense of peace, and the pages coming from the machines were what all that fuss in the office was about. Here he could see the purpose of it all. Martin had never experienced that before.

It was not the main printing room for Spiral, that was in the other wing of the building. That one never turned its lights off or rested its machines, but this room was for specialist printing, short runs. Some of the machines in this room were not being used and were encased in protective fabric covers with big white zips on the side. There were no mysteries, no unseen agendas in this room. This was where Martin wanted to be.

He had to change his runs to the evening. By the time he got home and got changed and was back out the door, the sun was going down. There was more traffic at this time, cars coming back from the city, pulling into driveways, the lights in the houses going on. There was more pedestrian traffic too, people coming up the hill from the train station. A new fence had gone up and heavy machinery was appearing, but it was quiet and still by the time he was running. He started to get used to it being dark by the time he was coming back up the hill the second time.

Then he would get in and shower. As he dressed himself in the bedroom, sometimes he would stand still and listen, trying to hear the rumble from the motorway. It wasn't always there. Sometimes he would stand silently for more than a minute and hear nothing except the creaks of the pipes in the house and some cars passing outside. Other times he could hear it once he had stilled himself, that deep undercurrent of sound.

Food was less of a priority now, and dinner tended to be something he or Alison could throw together quickly before they went back to the sofa. Alison would tell Martin about the other people in the company, about their personalities and quirks and behaviours, about who she got on with and why she didn't get on with others.

Some nights Martin would take himself up to the writing room with a glass of wine and sit amongst the piles of paper, the pages on the walls around him covered in sketches, hand drawn maps and timelines with words or phrases circled and underlined, and he would open up his file and reread what he had sent to *Noire*.

He had finally pressed Send. That was weeks ago. He'd received no reply. He hadn't told Alison. He would stand with his back to his desk, looking out the window, toward the dark shapes of the hills beyond against the night sky. One night Alison came into the room and stood behind him, wrapping her arms around his waist and putting her chin on his shoulder.

"When will it be time?" she said. "It's got to be time sometime."

Martin didn't say anything. One of the papers stuck to the wall had a sketch of Henry. His hair was unruly as if he was in a strong wind, and he was wearing a suit jacket and jeans. His eyes were just black dots. He had stubble, little black pen marks all around his jaw and chin. The paper was curled at the edges. Martin guessed it was four years old. Older than the house they were standing in. He couldn't remember drawing it. He thought it was like a police sketch of a missing person. People go missing all the time. Sometimes they are found, sometimes they are not.

"Do you fancy going out for a drink?" Martin said.

"Now? I'm ready for bed."

"I'm going to go out. I need to go out after that week. Isn't that what working people do? Go out on a Friday and let their hair down? I'm going to catch the next train."

Twenty-five minutes later he was stepping into the train carriage. It was dark outside and the windows showed him sitting with his jacket buttoned right up to his chin and a winter hat pulled low over his brow. He sent a text to Ozzy, *You working?* Just before the train pulled in to the station he got a reply. *Yes I am.* Martin went straight to ICE.

The queue was about fifty people long, so he walked to the front, but didn't recognise the doorman. *I guess it's been a while since I've been here,* he thought, as he walked back and stood last in line.

The group in front of him were mixed boys and girls in their early twenties. They were laughing and shoving each other. A few of them had tried to pull a fast one on one of their friends, telling him that the club night was a gender bender night and that they were all going to turn up in drag, in the hope that he'd fall for it and be in a skirt and heels when they met up. He didn't fall for it. All he had to do was check the venue website. The funny thing was though, that his Dad was a transvestite, so had it been a gender bender night he would have had a selection of outfits to choose from. That was why his Mum had left them when he was thirteen. There was more laughter in the group and some smart comments from the guys, like father like son, and one of the girls moved next to the guy and put her arm around him. The queue moved on. From behind him he could hear a conversation, *Well I just hope Kyle isn't in tonight, he always makes a cock of himself. Do you remember the time he took a shit in a glass?*

Across the road was another queue for another club, another line of people disappearing slowly through the dark doors, dressed for the hedonistic ceremony, a steady feed of young flesh into a mouth of the old city.

When Martin finally got through the doors of ICE he went straight to the bar. He spotted Ozzy mixing cocktails at the far end and headed there. He squeezed past girls in tight tops and guys with their biceps and bulked chests straining against their thin t-shirts.

Ozzy spotted him. He winked at him as he spun the mixer into the air and caught it as he spun a bottle in the other hand. There were whoops from the people at the bar as he threw ice into the air, stepped forward, and caught the ice in the glass behind his back. Martin knew that it would be a while before Ozzy would be finished with his performance and when he was he'd have a list of orders to get through and a crowd of people wanting more. His goatee had grown and was now even more groomed and waxed, like a Victorian magician. His bandana was a bright orange and his eyes and smile looked as mischievous as ever.

Martin ordered a drink, a brandy and coke. The bar lady asked did he want a double and without hesitation he said yes. He handed his money over, took his glass and tried to find a place to put himself. He ended up against the back wall, at the far end of the bar. When Ozzy finally came to him, he was grinning broadly and carrying a tall frosted glass with a straw. He put it in front of Martin.

"For you, on the house, try it out."

"What is it?" Martin asked picking up the glass and smelling it.

"Something special I threw together."

"Well, okay then, cheers," Martin said and took the straw in his mouth and sucked. His mouth was awash with a liquid that was cold, smooth, and dark. He could taste caramel and almond. Then the undercurrent of whiskey kicked in, rich and earthy. He thought of the weeds and nettles creeping over and through the new clean fences of New Acre. "Mmm, this is dangerous, I can tell."

"The ones that taste the best are always the most dangerous," Ozzy said and slapped him on the back. "I see you've ditched the hermit in the cabin in the woods look. You've lost a bit of weight. Now it's more of a …" he leaned back from the bar and cocked his head to the side, twisting his mouth and tugging at the end of his waxed 'stash. "More of a moderately successful mid-management with a pad in the city type, out on the town looking to make a love investment."

They laughed. Four men bundled to the bar and Ozzy snapped to attention.

"Gentlemen! What can I get for you?"

"What's going to get us drunkest, fastest for cheapest?" said one, and the others all laughed. Ozzy shot a sideward glance and a raised eyebrow to Martin, who put the straw back in his mouth and looked down.

Martin liked watching Ozzy work, how he spun the bottles, snapping them into position high above the glass when he was pouring. How he moved quickly and surely, with confidence and how he always stopped for a moment to gauge the customer's reaction when they took their first taste of the cocktail he had prepared. Martin could tell when Ozzy fancied the girls he was serving from the way he leaned forward, one hand on the bar and his other hand behind him on his hip, or how he stroked his goatee as they ordered. He lined up a row of shot glasses for the group of men and poured.

Martin could feel the noise and heat of the club getting into his skin. As he sipped at his drink he was sure it was unlocking something at the base of his skull, right where his spine stopped. It felt like a thick liquid was seeping forward, slowly filling up his head. He liked it. His straw made a rattling sound and he put his empty glass on the bar. When Ozzy came back his way, Martin winked and pushed the empty glass toward him. Ozzy smiled and went off to prepare another one.

As the night wore on Martin stayed in his position at the end of the bar, drinking frosted glass after frosted glass and feeling his head fill up with thick slow-moving liquid. By the time Ozzy said he was going to take a break and go out back for a smoke, Martin felt unsteady on his feet. In the staff car park Ozzy rolled a cigarette and passed it to him. The night was cold and Martin clutched his coat around him as he puffed.

"So, are you out for the night? You want to crash at mine? Do you have an agenda beyond drinking?" Ozzy asked as he rolled another cigarette.

Martin threw his half-finished cigarette to the ground. It had started to make him feel ill. The smoke inside him had reacted with the heavy alcohol. He felt like a swamp.

"No, I've got no plan. I guessed I'd get a taxi back, unless something happens worth sticking round for."

"Well I'm here till three and then I got to close the place down, so it's going to be four before I can do anything crazy."

"I don't think I'll stick around till then, although I am enjoying those cocktails."

"Is Alison expecting you back?"

"I guess so, we didn't really talk about it."

Martin pushed his hands into his pockets and started gently kicking the wall. It was cold standing still. Ozzy puffed a big cloud of smoke into the air.

"How are things with you guys? She got a ring on her finger yet?"

"Ring? Fuck no." He laughed for a second. Its sound was forced and it reverberated around them, like a dog bark. "Why do you ask that?"

"Well isn't that what she's expecting? You to pop the question? When things last a certain time, that's the next step, isn't it?"

"I don't believe I'm getting relationship advice from you, of all people."

"No, no, I wouldn't give advice, I'm just asking. I mean it's just a matter of time right? A baby or a big white dress, that's what they want."

"Ozzy, you should stick to mixing drinks and shagging skinny drunk girls."

"Well, now that you mention skinny drunk girls, did you see the two in the denim shorts? One brunette, one blonde?" and he continued to talk about the chances of getting them both into bed. Martin laughed along but couldn't help feeling discomforted by what Ozzy had said about Alison. He started to feel the cold of the night get under his skin. By the time they went back inside his teeth had started chattering.

When he resumed his position at the bar he realised how drunk he was. Ozzy asked him did he want another and he said yes.

As he was waiting he thought again about Alison. What did she want of him? They had been out for a meal during the week, to celebrate Martin's job. They didn't go to the usual Italian place, they came right into the city, to a place called Twin70. Alison had been told about it in the office. Martin told her how much she meant to him, how appreciative he was of everything she'd done for them. All this time he'd been working on the book it had seemed like she'd been the one providing everything. At least he had something of his own now, the job. He had somewhere of his own, the printing room. The book was nearly done, he would be done soon. He didn't tell her he hadn't written anything in months.

The young guy from the queue with the transvestite dad appeared at the bar. The girl who had put her arm around him was there, too. As they waited for their drinks they kissed. Martin heard her say something about him trying her clothes on if he wanted. The guy's hands moved down her back and clutched her bum. She moved even closer to him as he reached lower and put his fingers to the edge of her short skirt. She reached behind and took his hand and moved it round the front. As they kissed more passionately, she massaged his groin and his hand disappeared up her skirt.

Ozzy clunked two bottles down on the bar in front of them and coughed loudly. They broke off and the guy paid for the drinks before they moved away from the bar and against the back wall next to Martin. They resumed kissing. Now that they were next to him instead of in front of him Martin couldn't see exactly what was going on but he could hear the girl's breath and high pitched squeaks get more intense. He turned away so his back was to them.

Ozzy slid another frosted glass in front of him and said, "Don't get too close." Another girl came to the bar next to him with some friends and was saying, "So, I'm never going to go to Madrid again, not after that, he wasn't exactly a good ad for the tourist board," and they all laughed. One of the group looked like Zoe, but Zoe if her parents had stayed together and she had stayed at school and she had met somebody who loved her, even for a while. Maybe it was. Behind the group of girls two guys were trying to talk above the sound of the club, shouting at each other.

"Heart attack," one was shouting.

"Catheter?" the other shouted back.

"Heart attack."

"Panther? That's how he died?"

"Heart attack."

"Yeah, cat attack, weird, panther, wow."

"Panther?"

"What?"

The moaning beside him was getting louder. The group of girls were lining up their drinks on the bar. Zoe looked so pretty as she waited for hers to be poured, and so happy to be with her friends. Martin picked up his glass and felt the room warp as he sucked and sucked on the straw. He leaned over to the group and said, "So what happened in Madrid?"

The girl who had been telling the story said, "What? What's that?"

"Well, I used to live there, in Madrid, I have contacts, you know, I might know him."

The girl shot a look to her friends and said to him, "Not likely," and turned away. The rest of the group angled themselves away from him, too, and one of them gestured to the other side of the bar. As they gathered up their drinks, Martin saw a tattoo on Zoe's shoulder, bird silhouettes flying in a V formation. He leaned over again, stretching so that his face appeared over her shoulder and he said, "Who are your friends?"

She flinched and said, "What?"

"Are you going to be hanging around with them all night?"

She didn't even look at him again, just moved away, joining with the group as they moved away, slipping through the gaps between bodies in the crowded club. Martin was left leaning into space for a moment, but in seconds the space had filled with others, and he disappeared again.

The bodies and reaching limbs and jerky heads were all anxious to get to the bar, where Ozzy was still spinning bottles and juggling glasses. Martin straightened up and turned to the bar. Ozzy caught his eye and held his hand like a gun and shot it at him. Martin sucked on the straw until the ice rattled again, and slid the empty glass across the bar. Ozzy winked and soon it was full again. As Ozzy put the full glass in front of him he said, "I see you haven't lost your touch with the ladies," and then he was at it again, straightening to attention and taking orders, dutifully facilitating the indulgence that the club encouraged, with every pour pushing the clientele closer to the brink, and doing it with charm.

It was before three when Martin leaned over the bar to Ozzy and announced he was going to go. Ozzy broke off from talking to the blonde in the denim shorts and straightened up. "Are you sure, mate? You're welcome to hang if you want." Martin declined with a wave of his hand and a bow of his head and made his way to the door, bumping into people as he went. When he got outside he put his hands in his pockets and his head down and started to walk. He walked away from the clubs and the late bars and hailed a taxi. One stopped and he climbed into the back and asked, "Do you know the Sugar Club?"

The driver said, "Up on Church Way?" Martin agreed and they were off. It was warm in the taxi. The driver had the radio on, a voice in a language Martin didn't understand. Martin felt comforted by the rhythm of the speech, it wasn't rushed, it didn't sound dramatic, it felt like it skipped along with the slow rhythm of a nursery rhyme. He was sure that if he knew what the voice was talking about it would soothe him, reassure him.

Then they were taking the turning at the boarded-up pub on the corner and then they were there, and Martin was paying the driver and standing in front of the door. There was the five-point star. Martin heard the taxi pull away and stood for a moment more.

He turned and started to walk away. He got to the corner and stood in front of the boarded-up window of the pub. There was graffiti on the wood. Judy's a slag. Don't run from the gun. Southerners take it up the ass. A stencil of a tiger on top of a turntable with Roar Records written underneath it. Call me for a good time with a number. He put his hand in his pocket and touched himself.

He turned back and walked back to the Sugar Club door. He knocked. It was opened by the bat-eared bouncer. Martin smiled and said, *Hi.* The bouncer said, *No single males after eleven thirty,* and closed the door. Martin knocked again. When it opened he started to say, *I'm just looking for*—but the bouncer said, *I'm not going to tell you again to fuck off, you're not coming in. Fuck off,* and closed the door again.

Martin stood alone and cold on the pavement. He put his hand back in his pocket and squeezed. He walked the other way, away from the abandoned pub. In the back of his mind was the idea of finding

another way in. He thought of all the people in the nightclub, all of
the connections being made. He thought of the club with Andre and
Cassandra, and all of the shaking of hands and exchanging of cards.
He needed to make contact, some kind of contact.

He ended up walking and walking, further and further into
housing estates, across roads with cars parked tail to tail on either side,
past shops with shutters down and lights that flickered and shone on
an unmoving street. He didn't see anyone. *How am I the only one moving?*
he thought. He passed parks and basketball courts and school gates
and fences and driveways and flats and houses and terraces.

Ahead of him he saw a figure cross the road. The figure wore a
long black coat, and walked in high heels. At a crossroads ahead, it
turned left. Martin picked up his pace and when he got to the
junction looked to the left, and there was the figure, closer now but
still walking away. A wind came rushing up the road. It blew strong
into his face and blew the long hair of the figure into the air for a
moment. Martin faced the wind and followed the long dark coat
and thin heels clicking on the pavement. The figure glanced over
its shoulder and then started to run. Martin took his hands from
his pockets and started to run, too. The figure stopped at a parked
car and opened it, then climbed in and started the engine. The lights
shone straight at Martin, and as it drove past him, he put his hands
back in his pockets, and ducked his head into his chest. He felt an
ache deep inside his stomach. Then the car was gone and the streets
were quiet again.

He walked and walked until he could hear the sound of gulls
above the roofs. The sharp calls reverberated around the buildings
around him. They were like sudden spontaneous utterances of truth
breaking through the weary city. If only he could understand them.
He walked closer to the calls and they were overtaken by the sound
of engines passing, each one an aggressive crescendo then a trail of
noise, fading with a disappointed whine. He came to the main road
and lifted his hand until a taxi stopped.

By the time he got out at New Acre the sky was getting bright.
As he climbed into bed Alison sat up in the half-light and said, "It's
nearly morning, where have you been?"

He fell into bed. Within seconds his breathing deepened and
slowed and he started to snore.

CHAPTER THIRTY-TWO

When Spike wakes he's strapped to a chair in the kitchen. He's looking at the ceiling. The room comes into focus and he realises he's on his back. His arms are squashed between the chair and the floor. His wrists are bound with thick plastic binds and his ankles strapped to the chair legs. There's a belt around his chest. He cranes his neck back and sees Gregor just about to lift the chair up. Gregor sees he's awake.

"So soon? You are quite something, Spike."

He starts to strain as he lifts the chair into an upright position. When the chair is up, Gregor exhales loudly and walks around in front of him.

"And so heavy!"

He has put on a thin plastic apron. He is wearing surgical gloves. There is a table next to him; it's a plastic fold away table, made for camping. In the corner is a lump hammer. Spike tries to focus on what is on the table, but cannot. The room feels unstable.

"I thought there was a change in you, Spike. I guess I was right."

Spike tries to lift his hands and stand from the chair, but he cannot. He's looking around to see who else is with Gregor. *Surely he is being forced to do this,* Spike thinks. *He can't be doing this on his own. Or this is not Gregor.* He looks again. *Is he travelling?* He feels like he is in the belly of a boat, the floor seems to tilt. There is an over-powering smell of chlorine. Then Gregor speaks again. It is him. It's the real Gregor.

"I thought I could trust you with Lucy, but obviously not."

"Obviously not? What?" Spike is spitting when he speaks, his throat feels swollen. It doesn't sound like his voice. He shakes his head. He feels off balance, as if the room is moving. But he is in the kitchen of the house where Spiral was being made.

"What are you talking about?"

"Come on Spike, giving her and your little piece Spiral, then fucking them. It was super strong that first batch, we had to amend the formula, it was way too strong. But probably just right for what you wanted. I guess I should have listened to what you said in the Church club. If she's like this now, imagine her on Spiral. It was too tempting for you, wasn't it?"

"Gregor, she's playing you. I didn't touch her. I didn't give them Spiral. She's playing you!" As his voice raises it sounds more metallic, less real.

"Come on, what could she gain from lying about you? Why would she make that up? Did you enjoy it? Having the two of them? Was it like you thought it would be?" Gregor picks up a syringe from the table. It's full of a yellow liquid.

"Fantasies coming true don't always work out the way they do in your head. I mean it's one thing actually fucking your daughter—"

"She's not my daughter! Gregor, please listen, I didn't …"

"As close as you can get though, Spike. Some things are taboo for good reason, you know. But you obviously like testing boundaries."

"She told you then? Lucy told you about Kayleigh?"

"Oh yes, she told me all about what you put them through. On your daughter's sleep over. You fucking sicken me."

"Gregor, you know me, please, please you know me."

"Do I? I thought I did. How long have you been fucking your little piece? How many years have you been grooming her? This brings out a whole new side to you, Spike, a whole new side. You see, now I don't know whose side you are on. If you can take Lucy just to satisfy your dick then what else have you taken over time? I thought I could trust you."

The room has stopped moving for Spike, he can feel his balance stable on the chair. He shakes his head again and clears his throat.

"It's Lucy. Gregor think about it! Do you know who she is? Who is she?"

"She's a no-one. She's just a kid, a ghetto kid."

"How do you know, Gregor? You don't know who she could be working for. What do you know about her?"

"Working? If she was working for someone, she hasn't done a very good job, the deal went smooth. It's all done."

"Gregor, it was too smooth. Who have you sold to? You could have just put the stash right in Stranstec's hands. Where's Ali?"

"Thinking is not your strong point, Spike, you'd best not strain yourself."

"She's playing you, Gregor. I didn't touch her. When I got back from tracking Ali, they were already off it. We spoke on the phone. She's playing you!"

"Who did you call?"

"What? When did I—"

"Who did you call outside?"

"That's a personal thing, it's got nothing to do with ..."

Gregor picks up Spike's phone from the table.

"Shall I call it now?"

"It's an investigator, Maya's disappeared; I need him to find her."

"You could have asked me, you could have told me, Spike. You know I have resources. You know you can trust me, Spike. But now I think you and I have fallen out. You could have told me, but I can see why you want to keep this secret. It shines a light. It shows how sick you are."

"It's personal, it has nothing to do with—"

"You've been sticking your dick in your wife's daughter. Then you thought you'd have some fun with Lucy. Well we can have a little fun now."

"I didn't—"

"I have an experiment I've been wanting to try."

Gregor puts the phone back on the table and raises the needle in the air. The light hits the liquid in the syringe like gold. Scorpion heaves his hands and his legs, but cannot break the bonds. Gregor sees him trying. He watches him struggle, the chair is shaking under the strain.

"Wow, you nearly did it then. You know, Spike, in all the years I've known you, I am still always taken by surprise at just how big you really are. I can never get used to it. And now, all tied up like this, you are quite a monster."

"Gregor, don't do this. She's playing you!"

Gregor puts the syringe down on the table and picks up a roll of masking tape. He stands behind Spike. Spike starts to shout. Gregor covers his mouth with the tape from behind, pulling it tight, and wrapping the tape around his head, over his ears, twice around before breaking it. He walks back in front of Spike, slowly putting down the tape. Then he picks up the lump hammer.

"You're nearly there, nearly breaking out, Spike. This is just a precaution. Careful now, it might sting a bit."

Gregor raises the lump hammer high before swinging it down onto Spike's ankle. There is a loud crack of breaking bone. Through the tape Spike screams, a single short shout. Gregor does it again, back-handed this time, putting all his weight into the hammer, smashing the other ankle. Spike gives another scream of pain. The bone protrudes beneath the skin on the inside of his foot. Gregor steps back and considers Spike for a moment before putting the lump hammer back in the corner and picking up the syringe from the table, holding it up to the light.

"Now, you probably thought it odd," he says, "when you saw me dressed like this, but you must understand this is an experiment. I don't know what will happen exactly. And I plan to celebrate the success of this evening's deal with a fine meal. I certainly don't want to mess my suit up. The doctor that was working in this kitchen gave me a new prescription he's been working on. An hallucinogen. A derivative of a deliriant, benactyzine, I think he said. Very strong and with tendencies for extreme paranoia and very sinister visual trips, which is why he stopped it. But I got a little batch from him anyway, for special occasions."

Sweat is running down Spike's face. He can't breathe properly. His ankles start to swell. He tries again to break away from the chair. His huge bulk is straining, the veins on his neck and arms are raised. He thinks he can feel the chair about to break. It rattles as he pulls his arms upwards.

"It's okay," says Gregor, "I've mixed it with 300 milligrams of amphetamine, so it should be quite a party. Now if you'll give me a moment, I just want to get something. Don't go anywhere, I'll be right back."

He puts the syringe back on the table and leaves the room. Spike heaves and heaves in the chair, straining with every fibre of his being. When Gregor comes back he is carrying a long thin mirror, which he positions against the wall opposite Spike. Spike sees himself, huge and helpless, in the chair. And there is Gregor, stepping next to him and looking in the mirror too.

He is slim and neat, with his plastic apron and gloves on, looking like a manager visiting the shop floor of a food factory. Spike sees how small Gregor is compared to him, just what a difference there is between them, yet he is bound fast to the chair, and helpless. Gregor looks at Spike in the mirror. He leans down so their faces are side by side. Even the difference in the size of their heads takes Spike by surprise. It's as if they are from different worlds, or different times. Gregor talks at his reflection.

"For when your trip starts. The visuals are quite disturbing apparently, so best to put yourself in the picture, don't you think? Now remember," he says, picking up the syringe again and moving around behind Spike's huge trembling shoulders, "don't move, we don't want to miss the vein and cause some serious damage."

Spike watches Gregor, standing with a look of concentration on his face, syringe in hand, considering his neck like an artist about to complete his greatest work. Spike tries again to tear his hands apart, to move his legs, but explosive bursts of pain shoot up from his ankles. Gregor pats Spike on the back and waits for him to stop then puts the point of the syringe to his neck, saying in a whisper, "Shhh, now, stay still, stay still now, I don't want to hurt you."

CHAPTER THIRTY-THREE

When Martin woke, he felt like he was still drunk. The whiskey had turned his head inside out. He could hardly bear to open his eyes. When he did open them the room trembled around him. When he closed his eyes again he felt like he was falling. He got out of bed. He went downstairs and poured a pint of water, drinking it back in one and refilled the glass.

"So did you have a good night?" Alison asked. She was in front of her computer, sitting at the table. "You were in quite a state when you rolled in."

"Yeah, sorry," Martin said between gulps.

"Well, you have to get yourself better by tonight, we've been invited to dinner."

"Really? By who?"

"Andre and Cassandra. So if you feel like you need more sleep, then get it now, because you look like you need it."

"What's the occasion?"

"I don't know, but we can't turn it down. Your suit's already in the wash, just drink more water and go back to bed. I'll wake you. You look awful. Ozzy is always bad news."

When Martin lay back in bed he started to remember walking through the suburbs. He had flashes of following someone. He felt the cold of the night and pulled the covers around his body. As his mind let go of consciousness he felt like he was falling into himself, and it was cold. He pulled the covers tighter. The chill was deep in him, coming from the inside. *How long have I been falling,* he thought, just before he went to sleep, *have I been falling without even knowing?*

o   o   o

Later that evening, sitting at a table in a restaurant with Alison beside him and Andre and Cassandra opposite him, he remembered being outside the door of the Sugar Club. It startled him for a moment and he paused in mid-movement, with his fork halfway to his mouth. The others looked at him. He said, "Oh, I just remembered something, something I haven't done. It doesn't matter."

Andre said, "Do you need to make a note of it? If it's inspiration don't ignore it."

"No, no, really it's fine. Sorry, what were you saying?"

"Oh just about that old Bucket O' Blood. It's the only one that won't budge on the docks development. I mean we have offered more money than the place is worth, more money than he's going to make in his lifetime running that place. Have you been in it?"

Martin shook his head.

"The place is a dump," Andre continued, "a nasty little drinking hole. All of its customers must be dying."

Martin wanted to say that every customer is dying, but instead he chewed on his food and nodded his head.

Andre didn't stop. "It's such a pain when people stand in the way for no good reason, and you've got to follow the course, you know, go through the steps. We don't have the freedom of the artist. I so envy you. You can make it up, but we have to follow the rules instead of being creative. The artist, you know, you're almost expected to break them."

Cassandra looked bored as she sipped her wine.

Alison said, "You've got to stop obsessing about that place, though. I mean, maybe the fact that we'll build around it and that it'll be the only remaining thing of the original docklands will be what makes the place a success."

"That's nice of you, Alison. Isn't she nice? But it won't fit into the new development. That place'll never be a success. The landlord is just too drunk to do anything. But he'll have to crack eventually. Now, hey do you want to know why I invited you guys out tonight?"

He took the champagne from the ice bucket, which was mounted on an elaborate steel stand beside the table, and refilled everyone's glass.

"Well, I've got to tell you that we've secured the contracts for twenty-six percent of the docklands, which combined with what we've got going on in the inner city and the Acre projects, makes us the biggest native property developer in the city."

Alison and Martin gave a little cheer, and raised their glasses. Cassandra raised hers too, and they all clinked.

"Now, the reason you're here is because I just want to thank you so much, Alison. You've done fantastic work, and I really think you've brought something very special and dynamic to the company. I'm setting up a team for the docklands contracts, and I want you to be the Project Development Manager. There is one particular investor I want you to deal with, very wealthy and open to creative suggestions, and you're the one I want him to deal with. You'll also have to pick a team."

"Oh, Andre …"

"Now, wait before you say anything. It'll mean a pay rise, but it'll also mean a lot more meetings, dinners, cocktail bars, premiers, grand openings, probably a few new backless dresses and power suits. You are my number one, and I'm not taking no for an answer."

Alison said, "Oh, Andre, I'd be delighted!" They all clinked their glasses again.

The waiter came and cleared the starter plates. Martin was starting to feel drunk again. He excused himself and went to the rest rooms. There was an elaborate figure of a man in a long-tailed suit and a top hat on the door, and as he pushed it open he could smell a strong cinnamon, soapy odour. He stood in front of a sink and splashed his face. There were freshly pressed face and hand towels in a basket next to the sink and he patted one on his face. It was soft and warm. The lights were low and there was quiet classical music playing gently around him as he looked in the mirror. His suit looked too big on him.

He went back out to the table. They were talking about him as he sat down. Alison was saying how he was slotting right into Spiral. Andre winked and said, "Well, there's a ladder for you to climb, you'll leave the others behind in no time."

Martin said, "Ted seems like a good guy. He said he wants to set up an art house wing, a specialist section of Spiral. That'd be good to be a part of."

"Well, he's definitely expanding, he's going to be moving to the docklands," Andre said. "He's put a bid in for one of the sites, the old fishery; it's a large plot."

The waiter appeared carrying their mains. As he put Cassandra's plate in front of her she said, "Isn't it lucky that Alison met Ted that night? It's great what a word in the right ear will do."

Martin looked at Cassandra, who was smiling now, and then to Alison.

"What's that? You and Ted?"

"Well, yes I did have a word with him."

Martin felt his stomach being pulled away, and a gaping hole started to grow within him. He saw that everyone at the table felt it, too. There was a second of uncomfortable silence, an extra beat, as if the scene had been badly edited. The job had come from Alison, all of that stuff that Ted told him was a cover. Ted was just doing Alison a favour. That's what he was. A favour. He felt his intestines and stomach slowly drop away into the darkness that was rising within him.

"What did you say? When was this?"

"I just mentioned that you could do with a start, you know, it was nothing, really, Martin, we were just talking."

Andre chipped in. "Well, he was the right guy to ask." He pointed a fork of meat at Martin. "It's a growing company with plenty of opportunity. And isn't there always a gap between the finishing of the book and the publishing? It'll give you a well-earned break." He started to cut the meat on his plate. "Hey Martin? How is the book anyway? You finished yet?"

Martin took a moment. His throat felt dry and tight. He concentrated on his plate for a second. The meat glistened in the light, there were baby carrots arranged in an arc and broad beans in a cluster with a light peppered oil drizzled over them. Between the food, the white plate was impeccably clean, as if this was the first meal ever to be on it. He wondered how he was going to eat when the darkness was squeezing his throat like this.

"I've … it's finished, I think … I've … well, I've stopped making things up."

Andre nodded, "That's what I'm talking about, now's the chance to refuel that creative engine." He raised his eyebrows and pointed his meat at Martin before putting it in his mouth. "Mmm, this is fantastic. Have you got the veal too? It's delicious."

Martin started to eat but all he tasted was grey. All of the colour had gone from his taste, and when he swallowed the emptiness crept up his throat.

Cassandra said, "What's the publication date?"

Martin looked at her. Her smile was wider now, more energised than he had seen it before. He wanted to cry. He said, while his insides shook, "Sometime next year, I don't know exactly, but the editor is very excited. And excited to see what will come next." He picked up his glass of wine and took a gulp.

Cassandra didn't stop looking at him, even after he had put the glass down and started cutting his meat again. Her eyes said, *I know you're a fake. I knew you were a fake the first time I saw you. A fake who can't even get a job without his girlfriend asking around for him.* Of course it had been too easy, Ted hadn't spotted something special in him at all. Alison had taken him aside. Or maybe not, maybe in front of everyone Alison had said, *Please give him a job, anything. He needs something, please.* She must have, why else would Ted have just welcomed him in like that? Was it purely charitable? Or what did Ted get in return?

All of those late working days, those extra office hours. Martin realized he really had no idea what she was really doing all that time. Every mouthful was getting harder to chew, the food was just a thick grey mess. Each swallow was more and more difficult. Andre kept talking, now about the timing of the renewal project, how this is just the perfect time, about how so much has to do with timing.

As the meal continued Martin took part in some of the conversation, but every time he spoke it hurt. His centre had been removed, and he knew Andre and Cassandra and Alison could feel its absence. He knew they could see it, that he was caving in.

In the taxi on the way home, Alison said, "You shouldn't take it so bad that I spoke to Ted about getting you a job. It just came up in conversation. I don't know why you are taking it so badly. I've done you favour."

"No, no it's fine," he said, but he knew she knew he was lying. Still he repeated those words. "It's fine." They were only words after all. Just sounds, there for a second and then gone, like a car passing in the night. They'll do for the moment they exist, they'll cover the silence for a second, they'll move things along to where they're going. They're necessary, but they don't amount to much in the long run. Best to just let things move along and follow them, making appropriate noises as you go.

When they got back to the house, Martin went into the writing room.

"Come to bed, babe," Alison said, "It's late."

"In a bit," Martin replied and closed the door.

The curtains were open and he could see the dark trees at the end of the garden. He saw beyond the estate to where diggers and earth moving lorries and scaffolds were standing behind aluminium fences, waiting for morning to come so that they could build, build, and build, and push the darkness back further still.

He picked up a bound copy of the book and the plastic box of memory sticks. He gathered all the loose paper, the notes, the drafts of chapters, and stuck them under his arm. He closed his laptop and picked it up. Then he went downstairs and put all of it in the bin.

He stood for a while in the kitchen, looking at the bin, before he took everything out again. He grabbed a plastic bag from under the sink and stuffed everything into it. He took an unused spade from the closet under the stairs, then walked to the end of the garden with his spade in one hand and the plastic bag over his shoulder.

Then, in that black space beneath the trees right at the back against the wall, in that last refuge for the darkness, he started to dig.

CHAPTER THIRTY-FOUR

By the time Gregor gets to the turning for his house, the smell of chlorine on his clothes is giving him a headache. He rolls down the window. The hedges on either side of the long narrow driveway block out the sky.

He has a bag of food on the passenger seat. Fresh veal, eggs, prosciutto ham, spinach and kale, and a carton of full cream. There are bottles of wine rattling in the foot-well. As he approaches the gates he presses the remote control on his key fob and they start to open. Just as his car crosses the threshold, he sees movement from the corner of his eye.

Headlights flash at him and he throws himself across the passenger seat just as he hears two gunshots ring out. He unclips his belt and reaches into his jacket for his gun. There are more shots, and glass breaks, falling on him in tiny shards. The eggs have broken and are leaking onto his shirt as he takes his gun in hand and turns over, so that he is on his back. He raises his pistol with both hands in front of him and aims just above the edge of the window.

There is the sound of footsteps and he sees the crown of a head just above the sill of the window. Straightaway he squeezes the trigger and there is a bang, and the head disappears from view. There is another shot which hits the seat.

He reaches behind and opens the door, pulling himself out of the car as more shots hit the body and the inside of the car. He looks under the car and can see a body lying on the ground, a man with his eyes open and a big red hole where the top of his head should be, like the top taken off a boiled egg. He sees the feet of another man who is approaching the car, stepping over the dead body.

Gregor crouches down and moves to behind the bonnet as the man gets close enough to see into the car. Then he moves around the front of the bonnet, standing, raising his gun and firing in one swift motion. There is an explosion of blood and torn muscle and the man drops to the ground, his ass a sticky bloody mess.

Gregor moves from behind the car and picks up the gun which has been dropped. He stands above the bleeding man. He's groaning and rolling from side to side. It's one of the men from the deal. The other one is on his back. His arms are spread wide and the top of his head is missing. The mess of skull and brain starts just above the bridge of his nose, and a thick pool of blood is seeping into the gravel of the driveway.

Gregor leans and drags him aside. Brain is spread along the driveway, and bits of gravel are sticking to the inside of his open head. Gregor gets back in the car and drives his car away from the gates. As soon as his car is out of the way they close. He opens the boot of his car and takes out a chain. He wraps the chain around one of the bars of the gate, pulling it tight, then goes to the man who is trying to sit up and is searching around for his gun on the ground. He leans down and grabs the man by the collar, pulling him up to a sitting position.

"You're going to tell me everything."

The man spits blood and saliva into his face. Gregor grabs the man by the throat and punches him in the face hard. He starts to take the man's clothes off. Within minutes the man is naked and Gregor is standing him against the gate and tying one arm to either side before moving down and securing his ankles, one on either side with the chain. Blood is running from the wound, coating his leg. Gregor gets some on his hands as he ties the man's ankle into place. He wipes his hand clean on the man's chest.

"I've never tried this before," Gregor says. "Now, let's see what happens when I press this." He presses the button on his key fob and the gate starts to open. The man's legs are spread wider and his arms are stretched.

"So Stranstec decides to buy Spiral and then steal back the money. But who's the rat? Who sold me out?"

The gate keeps hitting a point and starting to close, and Gregor keeps pressing the fob again and again. The man's body jerks each time he does it, and the mechanics of the gate whir and whine. It opens a bit wider each time. Gregor picks up a handful of gravel and steps closer, reaching underneath, and grinds the stones into the wound, then sticks his gun into the torn muscle, pushing and poking the grit further into the bloody mess. He presses the fob again, and the gates open out. He reaches underneath the man's groin and puts the tip of the blood soaked gun between his buttocks. He presses the fob again and the gates stretch the man's legs even further apart. He pushes the barrel of the gun into the man's anus. The man cries out and spits again. Spit drips from Gregor's face, but he doesn't wipe it away. Instead he moves closer.

"I could pull the trigger. Or I could go and get my dogs. They're out back. A couple of pit bulls. I don't tend to feed them very much. I'm sure that they'd have some fun with you all tied up like this. You've already got blood on you. That'd send them crazy. Or should I pull the trigger now? I could always pull the trigger and then get them. The thing about the dogs though, is that they can't think through what they're going to do to you. They don't think about maximising the pain. And that's the bit I like. That's the bit I like the most."

He presses the fob again and the gates open a bit more this time. The barrel of his gun goes a bit deeper.

"Tell me. Who's the fucking rat?"

"A ... a big guy, gold tooth ... Asian. He set the deal. I ... I don't know his name."

"He doesn't know where I live. Who gave you the address?"

Gregor pushes the gun deeper.

"Fuck you.... Aaah ... aaaah ... It was Stranstec's pussy.... She gave the address. A little blonde piece ... aaah ... take that fucking gun out ... of my ass you sick fucker...."

"When I let you down, you're going to call Stranstec and tell him that you're here and the hit was good. A bit scrappy and I got a lucky shot, but you're okay, and I am out. The hit was good. The blonde is here, and I'm dead in the car. The house is fucking full of

Spiral, more shit than you can carry. You got it? If you try and tip him off I'm going to feed you to my dogs fucking slowly. I'm going to tie you up so they can only reach your legs, and when they've ripped them off, I'll think about what to do next."

He presses the fob again and the gate's gears whirr and whine again, pulling the gates further apart. He hears a shoulder pop and the man cries out, gritting his teeth.

"I'll do it.… I'll do it.… Just get the gun out!"

Gregor stops pressing the fob and pulls the gun down. He puts it to the man's face and stuffs it deep in his mouth right to the back of his throat. The man gags. Gregor stares in his eyes for a moment, then turns away and rummages through the pile of clothes. He takes the man's underwear and puts the gun back in his mouth, forcing it as far as it will go, then stretches the underwear over his head, holding the gun in place. He goes to the dead body, pulls it back across the gravel drive, props it against his car in a sitting position, then starts to undress it.

He starts with the shoes and pants, then unzips the jacket and pulls the t-shirt over the bloody mess of a head. Gregor is sweating now as he steps out of his shoes, takes his own trousers off, and pulls and forces them onto the dead body, turning it over and tugging the waistband up. There are smears of blood and brain on his face and sweat drips from him as he takes off his own jacket and shirt and wrestles these onto the corpse. Then he steps back into his shoes, and, naked but for his underwear, socks and shoes, turns the newly suited corpse around on the ground so that his feet are close to the driver door. He opens the door and walks around to the other side of the car, climbs in and leans over to haul the body into the car, legs first. He moves from one side of the car to the other, pushing and lifting, dragging and pulling, puffing and heaving, the air around him clouding with heat, until the dead body is in the driver's seat, lying over the passenger seat, over the crumpled shopping bags, shattered glass, crushed kale, and leaked egg yolk.

Gregor picks up his gun and goes back to the man stretched across the open gate and tears the underwear from his head. Long threads of saliva drop and drool from his mouth, soaking the barrel and the butt of the gun. He retches as Gregor pulls the gun from his mouth, and gasps great noisy breaths as Gregor walks over to his pile of clothes. He wipes the gun on a shirt and then goes through the pile until he finds a phone.

He walks back across the gravel and puts the nose of the gun against the man's wound, pushing, and says, "Give me the code." The man moans out a number and Gregor turns away from him, entering the code on the phone.

He goes to the car and leans in, putting the gun in the corpse's hand, then steps back to take a picture. He pauses for a second. He walks around the car, leaning in the other side, and picks bits of gravel from the broken skull and bloodied brain, then wipes his hands on his sweaty sticky torso and thighs. He steps back again, taking a picture from one side of the car and then the other. He retrieves the gun and walks back to the gate. The naked man with his legs and arms spread, stretched on the iron bars, is still grimacing in pain and puddles of spit and blood have gathered beneath him.

Gregor steps back in front of him, his skin glistening in the moonlight. His face and body are smeared with sweat, blood, and brain. He smiles for a second, his teeth flashing white, then his face straightens again.

"I'm going to let you down and you're going to make the call. You're going to send Stranstec those pictures. That's me with my head blown off. You see? I'm dead. It's all done and I'm dead. He needs to come down here and see this place. It's full of Spiral. You will make the call. Don't fuck with me."

O O O

Lucy wakes up on the couch with the blanket still over her. The TV is off, and the house is dark. She stands up and wraps the blanket around her as she walks upstairs. It must be the middle of the night. There are no lights on and a silence which feels like it has been undisturbed for hours. The smooth banister feels cold, and the stairs seem to go on forever in the darkness as she goes slowly up step after step.

When she reaches the top she switches on the light and the chocolate carpeted corridor looms in front of her. The swirling paisley patterns on the walls are frozen and lifeless, all of the motion and energy in that purple and silver edged pattern has disappeared and she feels like she is walking into a flat photograph. She hears running water, the sound of the shower as she passes the bathroom. The water against the tiles sounds like static interference on an old radio.

When she gets into her room, the eyes of pretty girl on the verge of tears follow her and she walks to the window to draw the curtains. Below her, off to the right, she sees a glow. It's the barbecue. There is still smoke rising from it and she sees hanging from the side an edge of shimmering blue material. She kneels on the cushioned sill, cups her hands around her eyes, and presses her face against the window.

The security gate is open and there is a car she hasn't seen before parked next to Gregor's car. The shimmering blue hanging from the barbecue bowl is the dress she wore. She goes to her wardrobe and opens it. The hangers are bare, swaying slightly. Cold fear runs through her, and she knows she has to leave now. She turns again to the window. This could be it, he could have come at last, but she doesn't recognise the car.

The gate. The gate is open. She has to go now.

She runs to her door and pulls it open. The sound of the shower stops suddenly, like the radio signal being switched off. She runs past the doors and to the stairs. As she turns the crook of the staircase she hears a door open and close above her. She runs to the front door and it is locked. The lights go on.

She turns to see Gregor coming down the stairs toward her, naked, his skin glistening, still wet. His eyes are wide and intense and his hair is greased back away from his face, dark and shiny in the light of the hallway. There is still soap on his calves, running down to his feet as he gets closer.

She turns her head away and sees, through the door of the parlour room, a man tied naked to a chair with his head flopped forward. The man raises his head. He has tape over his mouth and his face is bloody. An eyeball is hanging out of its dark socket, touching his bloody chest. Her insides are torn from her as she sees that it is him. It is Stranstec.

She sinks to her knees as Gregor reaches her. She's holding her hands up in front of her face, starting to sob with fear. He grabs her by the hair and yanks her up, then pulls her up the stairs. She is half crawling, screaming and sobbing and he pulls her up step by step. When they get to the corridor he drags her to the door on the left, which has always been locked. He opens it and drags her inside. There is another stairwell, narrow and dark, and he climbs each step, pulling her behind him. Lucy is shrieking, her voice deadened by the close walls.

When they get to the top he lets her go and she crawls away from him, to the other side of the room, huddling against the wall, pulling her knees up to her chest. He stands opposite her, his naked body pale and shining, his head seeming too big for his body, like a grotesque ventriloquist's doll that has broken free and is ready to exact a terrible revenge.

There are no windows in this room, there is no bed. The walls are grey and there is a thin mattress against the wall. In the corner there is a small tin sink with a single tap. There is a small wooden table with a lamp on it. That is the only light source. Gregor is standing in front of the open door, the narrow staircase behind him.

Lucy tries to speak. "Please Gregor, please. I'm so sorry, I'll do anything," she tries to say, but her words are stolen from her by sobs and gasps for air.

Gregor puts his face right to hers and bellows, the force of his voice shaking the room. "You thought you could play me? You thought you could manipulate me? Me? No-one can manipulate me! No-one plays me! No-one! I took you in and gave you everything. Now I am taking it! I am taking it all away."

"He made me, he made me do it. He made me, he made wait at Archie's and said ... he said that you would never be able to resist me, but I don't want to be with him, I want to be with you, please Gregor, let me, please, please I'll do anything for you."

Gregor turns and leaves the room, closing the door. Lucy hears the key turn in the door and his footsteps on the stairs. Another door closes. There is silence.

The lamp light doesn't reach the edges of the small room. On the table are a small pouch and a deck of cards. She unzips the pouch. There is a small plastic bag, tied at the end, with powder in it. Between the pouch and the deck is a syringe. She picks up the deck. They're tarot cards. They feel old. They have been used over and over and over. She moves to the mattress and puts it flat on the floor, curling up on top of it and pulling her dressing gown around her. There's no sound, nothing at all.

She closes her eyes and cries and cries and cries. Months and months of tears flow from her and she sobs and heaves on the thin mattress. Time passes.

As she lies there, the silence pushes into her. She feels it forcing its way into her, through her skin. She tries to fight it. She tries to call up the memories of her father putting records on the turntable, dancing in the kitchen, singing along with the choruses, but the silence grabs them and tears them apart. Its force frightens her. She can't follow a memory through. She concentrates again. She just starts to hear a voice singing *I've got you under my skin, I've got you,* and sees the shadow of her father taking his hat off and putting it on the kitchen table, when silence lunges in again, and the images and sounds are ripped to pieces as if by a savage dog. She curls up tighter. Time passes.

Later there is a single gunshot from downstairs which explodes inside her like a flash of blinding light, and then the silence rushes back like flood waters filling her.

CHAPTER THIRTY-FIVE

Since that night thirteen months ago, Martin hadn't considered Henry again. He had concentrated on work at Spiral, and true to his word, Ted had developed an arm of the company to deal with Special Interests. This meant publications which found their way into the self-help shelves or the new-age shops. The publishers of these books, which were mostly short runs, liked to think that every link in the chain cared about the books and the words on the page, and the message they were giving. Martin was happy to go along with that and was Spiral's point of contact.

Ted was very happy with the progress and the amount of return trade Martin was building just by taking an apparently flexible and friendly position. And he agreed with the publishers when they said the best motivation is to create positive change in the world and he told them all he admired the work they did in helping people to know themselves better and ultimately love themselves and each other more.

Martin's emptiness was something he had lived with for over a year; he had let the momentum of events push him along, like a paper bag in the wind. The hole inside him was never filled. He still couldn't taste his food. The space that had appeared within him was old, like the darkness of the docks and the space beyond the New Acre fence; it had always been there, waiting to come back.

The year had been like a tunnel, and when Susan Purvis had approached with her proposition he sensed the end of it. He'd contacted Ted and suggested free proofs. Ted had given him free rein to do whatever he thought appropriate to nail the contract. Martin was sure that if he was able to act interested in contacting your angels by holding coloured stones, then he could do the Bible. Then Henry appeared.

O O O

On the way home, Martin stopped into The Bucket O' Blood. He nodded to the few drinkers at the bar and ordered a whiskey and soda. Seated at the window table gazing out through the shadowy glass to the road and the derelict buildings beyond was Henry Bloomburg. His glass was empty. Martin ordered another whiskey and soda. He walked across, put the drinks on the table, and took the seat opposite.

Henry pushed the empty glass away and pulled the full one close. As Martin looked at Henry he thought how different he was to how he had imagined him. Henry looked older, less refined. His eyes sagged gently at the edges; his shirt cuffs protruded from his black suit jacket and were scuffed and grimy. His hat was tipped back, exposing a craggy lined brow and he took a long drink from his glass. The air around him was thick with defeat.

"Thanks," he said, without looking up.

"Not at all," replied Martin. He looked out the window at the crumbling docklands. When he looked back, Henry looked up from his glass. Their eyes met and locked. For a moment, as they regarded each other, they were perfectly still. The last sun of the day threw a weak golden wash onto their table. Henry's glasses reflected the two of them, one in each dark frame, as they faced each other.

"I'd like to ask you a few questions," Henry said.

"That's a good place to start," Martin replied. "I've got a few of my own."

Henry dug his hand in his suit pocket and pulled out his phone. "Do you know Anna White?" He showed the screen to Martin and there was a picture of a woman in her early twenties, slightly overweight and with limp brown hair, holding a Yorkshire terrier like a mother feeding a baby.

Martin shook his head. "Who is she?"

"She was your house mate in number nine Shale Terrace."

Martin looked again at the picture. "Anna White?" Nine Shale terrace was the first place he moved into when he came to the city. There were five of them sharing a two storey terrace. Martin had spent most of his time hidden away in his room. "Was there an Anna in that house? There could have been, it was a while ago. That was ten years ago. And I don't remember a dog. Why are you asking this?"

"I'm just curious to see what you remember." He took the phone back and flicked some keys then held it out again. "How about her?"

It was Zoe. She was posing and taking her own picture at arm's length. Her eyes looked out at him from dark make-up.

"No," Martin said, "Don't know her either."

"Really. Don't you want to know who she is?"

"Not really, not if this is just going to be you showing me pictures of girls on your phone."

"How about her?" Henry asked and changed the picture again. There was Lucy, dressed in a short red dress, looking like she is about to go out on a date. There is an excitement in her face, her shoulders are lifted slightly, she has her hands in little fists, meeting in front. Her smile is so uninhibited, so natural, so full of life.

Henry said, "Julie Dray. You know her?"

"I don't, I don't know her. Julie? I've never seen her. Maybe, I ... I've imagined her, but I've never seen her."

The picture changed again. It was a woman in her thirties sitting at a table with a bundle of different coloured threads on spools, with an exasperated look on her face.

"No, I don't know her. What is this about? Why are you showing me these?"

"All of these women are missing." He changed the picture again. It was a young Alison. Martin leaned forward. No, it was a girl who looked just like her, but younger and slimmer. "She's not missing, she's dead. I found her in a shower with her stomach split open." He changed the picture again. A blonde in green combat shorts and a t-shirt with braces brandishing a giant water gun.

"Come on. I don't know these people. I mean how do I know they even exist?"

"Nicola Carson. Daughter of Stan Carson, the junior partner in the garage you lived above. Of course they exist, do you think I'd be here if they didn't? They're all missing and you, you're the common link."

"Do you know anything about me? Why do you think I might have anything to do with these girls? I don't know them. I never knew them. Who do you think I am?"

"Come on, Mr. Tripp, I think I know who you are. The question is, do you? You say you can't remember these girls. Let me try and jog your memory. Let's start with Nicola Carson—" Martin grabbed Henry's hand and pushed it and the phone to the table with a sudden aggressive force. Henry's hand felt thin and bony, like an old woman's hand as it slammed on the table top. Martin glanced around the bar, but no-one was paying them any attention.

"No, let's start with you, Bloomburg. Let's start with you. How long have you been following me and who sent you?"

Henry pushed his hat back further off his head and leaned forward.

"If I thought you had something to threaten me with, then I might answer you, but as it happens, you don't. So I'm not going to reveal who I'm working for. As for the other question, I've been following you for a while now."

"How about that scar? Under your eye? How did you get that? I've never seen it before, how did you get that?"

"The scar was given to me by someone who didn't want their secret found out. I got away lucky. It's funny, some people are happy to be found out, it's like a relief, but some, they'll do anything to keep it all hidden, even hidden from themselves."

"What do you know about Lucy?"

"Who is Lucy?"

"I've never met her, but I know who she is. She doesn't know me. What do you know? Where is she?"

"I don't know where Lucy is, Martin. I don't know where any of the girls are. If I did, they wouldn't be missing. But these are some of the other girls you have met, in fact more than met, isn't there? You and Anna got quite close a few times didn't you?"

"I don't know her. This is ridiculous."

"Didn't you go drinking with her on the May bank holiday? When she met up with Brian Venter? You two had started to go home when Brian rang her, and then she left you standing by yourself on the road? Asked you not to tell the others about her and Brian, then left you there on Walken Street?"

Martin leaned forward and spat out, "I'm leaving right now, you ridiculous piece of shit. You don't know anything about me, you don't even know where the fuck you've come from."

"Like I said, it's interesting to see what you remember."

"Get fucked, I've got nothing to remember." Martin stood and Henry looked impassively at him. Martin said, "You've never loved anyone. You've never lost anyone. You've always lived through other people's stories, you haven't got one of your own. Don't turn up now and start fucking with mine." Henry didn't respond. Martin swigged back his drink, stood up, and purposefully walked out of the bar. He didn't look back.

Outside it was dark and starting to rain. Martin got in his car and put the key in the ignition. For minutes he sat staring. The encounter with Henry had taken him by surprise. He had taken himself by surprise. He hadn't expected any of what Henry had said. Henry was not how Martin had written him.

O O O

Martin took out his phone and dialled Alison. It rang and then went to her answering machine.

"Hi baby. Listen, I fancy stopping for a few, okay? I'll get a taxi back. Okay, 'bye."

The rain was getting heavier, and by the time he made his way across the car park he was soaked.

Henry wasn't there, just the two empty whiskey tumblers. Martin went into the gents, it was empty. He looked around the bar one last time. The landlord was sitting behind the bar with a half empty pint glass chewing a pen and glaring at a crossword in a newspaper that looked about a year old, and the others in the bar were drinking silently with dull eyes.

Martin went back to his car. The river was dark and slow as he crossed over the bridge and drove out of the city. The rain was heavy and the car was noisy. The motorway was full of spray and headlights and brake lights. He was looking forward to the quiet of the house.

When he got in there were no lights on. He checked upstairs to see if Alison had gone to bed. The house was empty. He stood in the kitchen with the light off. Rain dripped from his jacket to the linoleum floor. After a while he took his coat off and hung it over a chair. He opened the fridge and took out a beer. He went into the front room, turned the TV on, and spent a while changing channels and drinking from the bottle.

He took out his phone to check if she had left a message. The phone looked blankly at him. He wrote, *Where r u?* and pressed Send.

As he changed the channels he saw people talking, running, sitting, laughing, fighting, singing, crying, hiding, falling, walking. Every new person he saw on the screen reminded him of how little he knew about anyone. He didn't know where Alison had gone. Henry Bloomburg had questioned him. What did he know about Henry? What did he really know about Alison? He finished his beer and turned the TV off. He thought of waiting up until Alison got home. It was quiet. He went to bed. Martin went to sleep and the rain continued to fall.

O O O

Alison was watching the red numbers on the meter of a taxi and hoping they wouldn't climb over fifteen. When it got to fourteen fifty she said, "This will do. Just leave me here, thanks." She was only a few streets away. It had started to rain. She held her handbag above her head and ran across the road. In the rain people moved quickly through the city with their heads down.

She didn't know this part of the city well. The big shopping streets were behind her and the roads narrowed; there were small restaurants and wine bars, couples were walking hand in hand, hurrying through the rain to their candlelit tables. There was Twin70. Martin had brought her here just after he got the printing job. She glanced in as she passed. It looked the same: plush décor, low lighting, a sense of time slowed down. That was the last time they had been out together like that, just the two of them; all dressed up and looking into each other's eyes.

After the waiter had taken her second plate away Martin took her hand. She had thought he was going to propose. He didn't. He was going to finish with the novel, one way or the other. *One last push, and if no-one will publish it, that's it,* he said, *I will put it in the ground.* She had been disappointed and relieved; then disappointed again. *You are so good to me,* he said. *One last push.*

Alison caught her reflection in the window of Twin70. She could have dressed up a bit more, but no, no this wasn't a date. She was just seeing a band. A bit further down the road was The Blues Club. There was a small queue at the door. She was relieved when she saw that the people who were in the queue were about the same age or older than her.

The club was low-ceilinged with a bar against the wall on the left. At the end of the room was the stage. All along the walls were framed photos of blues and soul artists, smiling, holding trumpets, singing, peeping out from behind double basses, eyes closed, lost in song. Between the frames wall lights gave soft warmth to the room, and there were candle-lamps on the tables.

As she stepped in she saw him straight away, standing at the bar. He wasn't looking over, he was ordering a drink, but she immediately started to feel nervous. He looked even younger without a suit. When she had been showing him round the properties earlier that day he had been wearing a dark, close-cut suit.

Andre had put her on this contact personally. This was a man who needed to set himself up, because he was planning to move his business interests to the city. *This is a guy with connections,* Andre said, *you can tell just by the way he talks. Treat him sweet,* Andre had said.

The properties were city centre apartments, at the top of the price bracket, so the fact that he was about the same age as her was unusual. He held himself straight and had seemed very serious until they started chatting, not about property but about reality TV. His shoulders relaxed and his smile opened. That's when he said *There is a singer that was on one of those modelling shows playing in town tonight, singing with her band, she's really very good. She wanted to be a model, but was voted off in the second round. Nisha Taylor. Oh, I remember her,* Alison had said, *she was gorgeous, I couldn't believe they voted her out. Just wait till you hear her sing,* he had said. *Oh, I might pop in then,* she had replied. She looked in his eyes and she saw an intensity. There was some kind of destiny, as if they were characters in a classic novel, meeting for the first time. She felt like he was reaching into her with those eyes, that he was going to find something precious within her.

Then she outlined the advantages of the spacious fifth floor two bedroom flat with *en suite* bathrooms and a hallway with generous storage space. She gestured out the window and said something about parking, but she lost her thread and her hand waved around. Now his eyes seemed softer as he saw her, and she walked toward the bar. He was wearing a t-shirt and jeans, and his smile opened up again. When they greeted each other she felt awkward, she couldn't call to mind anything to say.

"Are you here alone?" he asked. She nodded. He was taller than she was. Taller than Martin. She was going to make a lie about her friend cancelling at the last minute, but it seemed superfluous. His chest was well defined in his t-shirt, and a light dusting of stubble crept down his neck. Everything about him seemed in sharp focus.

"So am I. Here grab this stool, it's going to get full in here." He pulled a tall stool over to them. "Hang on," he said. He tapped someone at the bar on the shoulder. When he spoke it was confident and clear. The man nodded and said, *Of course,* and stood. He took the tall stool from the man and exchanged it for the one she had been about to sit on.

"Here," he said, "this one has a back to it." She sat. He offered her a drink and she accepted. All of the tables were full, and people coming through the door were moving in around the walls, standing in front of the pictures.

"Nearly show time," he said as he handed her her drink. "I got you two." His eyes gestured toward the bar where another two drinks waited, one more for her and one more for him. "They close the bar during the performance."

She thanked him and said, "You must come here a lot then?"

"No, but I always enjoy it when I do. Cheers." They clinked glasses.

Alison took her phone from her bag and checked to make sure she had put it on silent. A text. From Martin. She didn't read it. She turned her phone off.

As she put it back in her bag the lights dimmed. A hush moved through the room from the front to the very back. Alison looked to the stage. There was a drum kit, a piano, a double bass, and an electric guitar. Men in dark suits were taking their places at the instruments. The light at the bar went out and she was in the shadows. He was standing behind her.

There was an expectancy in the air; everyone was waiting for something to happen. In that moment she wanted to lean back and feel his arms around her. She felt protected just being close to him. There was a silent strength within him. He stood straight with his shoulders back. Martin, when he spoke, hunched forward. He scratched his face, rubbed his hair, folded and unfolded his arms. All of the artistry she had been attracted to when she first met him was still tangled up within him, keeping his head bowed.

In their years together he had not grown stronger, he had retreated further and further into himself. She felt the age difference between them now more than ever. In those years she had supported him, and he had become weaker. The way he used to speak to her, the insights, the poetic images, perhaps they had all been used up. Like the stories he wrote when they first met. Those were what had got the interest of the agency. But since then he hadn't been able to find the formula of words that had come so easily to him at the start. Maybe it was all gone from him. He couldn't see things the way he did at the start, his vision was all focused inward.

Alison knew she had more within her than Martin could ever see, and now in the hushed anticipation of this crowded room she felt such strength emanate from the man behind her; and this man, she was sure, could see everything she could be. She turned around and he leaned close to her. She thought again how good it was to be with someone her own age, but someone so solid and defined that he might have been carved from marble in the time of the great masters. The lights went right down, the stage was in darkness, and the only lights in the room were the low table lamps, around which dark shapes waited.

"Mr. Alskev," she whispered, as the club held its breath, "I feel such a fool, I don't know your first name."

He smiled and whispered in her ear, "Gregor."

A spotlight hit the stage and Nisha Taylor, a beautiful black woman, appeared from the wings. She wore a long sparkling silver dress, cut low to her breasts, reaching elegantly to the stage. Behind her neck was affixed a collar which rose up behind her head like a silver backdrop, accentuating her noble poise.

A release of applause and cheers clamoured the air as she surveyed the room like a queen viewing her subjects. She did not greet them with hello, but instead sang a single note so clean and soaring that it took flight around the room and lifted the heart of everyone who heard it. A space which had never been before was created. There was a moment when she stopped and the note hung in the air.... And in that gap between the note and the silence, in that newly created space, Alison's future changed. Nisha Taylor counted the band in, and with a cymbal crash that new future began.

CHAPTER THIRTY-SIX

I n the morning Martin sat in front of his cereal. He didn't eat it, just watched as the cereal absorbed the milk and became sticky in the bowl.

Through the rain-flecked window he saw the trees at the back of the garden, bushy and thick, their branches reaching low to protect what was in their shadow. He went back upstairs and into the bedroom to kiss Alison goodbye. He moved her hair gently from her face and kissed her on the cheek. Without opening her eyes she mumbled, "Have a good day," before putting her face back into the pillow. He wanted to ask her where she had been, but instead he just looked at the back of her head for a moment before walking quietly out the door.

It was cold outside. As he sat in his driver's seat waiting for the car to warm up he noticed words written in the condensation on the windscreen. NOT HER. Then the condensation was gone and so were the words. It was seven fifty-six. He pulled out of his driveway. He pushed the accelerator down quickly, reached the roundabout, and then everything slowed.

In the car next to him on the dual carriageway there was a woman in her forties and a woman in her early twenties. The older one was looking out the window with her chin on her hand, and the younger had earphones in and was flicking through her phone looking vacant. Martin looked ahead again, craned his neck to see if there was any movement in the queue of cars, and there in the distance he saw the dark suited figure of Henry, coming toward him. Martin watched as Henry walked along the middle of the road between the steel and glass carriages, between the lives living in a hurry moving slowly. The road stretched on and inside the cars there was no colour amongst the dark shapes. Everyone was facing the same way. Only Henry was moving against this steel tide. As he got closer Martin could see that his suit was creased and his hat was pulled low over his eyes. He looked even older than the night before, as if years had passed. The cars moved slowly forward, closing the distance between Martin and Henry.

When he reached the car Martin leaned over and opened the passenger door. Henry sat in. He didn't look at Martin. He put the seat belt on, clicking it into place, and then sat looking out the window of the car. Martin looked at Henry's profile. His skin hung from his cheekbones and his chin, like an old sheet hanging out to dry. *His face had dropped from his skull,* Martin thought. He is coming undone. Henry tapped the window next to him with a bony finger, pointing at the car alongside.

"Mother and daughter?"

The traffic slowly moved forward again. Martin closed the gap between his car and the car in front. The gap behind him closed just as fast. Martin didn't reply. Henry said, "Must be, otherwise that would be just rude."

"Am I just going to have to get used to you?"

"I'm here, you're here, we might as well talk. This where you live? These your neighbours?"

"I live back up the hill."

"Nicer than Lomax."

"What are you talking about?"

"Lomax. You were busy when you lived there. How about up at New Acre? You keeping busy?"

"What do you want to talk about? You trying to pick me apart? With questions that don't make any sense? I don't know what you mean. If it's about those girls, I don't know any of your girls, so you can keep your pictures. I'm not going to answer questions about people I don't know; girls I've never met."

"I've read some of your stories."

"Ha, ha. Well, what do you think of that?"

"I think you're sick, Martin. I think that you have a lot of questions to answer. I think you're desperate. Desperate to change because you know you're sick."

"Well, fuck you, I'm not answering anything."

"What about god? Are you into that? A creator?"

"What? What the fuck? You don't care about god."

"Is god on the inside or the outside?"

"I'm too busy to think about god."

"Too busy? Isn't that what these books are going to be about that you're going to print? God, a creator? The power of god and the responsibilities of man? Is it that way round?"

"Well, okay. God has got to be on the inside, if it was on the outside everyone would know for sure. But nobody really knows. There are interpretations of god, but it's not observable like the outside. Nobody knows the inside."

"Especially not you."

"Especially not me."

"Too busy looking up your own inside."

"Very good. And why are you here again?"

"To see how much you remember. To break your denial. So, on the inside anything is possible?"

"Shit, I'm in the wrong lane."

"You didn't indicate."

"Come on, no-one's moving anywhere, there's no surprise."

Martin eased the car from the body of the steel snake onto the slip road. The radio announcer ran through the headlines again, and promised more detail on the hour. Then they were on the long avenue of the Crown Estate.

Martin said, "I'm late."

"You need to remember what you did with these girls."

"I don't know anything about any of those fucking girls! I told you that last night." Martin was shouting. He realised this and lowered his voice. "I don't know anything. Whatever you're into has nothing to do with me. I need to get to work."

He pulled into the parking lot and got out angrily, slamming the car door.

O   O   O

When Martin got in he went straight to Beth at the desk.

"Has anyone been in for me?" he asked.

"No," she said, "but a courier did drop these off from *Goodbooks*." She handed him three large heavy envelopes. "And who is this? Your father?"

Martin looked at Beth and then looked to where she was looking, beside him. There was Henry, who took his hat from his head and smiled and said, "Yes, Henry Tripp, nice to meet you."

"Yes, yes, sorry, Beth, yes my dad popped in to see me, so I thought I'd show him, well, show him Spiral. He won't stay long. Could you sign him in please?"

Beth handed over the signing-in folder and Henry smiled and filled it in.

"Well, lovely to meet you, Mr. Tripp. You were here the other day, too," she said. "I can see the resemblance, I knew it as soon as you walked in."

Henry handed back the folder and they walked through the foyer and to the lift. Martin didn't speak. Henry put his hat back on and followed Martin as they walked to his office. When they got there, Martin went in and slammed the door closed. The envelopes were prints of the cover and illustrations that *Goodbooks* wanted for their first print. There was an email waiting for him, sent the evening before, from Susan Purvis. The attachment was a proposed contract.

Martin drank his coffee and settled into his chair before opening it. As he read, it felt like caffeine spreading through his system. His skin felt electrically charged. The contract looked good. *Goodbooks* had secured a release for extracts to be published in a Sunday paper and were ready to go with the first two books: *The Old Testament Today*, and *The Koran for Everyman*. He prepared his response. Martin sweated.

Hi Susan, thank you so—

He deleted.

Miss Purvis, it is with gratitude—

He deleted.

Susan, I have read the contract and—

He pushed his chair back and stood up.

He thought about Alison. He pictured her at home, getting ready for her work day, looking at herself in the mirror, pulling in her belly, and flicking back her hair. She picks up her work folder and handbag and checks herself once more before leaving the house.

O   O   O

Lucy lies in a cold dark room, waiting for someone to save her. Her breath is shallow. Her pale skin is almost transparent and her lips have turned blue. She tries to make a fist, but her fingers will not respond. Her eyes are closing.

O   O   O

Susan Purvis is in her office. She's on the phone. She is speaking with clarity and conviction. Outside her closed office door someone is waiting to see her. As she speaks she moves her hands, rotating from her wrist open palmed, wide fingered in a circular motion, creating momentum. Things, unseen, are changing.

Martin sat back down and typed the acceptance of the *Goodbooks* contract and requested a meeting to sign the contract.

O   O   O

When Alison got to work, there were two messages for her. One was from a Mr. Bloomburg, requesting a meeting. The other was from Gregor Alskev. He wanted to view more properties, and was interested in office properties in the docklands project. Alison returned the calls. She left a message with Mr. Bloomburg, and spoke to Gregor Alskev and arranged to meet him in the city centre.

When she saw him again, suited so smartly and walking through the street with such confidence, she felt a rush to her heart. Surely the timing of this man's entrance to her life was no accident. Perhaps all of her time with Martin had just been preparing her for this moment. All of the romanticism in which she wrapped Martin, the creativity which she once admired, she now saw as a force that was binding him and making it impossible for him to move on.

She had stopped reading his work a long time ago because she saw how he took what was real and bent and coloured it to fit within his fictional design. It disturbed her to see what was recognisable distorted in such a way; it felt as if he was using his life and hers to embroider an elaborate lie.

Now here was a man whose strength was there for all to see, who was not afraid of money, whose ambition was not cloaked in some elaborate artistic ideal, someone who lived in her world, the real world. When she had been preparing the folders on each property, she had been imagining Gregor in them, and then imagining her with him. Sitting at the four-point black tiled breakfast island as he walks through the spacious hallway furnished with exotic wall hangings lit by adjustable in-wall lighting; or standing at the triple glazed full wall tinted window of the sixth-floor open plan apartment with the view of the river and the south-end markets the morning after a festival when the city is waking up slowly and the barges are moving sleepily down-river, sending shivers through the gold ribbon reflection of the morning sun, and him standing behind her, wrapping his arms around her, gently moving her hair aside and kissing her neck, thanking her for a fantastic night. Alison smiled as he approached and his smile beamed back at her.

Over the afternoon they attended four different properties, all bigger than the previous day, before Gregor invited her to lunch. They sat opposite each other in the little Italian restaurant and Gregor encouraged her to try some of his. As they ate they swapped dishes back and forth, and the textures and tastes of fried calamari, roasted artichoke heart, strascinate in tomato and chilli, seasoned flatbread with wild boar pâté, and rich red wine filled her senses.

Gregor asked her about her life, where she lived, who she lived with. She told him about Martin. She said he was a novelist. She didn't say he'd never been published. He asked would she marry him. She said no. She asked him had he anyone. *Once,* he said, *but she had drug problems which made the relationship impossible.* Although he felt bad about the ending, there was nothing he could do. *You can't change people to be what you want them to be. There comes a time,* Gregor said, *when it is impossible not to make a choice. Life stands in front of you and challenges you and the things you once decided were the most important become the things you can't carry with you any more.*

O O O

That night in bed Martin listened carefully to Alison's breathing. It was slow and regular. He thought about what she might be dreaming and then about the futility of that.

He opened his eyes and looked into the darkness of the room, closed them again and looked into the darkness behind his eyelids. Two small pieces of skin to separate the outside from the inside, but in the dark it made no difference. The rumble of the motorway was there in the room with them.

Alison had stayed out late again, not coming back from work until nearly nine. *Meetings and administration,* she said, *very boring stuff.* Martin had spent the time cleaning, wiping the counter tops and the table, sweeping the floors, adjusting the edges of the sofa throw, and placing and replacing the cushions. He had turned the TV on and off and on again. He felt like he was only touching the surface, like an insect sitting on the water of a stagnant lake, just light enough not to break the thin film.

Alison turned over in her sleep, throwing an arm over him. He carefully lifted it from his chest and got out of bed. Without turning on a light, he stepped into his office room. The curtains were open. He stood at the window and looked onto the garden.

When he had moved in with Alison they had spoken about putting in a little fish pond near the end of the garden and a patio area by the house, big enough for a table and chairs, somewhere to sit out in the summer. A bird table and a flower bed. How they had imagined all that would fit in that little patch of grass. It seemed too small for anything now.

He turned and switched on the computer. He looked again at the message Susan Purvis had sent at six forty-three. She was going away on business on Friday morning but had time tomorrow evening to sign the contract. *How about a celebratory dinner at Twin70?* Martin had replied: *Seven thirty at Twin70 was fine. Looking forward to seeing you then. Regards.* He read through the correspondence once again, then turned the computer off. He lay back in bed. He didn't sleep.

O   O   O

In the morning he kissed Alison goodbye and left the house without eating. He took his suit, still on the hanger, and put it in the back seat. The emptiness which had become a part of him now reached through to the tips of his fingers, right to the backs of his eyes. There was nothing inside him anymore.

When he got to the roundabout he took the third exit instead of the second. He sat in another queue of cars, just facing in a different direction. For the next eight hours Martin drove around the bypasses, ring roads, and industrial estates of the city. He didn't want Henry to find him again, so he went where he had never been, taking turns he had never taken before. All of the roads led him past iron fences to roundabouts and car parks, business estates just like the Crown Estate, all of the buildings named with a letter and a number, rows and rows of cars outside buildings exactly like his printing building. He drove and drove. The warmth of the car, the traffic so slow, the radio turned way down low, and the decision that he had made to go nowhere at all comforted him as he drifted in and out of semi-sleep.

The day passed quickly with only the unchanging news headlines to mark out the hours. It was after five before Martin finally pulled into the car park at Spiral. He walked into his office to get the paperwork he needed for the meeting, then straight back out again.

O O O

Martin checked his hair again in the rear view mirror. He reopened his briefcase. The contract was still there, a promise waiting to be fulfilled. He closed the briefcase and got out of the car, straightening his suit jacket as he walked across the car park. As he walked through the doors of Twin70 he could see couples dining in the low lighting, hands touching, eyes widening. He was early. He said, "Reservation for Purvis," and the waiter led him to a booth toward the back of the room.

"There you go, Mr. Purvis," the waiter said.

As Martin sat down he ordered a whiskey and soda. The waiter nodded efficiently and turned away. From this table near the back of the room the noise of the restaurant was muted and comforting, like a familiar television programme in the background. Martin unbuttoned his suit jacket. He placed the briefcase on the seat of the chair next to him, then moved it to the ground, leaning it against the leg of the chair. He rubbed his eyes. The waiter brought the glass.

He had finished his whiskey when Susan Purvis arrived. She was wearing a suit jacket, with a skirt and heels. Her walk was purposeful and even, and the fabric of her skirt stretched slightly across her hips with each step. Over her shoulder was her embroidered bag. Her hair was tied up. Her neck was elegant and pale. She smiled as she approached. He stood and pulled out her chair.

"Thank you," she said. "I'm sorry I'm late. Just organising everything before my trip. Details can take up so much time." She reached into her bag. "Shall we—"

"Sign now?" said Martin.

"Before we eat?"

"Yes, let's." Martin beckoned to the waiter and smiled at Susan Purvis as he came over. The waiter stood straight and attentive. Martin ordered champagne without looking at him. Susan Purvis took her papers from her bag. They exchanged papers and signatures. After the waiter had poured they held their glasses to each other and he looked into her emerald eyes.

"May this be the beginning of a long—"

"—and prosperous"

"—a long and prosperous relationship. Cheers."

"Cheers."

As the evening turned Susan Purvis talked about her travels, her business, her plans. Martin found himself wanting to get closer. *Maybe,* he thought, *people are at their most attractive when they talk about their aspirations, their ascendant futures, when they are filled with the blank wonder of possibility.* She had a confidence, a glowing promise, that Martin was now a part of. His signature was next to hers.

Susan Purvis talked about the innate goodness in people. *The child in everyone that needed a guiding hand, how uncomplicated the good truth was. It only had to be presented to them in terms they understand.* He leaned closer. *People's attention spans are so much shorter now,* she said. *The language used must be so much more emphatic. These handbooks can provide a more immediate understanding of god so ordinary man can form a relationship with the creator much quicker. Everyone needs redemption, and only the creator can redeem.* Goodbooks *can help.*

Martin felt comforted and lonely at the same time. He found himself focusing on her lips, her eyes, the crucifix which hung around her beautiful neck catching and reflecting the light, and her hands, always in motion when she spoke.

The waiter was returning with a bottle of wine when Martin mentioned that he had been a writer, had written a book. Susan Purvis said, "I hadn't guessed."

"Yes, but I got better." They both laughed so loud the noise they made took them by surprise. The waiter stepped back for a second then leaned in to pour. He smiled at them both. By the end of the meal Martin counted that they had got through a bottle of champagne and a bottle of wine, as well as a couple of brandies each with their coffees. He put his card on the silver tray without looking at the bill and nodded as the waiter smiled and took it from their table. There was no-one else left in the restaurant.

"Well, if you have to be away early in the morning—" Martin began.

"No, well, the afternoon, but there is still so much to do before I go. I should get my head down. I am glad that we have had the chance to get—"

"—to know each other. Let me get you a taxi," Martin said as they stood up.

"It's not far, I can walk."

Martin thought for a moment about offering to walk her home, but a clean good-bye now would be better. As he held open the doors of Twin70 Martin said, "No really, let me get you a taxi, it's late."

It was quiet on the street but for the sound of muted music coming from The Blues Club. Martin could just hear a dull steady thud and a three note bass line repeated over and over. Soon people would pour from its doors, some of them arm in arm, with rhythms and movements of music still in them.

Martin and Susan Purvis walked together down the narrow streets leaving the noises of the club behind and onto the wide main street. Martin waved a taxi down. He held the door open for her and said good night. He stood watching the lights of the taxi getting smaller as it drove away. Then he walked back to his car. He climbed in and put his briefcase on the passenger seat and rested a hand upon it. He was touching a future. A trajectory. Action which would cause consequence. Something that could make a difference. When he had asked Susan Purvis did she not feel that she was interfering with the word of god in some way, she shook her head. *The word of man, interpreting god,* she said. *The word of man, which stands between god and man. The fewer words the better.*

O   O   O

When Martin got out of his car at New Acre he could see the shapes of the diggers and scaffolds popping up behind the fences in silhouette.

He could feel the touch of the moonlight on his skin. A wind had picked up, slow and insistent, like a wave coming in to break. The noise was like a train in a tunnel, approaching, finally reaching him. Martin stood listening for a minute to the growing sound before unlocking the front door and stepping in, closing the door and locking himself into the silence of the house.

As he entered the kitchen he flicked on the light. There, standing on the other side of the kitchen, leaning against the worktop, was Henry, in his black suit. Martin closed the door. Henry didn't move. His neck was thin in his collar and his face had aged so much it seemed that his bones had withered. Martin opened the fridge and took out two bottles of beer. He opened both and gave one to Henry. Henry took it and nodded.

"Thanks. I didn't like to help myself."

"You look older."

"I am. I'm near the end, but there's just one more thing."

"One more thing? Well let's sit."

Martin turned the light off. All of the sharpness and definition disappeared. Henry let out a sigh. Martin pulled out two chairs and they both sat. Henry rubbed his forehead, tilting his hat back, and Martin saw his eyes blink slowly. Martin drank from his beer.

Henry looked so old, so old. Martin saw an old man with a wasted life behind him. A life spent chasing after other people's problems, revealing answers to other people's questions, finding out other people's secrets, making money from the misery of people's lives. The moonlight slipped through the swaying branches of the trees outside and onto the countertop.

"I still don't know why you're really here," Martin said.

Henry said in a quiet voice, "Yes, you do. You deny everything. All of your life, you have blocked things out, terrible things."

"Listen." Martin leaned forward. "I made you, you sad old man. And I can break you. There's nothing to remember. You, you are a fiction, looking for a mystery to solve. Well there's no mystery here, no matter how hard you try and cook something up, there's nothing, just me. Me, stuck in this place I don't want to be with someone who doesn't want to be with me, doing things I don't want to do. This is me, there's no fucking mystery."

"There is only one mystery I've never resolved. Do you know what that is?"

Martin sat back again and drank from his beer. "No, why don't you tell me."

"The Fly Guy."

"The Fly Guy is just a story."

"Like the others? Like the other stories? That's where you hide them, in your stories? Do you even know what you've done? What you're denying?"

"There is no fucking Fly Guy, that's the secret, you fool! Everything you've been chasing, there's nothing! It's all nothing. So you are nothing!"

"Then why am I here? You have tried to block it all out, but you can't any more. I found you. The time has come. You've been begging for change. Well, open your eyes. Now is the chance. I am revealing you to yourself, and now is the time. You have the power to stop, to change, to save. If you could save anyone, who would it be?"

"Myself. If I could save anyone I'd save myself."

Martin stood and filled a pan with water. He turned the knob for the gas hob. A hiss and click. Then there was a blue flame shivering. He turned it up full. He had to go to work in a few hours. He had to sit in traffic. He considered putting his face on the blue circle and wondered how it would feel. He put the pot of water on the flames.

When he turned back to Henry he could still see a blue circle in the dark. Henry was sitting rubbing his forehead. His hair had receded, his face had dropped some more, and there were deep shadows under his eyes. His hands were like claws protruding from the darkness of his suit. Martin saw how weak he was. He saw how easy it would be to break him.

"You had no-one to love. Is that it? Have you come here to get love from your creator? Have you come here to die? You're the one with the fucking baggage, you're the one who needs to come to terms with his past. I don't have a past. No baggage. See? Empty-handed. You've got the past I gave you and you've never made any connections, that's what's wrong with you. You're the one who has never had anyone." Martin opened the fridge and peered inside. "I thought we had eggs."

Henry still didn't say anything. The light from the fridge was soft. What Martin really wanted to do was lie down on the kitchen floor and feel it wash over him. Where could he find comfort now? How could he reach through all of the walls, the windows and doors, the frames, the constructions, the barriers between? Everyone was separated like specimens in their jars. He straightened up and walked over to Henry, stood in front of him. Martin could feel anger now. He felt it like it was the first time; it surged through him, filling up the empty vessel that he had become.

"What good are you here?"

"You must remember. What you did to Zoe, what you did to Anna." Henry's voice was old, too. It came creeping from his throat, barely audible. "Think again, if there was one person you could save, if the power was given to you. If you could save just one, who would it be? If you remember just one, the rest will follow. Allow yourself to remember."

"There's nothing to remember! You're a fiction and you are making fictions. This is all in your head. All in your fucking head. It's all fictions, everything I've done! And you are wrong! I have power, and I'm going to break you."

Martin drew his arm back and with all the strength he had, hit Henry on the side of the head with his beer bottle. The sound was loud and thick. The bottle didn't break. Henry's head wobbled and flopped. His hat tipped to a sharp angle. A sound like a door creaking open escaped his mouth. Martin dropped his bottle and grabbed Henry around the neck. He began to squeeze, hard. A red wound opened like a mouth above Henry's ear. Blood started to pour down his neck.

Henry suddenly threw his arms around, knocking the beer from the table. He tried to stand. He choked out the word *Stop*. Martin pushed down and squeezed with everything he had in him. Henry's hat fell off. He was choking and his feet were scrambling beneath the table. Martin could feel his fingers digging deeper into Henry's neck. He felt how frail his windpipe was and felt a surge of power when he knew he was crushing it. His hands seemed to grow the more he squeezed. Martin felt all of the hours and hours, all of the sharp edges, blank spaces and waste, all of the words and the yearning gaps between, all of it was rushing from his shoulders down his arms and into his hands. All of the past, real and imagined, everything he has done and has not done, everything he will do and not do, will converge onto this one act, and concentrate the pressure, the power, the real power he can feel in his hands.

I will kill you, Henry. I will it, I will it, I will kill. I will kill you, Henry, I will kill you.

And then he realises he has.

O O O

Alison pushes open the door.

"Who are you talking to?"

Martin is standing in the middle of the kitchen with the light off, with his back to her. He does not turn. Steam thickens the air. The fridge is open, spilling yellow light, oozing across the linoleum. On the stove, gas flames grip a pan with blue flickering fingers. The noise from the bubbling water rises and spreads. The blind is open. Through the window she sees the silhouette of the bare tree shaking manically in the wind and the moon through the agitated branches. The shadows in the kitchen move and shake, darting over the counters and tabletop, brushing Martin's slumped shoulders and the backs of his legs, sliding off the shelves and retreating into the corners, twitching.

She reaches for the light switch.

"Don't," he says, not turning around. "Don't turn the light on."

"What have you done? What's that on the floor? Martin?"

"Nothing. This is it. Go back to bed."

"Martin ..." He still does not turn.

Alison steps back out of the kitchen and closes the door. She knows Martin is drunk. It seems that beyond that door the whole room is drunk too, that everything around him is teetering on an edge, just about holding itself up. She doesn't want to be part of that. She pads back upstairs and back into bed. She knows that there is a natural end to everything, and the secret is to know when to step out, to avoid the cycle repeating.

She pulls the cover over herself and closes her eyes. She sees Martin with his back to her. He doesn't turn around, and in the place where she used to feel love she now feels pity. She sees Gregor from afar, tall and confident, looking at her from the doorway of an immaculately restored seventeenth century shop front converted into a luxurious three storey townhouse, and gesturing for her to come in, come in. She feels a rush of love, an excitement. It's suddenly easy to imagine life without Martin.

O O O

The back door of the house unlocks and then opens. Martin steps out. He drags Henry's old limp body to the back of the garden. He comes back to the house and goes inside. The wind still rolls and roars through the tops of the trees and underneath the shadows deepen and pulse. The moonlight ebbs on the dark suit and swells on the white face of a broken old man. Martin steps out of the house with a spade in his hand. He walks back across the moonlit rectangle of grass and disappears into the shadows at the end of the garden.

O O O

When Alison wakes in the morning, she looks to the other side of the bed. Martin isn't there. He hasn't kissed her goodbye. She gets out of bed and goes to the bathroom. The door to the office is closed. She opens it. Martin is there in the suit he was wearing the night before, sitting at the desk, typing on the keyboard. The light is on and the curtains are open. He doesn't turn his head or acknowledge her in any way. There are streaks of mud and grime in his hair and his hands are grey and chalky. There is a pile of papers on the desk beside him and soil on the floor around him. The pages she can see have thick black marker lines crossing diagonally over the typed text. The computer screen in front of him is filling with words.

"Martin," she says, but he doesn't stop typing or take his eyes from the screen. She steps back out of the room and closes the door. From the other side she can't hear anything. She listens for sounds of his fingers on the keyboard or heavy breathing, but there is nothing. She sees the mud on the floor, the footprints on the stairs. She puts her ear to the door. Nothing. She opens the door again. There he is, the words are moving along the screen.

"What about work?" she says. He doesn't reply or even make any sign that he's heard her. It is as if she isn't there. She isn't there, or she is there and he is not.

CHAPTER THIRTY-SEVEN

Lucy. Anna. Zoe. Nicola. Marketa. Susan. *Lucy*. I've been watching you for so long. I have always been watching you. I have heard you knock on the walls and wail, I have watched your aching hours pass. Who you have been, who you are, who you can be, the possibilities reverberate around you, all with the tone of tragedy, as if all of the voices you have and will ever have are entwined, threading into each other, crossing over each other, winding into a chord that binds with a song of grief. Even when you sleep the room holds the echo of your sorrow. I have been watching and writing, and my heart breaks every time I write. I have seen and felt everything and yet still I condemn you. If there was one person, just one ...

Now your back is to the door. You are sitting on the floor. The room is dark, the only light on is a small desk lamp on the floor next to you illuminating the tarot cards. Beyond the small pool of light the floor of the room is grimy and the flash of crumpled silver foil reflects from a corner. In the other corner in the shadows is a small bundle of naked plastic dolls, some missing limbs or their heads or with their torsos twisted around. Near the mattress is a cut up set of clothes, strips of a small red dress and tattered cuts of denim lie in a heap.

You have cut the deck into three piles face down, and now you take the top one from each and place them in a row before turning them over. You are singing softly to yourself, *the way you wear your hat, the way you sip your tea, the memory of all that, no they can't take that away from me.* Your skinny hands are pale and elegant. Your skin has a luminescence in the lamplight. You see the Magician, the ten of wands and the Chariot. Your hands move delicately over the cards, changing their order. The ten of wands, the Chariot, and the Magician. You stop singing and turn your head.

There in the door is my silhouette. My frame is thin and my shoulders are slightly hunched. My jacket does not fit me and my wrists and hands protrude from my sleeves, hanging loose, redundant. Your eyes are glazed. In a weak voice you say, "Have you brought something? Have you got it? Something?" I hold my hands out, empty. You say, "You said you'd come back with it. You said. I feel like I've been dying." You bend forward with your arms folded and put your face on the ground. I take two steps into the room. My movement is odd, jerky, as if I have extra knees and elbows, or there are frames missing from the film. I speak.

It's me. I've come for you. You look up again and this time rise. You are weak. In the half-light of the room you are like a ghost, almost not real. You float just above the floor and sway.

"What's wrong with your eyes? Which one are you?"

It's me. I'm Martin. I love you. At last I can save you.

ABOUT THE AUTHOR

Irish born Colum Sanson-Regan, who now lives in Cardiff, Wales, has spent most of his adult life as a musician. He fronts his band, Goose and is a well known face around Cardiff's live music scene. Colum is best known in the pop-culture scene as the body double for David Tennant on *Doctor Who*.

Colum studied Creative and Professional Writing at the University of South Wales, where he received the Michael Parnell Prize acknowledging his writing abilities, and went on to get his masters in Creative Writing, where the idea for *The Fly Guy* was born whilst writing his final dissertation.

OTHER WORDFIRE PRESS TITLES

Our list of other WordFire Press authors and titles is always growing. To find out more and to see our selection of titles, visit us at:

wordfirepress.com

9984556R00173

Printed in Great Britain
by Amazon.co.uk, Ltd.,
Marston Gate.